“When I first picked up *Knuck*
Sunday night. As Sunday night started
Monday
morning, however, I had to force myself to put the book down and go to sleep. The story just sucked me into it, hitting home for me in a lot of ways. I never thought I could enjoy a knuckle sandwich so much.”

—BRIAN “HEAD” WELCH, musician;
author of *Save Me from Myself*

“I swear I know these people! *Knuckle Sandwich* took me back to those great days in high school and college when all my friends were in bands. This is a funny, nostalgic, and meaningful tale, told in Adam’s entertaining style that will be music to your ears!”

—JEDD HAFER, coauthor of
Bad Idea and *From Bad to Worse*

KNUCKLE SANDWICH

A NOVEL

ADAM PALMER

TH1NK
P.O. Box 35001
Colorado Springs, Colorado 80935

www.navpress.com

TH1NK is an imprint of NavPress.
TH1NK and the TH1NK logo are registered trademarks of NavPress. Absence of ® in connection with marks of NavPress or other parties does not indicate an absence of registration of those marks.

ISBN-13: 978-1-60006-048-9
ISBN-10: 1-60006-048-X

Cover design by The Design Works Group, Wes Youssi, www.TheDesignWorksGroup.com
Cover image by Shutterstock
Creative Team: Nicci Hubert, Dave Lambert, John Kudrick, Reagen Reed, Arvid Wallen, Bob Bubnis

Palmer, Adam, 1975-
Knuckle Sandwich : sometimes rock 'n' roll hits back / Adam Palmer.
p. cm.
Summary: Three Midwestern college students, Jeremiah, Matt, and Liz, have very different reasons for forming a Christian rock band, but when they move from the youth group circuit to opening national tours, fame brings about changes that threaten to destroy them.
ISBN-13: 978-1-60006-048-9
ISBN-10: 1-60006-048-X
[1. Bands (Music)--Fiction. 2. Rock music--Fiction. 3. Fame--Fiction. 4. Interpersonal relations--Fiction. 5. Christian life--Fiction.] I. Title.
PZ7.P18094Knu 2007
[Fic]--dc22
2007008274

Printed in the United States of America

1 2 3 4 5 6 7 8 9 10 / 10 09 08 07

FOR A FREE CATALOG OF NAVPRESS BOOKS & BIBLE STUDIES,
CALL 1-800-366-7788 (USA) OR 1-800-839-4769 (CANADA).

To JDP,

for teaching me two important skills:

storytelling and harmonizing

CONTENTS

ACKNOWLEDGMENTS

This story is highly personal. I lived many of these episodes, though I've taken a lot of artistic license here in order to present a better overall narrative. (I also left out the very *Spinal Tap* moment when my band appeared on a local morning show as second banana to a gaggle of penguins.)

But because this story is personal, I have a lot of people to thank for helping me get it from my brain onto the pages you hold in your hands. First off: thanks to the *real* Knuckle Sandwich, a hard-core band from New Jersey that graciously let me borrow their name for my fictional group. I've never heard your music, but for this simple act alone, I must tell you: You rock.

Thanks also to my editor Dave Lambert, who did a fantastic job of trimming the fat from my writing and who showed me a thing or two about adverbs.

Thanks to my friend Jeff Gerke for helping me shape the story into something interesting.

Thanks also go in the direction of my friend and agent Jeff

Dunn, who understands the publishing biz in ways I never will. It's nice to have you on my side.

Gallons of thanks to the Brothers Hafer for being hilariously awesome writers in their own right. Your writing excellence challenged me to hammer on this book a little harder.

Many, many thanks to my former bandmates from The Embers, who lived a lot of these stories with me: Ryan Anderson, James McAlister, and Michelle Palmer. It was an honor to share so many stages with you guys, and I hope you don't mind some of the stuff I threw in here. I saved some memories for a future book.

I also must thank the guys from Echobase/Hermit Thrush/RedTwo/RedLeader/RedFive/Tow Truck/Handsome/Whitewash: Sterling Williams and Matt Wright. Some formative times of my life were spent jamming in your respective bedrooms (or attics). Thanks for your friendship, even if we could never decide on a name.

Thanks to all the gang from Adore: Whitney George, Aaron Davis, John Mitchell, and Shane Spicer. Boy, did I ever learn a lot of things about music from playing with you guys. I still use that quarter slide trick to this day.

Tons of thanks to Brian "Head" Welch, for letting me into your world as I worked on your book. I think God set it up, man. I needed to work on your book before I did this one, and it worked out perfectly.

Thanks to everyone in the worship arts at Believer's Church, who are too many to name here. It's a privilege to worship with you, and I look forward to what God has in store.

Thanks also to everyone I played with at Church on the Move and Oneighty, for giving me confidence in my playing abilities.

Thanks also to Danny Borrell and everyone at Faith Center for sowing into my teenage life as much as you did. Thanks for letting me perform my silly songs for the congregation, even when they were tenuously connected to ministry.

Thanks to Mark Keefer, David John, Justin Rice, and everyone else who's been on the button-pushing side of my limited time in recording studios. I never knew there was so much to learn.

Thanks to Mike Flatt and Khalid Winston, for seeing something there to champion, even if we didn't make it big. Thanks also to Tim Cook for giving us a place to play and for encouraging us to add some "soft brass." Sorry that never happened.

Thanks to Dav Steele for the recording studio shop talk. I used it verbatim, bro.

Thanks to Isaac Witty, for being my best friend at a very important time in my life. I couldn't have made it through those turbulent teenage years without our late-night walks in your neighborhood.

Boy, these are really starting to feel like liner notes, aren't they? I'm going to resist the urge to list a bunch of names with inside jokes in parentheses.

Many thanks to everyone who worked with me at Mardel for those six and a half years. Your acquaintance was and is treasured. I hope you guys don't mind me poking a little fun at my time there.

To my extended family of in-laws, the Rutherfords: thanks for all your support, for giving me work in the lean times, and for being such giving people. I'm glad to be a part of your family.

To my mother and stepfather, Carole and Patrick: thanks for the words of encouragement and for reading *Mooch*, though it wasn't really your thing.

To my family: thank you for giving me up for all those nights when I had to work on this book. I pray that God repays you for that time. To Marley, Emma, Noah, Dorothy, and

Sterling: I love you all, and I hope you get a kick out of reading your names in yet another book. To the Bean: you're probably born by now, but as I write this you are but a tiny child in your mother's womb. I hope you didn't cause too much trouble on the way out.

And lastly, to my wife, Michelle, the melody to my harmony: music brought us together, but God keeps us here. Thank you for living so much of this with me and for choosing every day to stick it out. You're my best friend and the greatest singer in the whole wide world—I love you dearly. You . . . are . . . my . . . biggest . . . fan.

PROLOGUE

When the two editors of *Contemporary Christian Rock Music Journal Magazine* fashioned their list of "100 Essential Christian Rock Albums of the 1990s" for a December 1999 cover story, I don't think anyone was surprised at their choices. Sitting at number one was Winnowing Fork's *Thresher*, which everyone assumed, given how many units it sold and how much coverage *CCRMJM* (affectionately referred to in the industry as "Cram-Jam") had given them when *Thresher* was released in 1997.

Just under that was *Armies of Darkness/Armies of Light*, generally considered the best of the five concept albums released in the '90s by industro-goth pioneers Deathlife. The early Christian pop-punk masterpiece, 1994's *Three Nails, Three Chords* from Shetland Barbecue, rounded out the top three.

I remember looking over the list, agreeing with some selections and disagreeing with others. Yes, Cross-Eyed's misguided *Funnel Vision* landed in Cram-Jam's top twenty, which I knew would happen (people love it, I think because of lead singer Jet

Reed's easily accessible—though excruciatingly cheesy—lyrics). They chose Angel Warriors' *Superman-tural* instead of *Piercing through the Devil's Darkness*, which surprised me, as the latter put Angel Warriors on the map, and the former seemed, well, more of a joke.

But when I got to the end, I was curiously disappointed that *A Fistful of Hollers*, the seminal debut recording from Knuckle Sandwich, had been overlooked. I wasn't expecting them at the top—or even the middle, really—but surely their tasty blend of chunky riffs and Matt Ripke's guttural, soaring voice merited a mention in the eighties. Low nineties at the lowest.

When I contacted Cram-Jam's Cincinnati offices and spoke to senior editor Linus Easley, he only clucked his tongue and said, "Yeah, they almost made it. We decided to put AstroHydro-AeroFighter's self-titled album in at a hundred instead."

"But that album just came out two months ago," I said. "And shoegazer's a flash in the pan."

"Yeah, it was more Charlie's deal than mine." He referred to Charlie Change, the *other* editor at Cram-Jam. "He's in a phase right now. Just bought himself some horn rims."

"How trendy."

Linus laughed. "Anyway, I'd say Knuckle would've been 101, if we'd gone that far."

Knuckle Sandwich, at number 101. Almost made it, but not quite. Sounds about right.

Adam Palmer
June 2007

CHAPTER ONE

CAMP LAODICEA HAS BEEN SUFFICIENTLY ROCKED

Jeremiah Springfield's life was completely changed through almost no action of his own.

His father, Bruce Springfield, was a consistently local jazz musician who provided for himself and Jeremiah by playing solo instrumental versions of "Misty," "My Funny Valentine," "It Don't Mean a Thing if It Ain't Got That Swing," and the like on his old-school Gibson hollow-body electric.

Bruce was known around town, and therefore Jeremiah grew up viewing his father as somewhat of a rock star. Everywhere they went together, someone recognized his dad from some gig somewhere, and they'd ask when he was playing next, and where, and whether it was a bar, and, on occasion, why a Christian man like Bruce Springfield would be frequenting a bar.

"Just so you know," Bruce had once told the young Jeremiah, "musicians like me are the only people who have to change their occupation when they get saved."

"What do you mean, Dad?"

Bruce smiled. "Music means different things to different people. To me, it's my job. I love it, and I do what I can to play for the Lord, but I gotta go where the money is." He smoothed down Jeremiah's hair. "Make sense?"

It didn't, but Jeremiah smiled and nodded anyway.

It was perhaps his father's lifestyle of recognition and polite notoriety that impelled Jeremiah on a musical career of his own. That, and an inheritance of his father's sense of humor and love for classic rock.

In the mid-'80s, Jeremiah's dad had often joked that he was one syllable away from having written "Born in the USA." And, early in life, Jeremiah realized that only his father's love for Three Dog Night had prevented him from being named "Buffalo" or "Dusty."

Like most children of musician parents, Jeremiah began learning guitar at an early age but lacked his father's natural affinity for chords. Every step on his own way to rock stardom was a difficult one.

Finally things fell into place for Jeremiah at the age of sixteen. His youth pastor, a progressive fellow who went by just "Darren," pulled Jeremiah's dad aside after church one morning. Jeremiah happened to be standing nearby.

"Bruce, I need your help," Darren said. "The bass player in our youth group's praise-and-worship band is leaving, and I need someone to step in." He adjusted his skinny, neon orange tie. "I know that's not normally your thing, but I'm a little out of options."

Jeremiah's dad put his hands up. "I don't think I can do it, Darren. You know I have a standing gig on Sunday nights."

"Well, what am I supposed to do?"

Both sets of eyes swiveled toward Jeremiah.

"Jeremiah could learn it," his dad said. "What do you think, Jeremiah? Wanna play bass?"

"Sure."

And thus, just like countless other musicians before him, he switched from guitar to bass simply because there was no one else to play the darn thing.

| | | | | |

Jeremiah's teenage years settled into a regular pattern of youth group, school, friends, and girls—not always in that order. On rare occasions, "friends" and "girls" got reversed. Youth group and school were always tops on his agenda, and he excelled at both. He loved playing in the youth-group band, went to every function, wore his Power Band everywhere, and accumulated a drawer full of Witness Wear. At school, he was an honors student who specialized in higher mathematics and British literature. He was, perhaps, the most well-mannered rock 'n' roller in the class of '93.

The only time the pattern broke was summer, when Jeremiah attended the inevitable week or two of church camp, all of which was a grand adventure. For there, in the red Texas dirt of Camp Laodicea in the summer of 1992, Jeremiah came the closest to rock stardom he'd ever been.

"We're first!" Jeremiah's friend Dan—and the lead singer of the Teens Ablaze praise-and-worship band—burst through the door of their starkly lit cabin, the hot Texas sun taking full advantage of the opening and temporarily turning the room into a bunk-bed-filled terrarium.

Jeremiah was sitting on the bottom bunk of the bed he and Dan had claimed earlier that day, unzipping the lid of his somewhere-between-teal-and-turquoise suitcase. "What?" Jeremiah said, stopping in mid-zip.

"Teens Ablaze is playing first this year," Dan said, panting through a mouthful of braces and Wrigley's Doublemint gum (two things his orthodontist found incongruous). He was wearing a generic Oklahoma Sooners cap that had already started forming a distinctive sweat ring.

Every year, the staff at Camp Laodicea asked different youth groups to handle the praise-and-worship portion of the nightly services. And this year, it seemed, Jeremiah's youth group, Teens Ablaze, was on the schedule for the first night, the inaugural outing, the kickoff of the camp experience.

"Dude," Jeremiah said, "we're setting the tone for the whole week!"

"I know!" Dan said, shutting the door and giving the room a reprieve from the direct heat. It did not, however, give the room a reprieve from its distinct odor of Comet and Teenage Boy.

This was an important gig; they would be throwing down the gauntlet to all the other youth group bands: Bring your "A" game or don't bring anything at all.

Of course, the competition was all in good Christian love. There was no prize at stake, no official recognition—only the admiration of your peers, which, to the quasi-nerdy adolescent boys who made up most of the bands there, meant everything.

Jeremiah took it all in. What it all meant. He tried to sum it up in words. "Dude."

"Yeah, dude," Dan said, sitting down on the bunk opposite Jeremiah.

It was the chance to impress girls. Girls from other schools, churches, cities—states, even. Girls who didn't know how dorky the boys really were, who didn't know the countless hours they spent in their bedroom closets practicing arpeggios and diminished sevenths. Girls who had no idea that, for most of these guys, the youth group praise-and-worship band was a welcome distraction from playing "Doctor Who" on flugelhorns while marching at halftime.

No, these girls only saw Summer Camp Musician Guy, and, for one week only, Jeremiah was looked up to.

Not only would Teens Ablaze be the first-strike musical commandos, but his coolness status would be as solidified as the mass of wavy, gelled hair that sat atop his skinny, Shakespeare-filled head.

The *chicas* would know, from day one, that Jeremiah Springfield was the baddest bass player roaming the prayer paths of Camp Laodicea. And summer camp would be rockin'. Thus spake he.

"What should I wear?" Jeremiah said, flipping open the lid of his suitcase to reveal a vast assortment of Christian T-shirts, each with a clever turn of phrase that almost always provoked a laugh or two from his youth pastor.

Jeremiah came with a new set of shirts every summer, and every year he planned on unveiling them slowly, starting off with something innocuous yet hip, like the one that said "Save the Planet" in one style of writing, then with an apostrophe and an "S" and the word "PEOPLE" tacked onto the end in a faux-spray-paint style. It was catchy, humorous, and it tweaked the environmentalists. At least, he thought it would—he didn't actually *know* any environmentalists to tweak.

He held up a shirt with a variation on the popular "Budweiser" bow-tie logo, but this one said, "Hey Bud, Wise Up!" He showed it to Dan. "This one's kinda rebellious. Makes me look like I'm advertising beer."

"Girls like rebellious guys," Dan said. "Remember that one episode of *Star Trek: The Next Generation*?"

"Yeah, that was a good one," Jeremiah said as he kept

flipping through his strictly evangelical wardrobe until he landed on the *piece de resistance*, his most prized apparel possession, one that had cost him twenty bucks last fall when he attended a Cross-Eyed concert at one of the many nondenominational churches that dotted the Tulsa landscape. It was, in fact, a Cross-Eyed T-shirt, a regular work of art that featured the band's trademark riveted-steel cross logo on the front, and all the dates of the "Eyes on the Prize" tour on the back. Jeremiah had practiced pointing out "Tulsa, 11/2/91" (in the second column, third one down) so he could prove that he had indeed been to the show.

He showed it to Dan. "What do you think?" he said.

Dan narrowed his eyes and nodded. "Nice."

"I was kinda saving it for the last day, though." Saving it for the last day was Jeremiah's way of going out on a high note, while still *seeming* flippant about the coolest thing in the world. Because truly cool people don't care about being cool. Right?

But being the first band . . . that was a big deal. It changed everything. Being onstage with this very shirt could cement him as temporary king of coolness all week long! It was a tough decision to make, and not one to take lightly.

"Well," Dan said, "if you want to save it, you could always go with Bart."

Jeremiah flipped through his collection and found a shirt that featured an off-model, copyright-avoiding rendering of Bart Simpson sitting in a pew, head bowed, with "REPENTANT AND PROUD OF IT, MAN" emblazoned in a not-quite-Matt-Groening font above it. It was the perfect mix of hubris and contrition for the occasion.

"Awesome."

After dinner (some sort of Sloppy Joe concoction), Jeremiah, Dan, and the rest of the Teens Ablaze band headed toward a big clearing at the edge of the campground to find the huge, roofed, wall-less structure by the lake where all the campers would be meeting morning and evening over the next week.

The powers-that-be at Camp Laodicea had decided long ago to call this meeting place "the Tabernacle," though it had no ram skins dyed red, nor hides of sea cows, nor acacia wood. No gold inlay anywhere. No goat hair curtains. Instead, it was a lot of concrete foundation, three sections of hard, wooden benches—painted maroon—and a tall, vaulted ceiling that appeared to be made solely of chip-board.

Instead of walls, vertical steel I-beams stood every few feet to support the structure, allowing campers to experience God amidst the wonders of his creation, including but not limited to: sunshine, tender breezes, the rustle of tree leaves, rain, gale-force-wind-borne dust, fresh smells from the lake (June to mid-July), stagnant smells from the lake (mid-July to August), and mosquitoes. It was a mixed bag of creation wonders.

Jeremiah made his way down the aisle of the Tabernacle and approached the stage, a foot-high platform that spanned about two-thirds the width of the structure and that also happened to be the only carpeted area in all of Camp Laodicea. He lifted his bass out of its case and strapped it on—a Peavey T-40 his dad had bought from a friend who'd given up the cash-strapped musician's life to become a realtor.

The beauty of the T-40 is that, while it has a decent tone, it weighs roughly five hundred metric tons. Every time Jeremiah hung it on his shoulder, he felt he was strapping on a redwood forest with four strings. He felt ready to rock. Adding to the weight was a pile of stickers bearing the names of Jeremiah's favorite bands. He'd plastered the stickers all over the guitar's body (taking care not to cover the pickups) and even on the neck (taking care to cut out slots in them to make room for the frets).

Jeremiah looked up to see Dan approaching, artfully tucking and then slightly untucking his crimson Oklahoma Sooners T-shirt as he walked. "You ready to rock tonight?" Dan said.

"You know it, bro."

At showtime, the campers (smelling of roughly equal parts cologne/perfume and insect repellant) filed into the Tabernacle, and soon it was time for Teens Ablaze to burn it up.

And burn they did. They kicked it off with their own reggae version of "Celebrate Jesus, Celebrate," followed by the funk-jam version of "Lord, I Lift Your Name on High" that featured Jeremiah's heavy slap-and-pop capabilities. As usual, Jeremiah took a backseat to the keyboard player (and vocalist) as they moved into the slower portion of their set—what was commonly referred to as the "worship" songs. Nevertheless, Jeremiah did his best to bob his head in time with the whole notes he invariably played on "To Him Who Sits on the Throne" and "There's Something about That Name" and the like.

When their set was over, Jeremiah caught the smiles of a few cute girls in the front row and determined that Camp Laodicea had been sufficiently rocked. He did his best to give a casual nod in the girls' direction, but it came out as more of a tense hiccup. Par for the course, as far as Jeremiah and girls were concerned.

See, the thing is that Jeremiah, while being easygoing and studious and charming in his own musically geeky way, always got a little tense around girls he was interested in. Or perhaps it would be more accurate to say, "girls who showed interest in him." The ones he was interested in always wrote things in his yearbook like, "You're such a great friend!" and "You're so nice—stay that way!" Very few remarks on his cuteness or his astonishing potential as a husband.

But on rare occasions, a girl *would* show interest in Jeremiah, and it was then that he suddenly took on the rigidity of his T-40 and his speech sounded roughly like the ground buzz his bass took on when he accidentally used the bad end of his instrument cable to plug it in.

So: tense hiccup to the young ladies in the front row.

Oh well. At least he had Bart Simpson to do the talking for him.

CHAPTER TWO

THE KID WITH THE WAY-COOLER TALENT

The next night, Jeremiah thought about debuting his Cross-Eyed tee, but decided to hold it in reserve. He didn't want to shoot all his fireworks at once. So he headed to the Tabernacle sporting his Budweiser parody shirt and a cautious, we'll-see attitude. The shirt was for all the other campers; the attitude was for Shekinah Fire, the youth group praise-and-worship band set to lead that night.

Jeremiah spotted Dan in a pew about halfway back and ambled in his direction, plopping next to him. "Man, we rocked the Tabernacle so hard last night," Jeremiah said. "Shekinah Fire has to be feeling pretty shaky, don't you think?"

"It isn't a competition, Jeremiah," Dan said, rolling his eyes.

"Sorry, I can't resist comparing," Jeremiah said, holding up his hands in mock protest. "It's in my blood. I get it from my dad."

"Your dad doesn't think like that."

"Hey, his bio says he's Tulsa's foremost jazz guitarist," Jeremiah said, campers beginning to fill out the pews all around them. "And if you're a guitar player, foremost or not, you compare stuff."

Dan seemed unimpressed. “Maybe.”

“Haven’t you ever heard that old joke? How many guitar players does it take to change a light bulb?”

“No.”

“Ten. One to do it, and nine to say, ‘I could do it better.’”

Dan gave Jeremiah the stink-eye for a half-second, then broke up laughing.

Jeremiah pointed at him with teasing accusation. “See,” he said, “it’s funny ’cause it’s true.”

The conversation was interrupted by a jangly, wimpy “G” chord from a thin-sounding acoustic guitar. Dan whipped his thumb toward the stage. “Well, they’re starting. So I guess we’re about to find out.”

Jeremiah looked at the tiny stage and was immediately relieved at what he saw. Before Shekinah Fire’s band had even struck a note, Jeremiah knew they weren’t going to rock as hard as Teens Ablaze; he could tell by their clothes.

“These guys are wearing way too many button-down shirts and loafers,” Jeremiah said as the band kicked into their own fairly straightforward version of “Celebrate Jesus, Celebrate.”

“Just get into it, man,” Dan said, clapping along. “We’re supposed to be worshipping God, not checking out the band.”

Jeremiah began to clap as well. “You bet,” he said, relaxing enough to get into it. The band wasn’t bad; just not as good as Teens Ablaze.

It dawned on Jeremiah that no one was singing yet. And then it dawned on him that, while everyone in the band had microphones, there was also a mic on a stand, front and center. This filled Jeremiah with unnerving dread.

He pointed it out to Dan. “What’s up with the empty mic? That’s weird.”

“Why?”

"I don't know," Jeremiah said with a shrug of his shoulders. "It just is."

And then, bounding in from God's creation, came a young man with longish black hair, hollering indistinctly. Jeremiah had a difficult time seeing him clearly, and when everyone in front of him threw up their arms to cheer the new arrival, Jeremiah couldn't see him at all.

It wasn't long before the kid had jumped onto the stage and grabbed the empty microphone. "Come on, Camp Laodicea!" he said. "Let's make some noise for JESUS!" He sang the "JESUS!" part, a broad, soaring note that rang clear in the evening air. The campers responded with hefty shouts, much clapping, and a wide variety of "WOOO!" type exclamations.

"I hope you're clapping for the Lord!" the kid said. "It's all his! Praise him, Camp Laodicea!"

The band seemed immediately energized by the kid's coolness. They began to play with more fervor, the keyboard player putting more emphasis on accented notes, the drummer swinging his arms a little more loosely, the bass player adding some passing notes to his lines.

Then the kid began to sing, and Jeremiah's concern over who was more rockin' at Camp Laodicea was renewed with intensity.

The kid was great. He sang with little to no effort, his voice grounded and soaring at the same time. He had an awesome rock growl, but tinged with a little bit of soul. It was simultaneously edgy and tasty, like being punched in the mouth with a fist that had been battered and deep-fried.

Grudgingly, Jeremiah had to admit that Teens Ablaze and Shekinah Fire had played to a draw. While the Teens Ablaze musicians outplayed Shekinah Fire's, there was no denying that Shekinah Fire's singer was far better than Dan.

Jeremiah turned toward Dan, ready to tell him that this upstart kid from Shekinah Fire had nothing on him, when he saw that Dan was getting into the music more than he ever did when he led Teens Ablaze.

"This kid is awesome!" Dan hollered over the noise.

Jeremiah cocked his head, bewildered. "Yeah," he said, "I guess he isn't bad."

"Are you kidding me?" Dan said, clapping along to the beat. "He's intense. You can tell he really *means* it!"

"Don't *you* mean it?"

Dan shrugged. "Yeah, but . . . well, not *that* much," he said without taking his eyes off the stage. Suddenly, he gripped Jeremiah's arm and pointed. "Dude! Check out his shirt!"

Jeremiah stepped out into the aisle to get a better look.

He couldn't believe what he saw.

Cross-Eyed. "Eyes on the Prize."

| | | | | |

"Man, that dude was *awesome*!" Dan said as he and Jeremiah walked back to their cabin after the evening service.

"Yeah, you mentioned that," Jeremiah said, his head hanging like a chagrined Charlie Brown. He booted a small stone he spied in the moonlight. It didn't go far.

"What's the deal with *you*?"

Jeremiah looked up. "Huh?"

"You're so . . . pouty."

"No I'm not!" Jeremiah said, and the second it came out his mouth, he knew it sounded defensive. And pouty. Dangit.

The two walked in silence for a moment, and then Jeremiah said, "Okay, it's just . . . why'd that guy have to be *so* good and, you know, wearing the same shirt as mine?"

Dan stopped walking, so Jeremiah stopped, too.

"What?" Jeremiah said.

"Are you serious?"

"Well . . ." Jeremiah's head drooped again. "Yeah."

Dan chuckled. "That is so . . ." he said, glancing skyward as if trying to read the appropriate word in the stars. Finally, with a laugh, he said: "Stupid."

Jeremiah gave a soft laugh and began walking. "Yeah, I guess you're right."

"You know I'm right. I'm always right."

Jeremiah decided against setting Dan straight on his level of rightness. Instead, he walked on in silence, taking in the ethereal natural beauty of Camp Laodicea at night.

"Yeah, that kid *does* rock," he finally said.

||||||

The next morning, Jeremiah and Dan tracked down the Kid Phenom from Shekinah Fire at breakfast. Surprisingly, he was sitting by himself.

A note about the dining hall at Camp Laodicea: Imagine a large, magnificently cavernous room with splendid accoutrements everywhere and tasteful, indirect lighting in all the right places, making it feel cozy and spacious at the same time, like the dining hall at Hogwart's.

Camp Laodicea's dining hall was the exact opposite of this. It was *just* too small to handle the camper-load that demanded its services, and consequently was always packed with people. To many of those people, the extra personal hygiene that adolescence required was still a foreign concept. Tack onto that the rows of bare tables, the hard plastic benches on either side of them, and the dull fluorescent lighting that added a harsh bluish tint to everything, and you had a setting that matched the camp's food.

So, there sat the Kid, conventionally handsome but with heavy eyebrows, quietly eating a bowl of Crunch Berries—at least, it looked like Crunch Berries in the weird blue lighting—by himself, the rest of his band still in the serving line. The Kid didn't see Jeremiah and Dan as they snaked through the labyrinth of tables to him. Jeremiah did notice the Kid smile through a bite of Berries and nod in the direction of the serving line. Out of curiosity, Jeremiah followed the Kid's look and noticed the girls who'd waved at him, at Jeremiah, two nights before. They were now giggling and casting looks in the Kid's direction. One of them snuck a half-wave at him.

They'd reached the table, and as Jeremiah returned his attention to the mission at hand, Dan was already introducing himself.

"Hi, I'm Dan. From Teens Ablaze." Dan had his right hand extended and practically buried to the knuckles in Crunch Berries.

The Kid put down his spoon and took Dan's hand, shaking it enthusiastically. "Hey, Dan. I'm Matt."

Dan gestured to Jeremiah. "This is Jeremiah. He's our bass player."

Matt reached over and grabbed Jeremiah's hand, which Jeremiah hadn't even realized he'd half-heartedly extended. "Awesome," Matt said. "You're really good, man."

Jeremiah's eyes bounced around the room a bit. He didn't understand enough about his emotions to know, but he was simultaneously embarrassed and flattered. It felt to him like eating Crunch Berries. With milk that was a week past its sell-by date. "Uh, thanks," he said.

Matt motioned toward the benches opposite him. "You guys can sit down, if you want."

Dan practically leapt into the bench and leaned in toward Matt, resting his arms on the table. Jeremiah took a little longer getting himself situated, resting his elbows on the table but hanging back a little.

Matt took a bite of his cereal, looking back and forth at them as he chewed. He swallowed, wiped a dribble of milk from his chin, and said, "What's up?"

"Nothin'," Jeremiah said.

"You're awesome, man, that's what's up!" Dan said. "How'd you get so good?"

Matt gave a small laugh, looking genuinely embarrassed. "Thanks," he said. "I don't know." He pointed toward the ceiling with his plastic spoon. "God, I guess." He put the spoon to his mouth and absentmindedly bit it with his incisors. "I don't know. I just feel it, you know?"

Dan pointed at Jeremiah. "That's what I said to him!" He looked at Jeremiah, his eyes wide as CDs. "Remember, I looked at you and said that he looked like he was *feelin'* it?"

"Yeah," Jeremiah said, backing his head away from Dan's enthusiastic encroachment on his personal space. He caught himself as a memory flashed in his mind. "Actually, I think you said that you could tell he *meant* it."

Dan brushed off the correction. "Same thing." He turned his attention back to Matt. "So, how long have you been singing?"

Matt finished his last bite of cereal as he considered the question. Jeremiah noticed that Matt had the same Crunch Berries-related quirk as he did: He ate all the regular Cap'n Crunch first, saving the berries for last. Jeremiah was just orderly like that. In his mind, the berries had a superior flavor and thus were the last taste he wanted to give himself before finishing breakfast (which ultimately ended, of course, with guzzling the remaining milk from the side of the bowl).

Still crunching, slight bits of berries spritzing from his mouth, Matt answered Dan's question. "Since I was a kid, man. I've only been in the band for a couple months, though."

Dan smacked the table with his open palm. "You're lying, man!" he said with a broad grin.

Matt looked back down at his bowl, shaking his head. "Nah, it's true."

"Really?" Jeremiah asked.

Matt nodded.

Jeremiah wondered if it was true. Matt had looked so natural onstage, so comfortable. Was it possible that he had been doing it for only a couple of months?

Or maybe he really *was* that good. Maybe he was just naturally talented at singing and performing. Gifted, you know? Like how Jeremiah had an innate understanding of sonnets. Except, well, Matt's natural talent was way cooler.

"Dude, I can't believe that!" Dan said.

Matt gave a shrug. "That's just how it is. I guess . . ." He trailed off, narrowing his eyes thoughtfully and looking beyond Jeremiah and Dan, as if searching for a good way to say whatever he was about to say. "I guess God just gave me this gift, you know? And I want to use it for him. I just love to sing songs about God. And to him." He picked up the Styrofoam bowl, put it to his lips, and downed its milky contents. "I just love God."

Jeremiah could tell he meant that, too. Even though he had a droplet of milk running down his narrow chin.

CHAPTER THREE

IN WHICH THE LADS FIND COMMON GROUND

Jeremiah and Dan became fast friends with Matt during the rest of the week. Jeremiah discovered that Matt was a huge Cross-Eyed fan, just like himself. They spent many an afternoon discussing the "Eyes on the Prize" concert tour, as both of them had attended—Jeremiah in Tulsa, Matt in Oklahoma City.

The show had affected them equally in their musical aspirations. Matt had been taken in by Jet Reed's command of the stage and seemingly effortless vocal delivery. Jeremiah had been floored by Lance Stanley's impressive bass amp, one of those big towers of speakers that seemed taller than Stanley himself. And, of course, the sound that came out of it, an intestine-liquefying, round, deep tone that Jeremiah had physically felt in his feet, was something Jeremiah could only dream of. Such earthquake-starting bass was frowned upon at Teens Ablaze, and indeed unachievable on either the church's or Jeremiah's current equipment.

Still, the pair fundamentally agreed on Cross-Eyed's collective awesomeness.

"I just love the lyrics Jet wrote for 'Kill Me,'" Matt said one day as he, Jeremiah, and Dan munched on ice cream cones they'd picked up at the Snak Shak. (Oh, how those missing Cs bugged Jeremiah!) "I mean," Matt continued, "'Annihilate every sinful breath / come on, Lord, put my flesh to death / Spirit won't you come and fill me / I can't truly live until you kill me.' How awesome is that?"

"It's totally stinkin' awesome," Dan said.

Jeremiah frowned. "Dan, you don't really like Cross-Eyed that much."

"I like 'em enough."

"Why are you saying how awesome Jet's words are?"

Dan adopted a very "well, duh" tone to his voice. "'Cause I've never really listened to them before."

Jeremiah shrugged.

Matt licked his ice cream below the rim of the cone. "I tried to talk the Shekinah Fire band into doing that song for praise and worship."

Dan had his CD eyes again. "NO WAY!"

Matt nodded matter-of-factly. "But no one would let me."

"Dude!" Dan said. "Homey don't play dat!"

"You're telling me," Matt said.

Jeremiah decided to inject some much-needed balance into the conversation. "Why wouldn't they do it?"

Matt took a bite of the sugar cone. "I don't know. None of them are really very big fans of Cross-Eyed. Or rock, really. They like mostly lame worship stuff like, um, all that Harvest Gold stuff."

Dan and Jeremiah both recoiled. Harvest Gold was an eleven-piece worship group that featured a lot of soft brass and mellow twelve-string guitar, sort of a combination of big band and Crosby, Stills, and Nash, a comparison Jeremiah was only able to make after a guided tour through his father's vast collection of LPs.

"Yeah," Matt said simply. "So . . ."

"Wow, uphill battle," Jeremiah said. "How did they even let you be in their band?"

"Oh, that's easy," Matt said, grinning. "My dad's the pastor."

Jeremiah and Dan nodded. That solved the mystery, then. Jeremiah hadn't understood how all those preppy guys had allowed a cool rocker like Matt in their band. Shekinah Fire was a big youth group, and their church was big, too—there had to have been a singer who was more along the lines of the rest of the guys in the band *somewhere* in the church.

Yes, youth-group praise-and-worship personnel are volunteers, and yes, usually the praise-and-worship leader generally takes whomever he can get to play. Jeremiah had figured that, with Shekinah Fire, Matt had been the main guy and had assembled his band out of whoever was available. To hear that the band had already existed, and that Matt was toiling away with these square dudes at the behest of his father—well, it made Matt somehow even cooler.

Dan must've been thinking the same thing. "Man, I'm sorry you got stuck with such a lame band. Why'd your dad put you in, anyway?"

"I asked him if I could find a place to sing for God somewhere," Matt said. "I don't know—I just love to worship God, guys."

"Yeah, me too," Dan said, enthusiastically.

"Same," Jeremiah said, attempting to match Dan's enthusiasm.

It was true, to a degree. Jeremiah did love playing music, and he especially loved playing in Teens Ablaze, so that meant he loved to worship God, right? Of course, if he was honest with himself, he knew that it wasn't really worship he was after—it was fun. And maybe a few smiles from the cuter girls in youth group.

Not that he didn't love God. He did, intellectually. Jeremiah had grown up in church—he had all the Christian stuff down pat. He knew what the Bible said (mostly). He knew all the right things to say to everyone, and he knew the right shirts to wear and all that stuff. He knew *about* God.

But did he *know* God?

Sure. Why not?

Here's what Jeremiah knew: Shakespeare, math, and how to play music. Those were things upon which he had a firm grip. God, girls, grownups—these were concepts in which he had varying degrees of confidence.

Dan was definitely farther down the "I just love to worship God" road than Jeremiah. His exuberance over Matt's statement was genuine. On this particular journey, Jeremiah considered himself driving more on the "I love to play music in a worship band" frontage road, which ran parallel to Dan's "I love God" highway. For now, anyway.

But where Dan had a passion for God, Matt seemed to have a passion for God *and* the stage presence to showcase it. He was a nuclear warhead on stage; Dan was a car with no wheels: He had the passion, but not enough talent to make that passion go anywhere.

Jeremiah blinked out of his reverie; Dan and Matt were conversing excitedly about different worship songs. As he looked at the two of them, he allowed his mind to wander just once more.

Maybe he could be in a band with Matt one day.

Nah. Never happen.

||||||

As always, summer camp was over seemingly before it began. A week was never long enough. Soon, claps on the back were being given (boys), tears were being shed (girls), promises to keep in touch were made with every intention of keeping them (boys and girls), and promises to keep in touch were made with the realization that they most likely wouldn't be kept (camp staff).

Jeremiah, Dan, and Matt said their good-byes early that last day. They met for breakfast (the dining hall always went gonzo on the last morning and served powdered eggs, floppy bacon, flavorless biscuits, *and* flour-heavy gravy—it was a veritable feast), then shared one last moment of solidarity next to the Teens Ablaze van, the standard sixteen-passenger number with a white, die-cut vinyl sticker on the side window featuring the words "Teens Ablaze" in a ten-inch-tall, youth-friendly font.

"All right, dudes, I gotta head over to the Shekinah Fire van," Matt said, checking his wristwatch. "We're supposed to leave in ten minutes."

"All right, man," Jeremiah and Dan said simultaneously.

Matt gave them each that handshake where you shake the hand, then pull the other person in for a quick clap on the back before releasing just as quickly. He looked intently at each of them, then said, "You guys mind if we pray real quick?"

Dan and Jeremiah looked at each other. Dan's eyes were saying "Yes!" Jeremiah was fairly certain his eyes were saying, "Uh—sure . . ."

"Yes!" Dan said.

"Okay," Jeremiah said.

"Great," Matt said. He placed one hand on Jeremiah's shoulder and one on Dan's, then bowed his head slightly, closing his eyes on the way down. "Heavenly Father, I pray for my brothers from Tulsa here. I pray, God, that you'll give them a safe trip home, bless them with traveling mercies all the way back to Oklahoma. Bless them as they enter their senior year in high school. And God, I just pray that you'll show yourself to Jeremiah and Dan, show them how much you love them, and how much you care for them, and how much they rock. Thank you for their musical talents, God. I pray they'll always use them for you. Amen."

Wow. Jeremiah was surprised that such a heavy prayer had come out of his new friend. Here's something that *didn't* surprise him, though: how quickly Dan responded with a prayer of his own.

"Dear Jesus, thank you for our new friend Matt. I pray that you'll also be with him and his crew as they head back to OKC, and that you'll just bless him in that band, God. Thanks for giving him a way to sing for you, and I pray that you'll just give him bigger and bigger platforms to sing on. Amen."

When he looked up, Jeremiah could have sworn Matt's eyes were a little misty. "Thanks, man," he said to Dan. Then, to Jeremiah, "Both of you."

"You're welcome," Jeremiah said quietly.

Matt's hands were still on their shoulders. He gave them both a squeeze, then dropped his arms back to their sides. He gestured toward the Shekinah Fire van (sixteen-passenger, vinyl sticker, etc.). "I better get going." He headed off toward his fellow Shekinah-ites.

"Take it easy," Jeremiah said.

Matt turned around and kept walking backward. "You, too. Both of you." He waved one last time and turned to face forward, never breaking stride.

Dan was watching Matt leave with an unmistakably bummed look on his face. Jeremiah gave him a playful smack on the chest. "Come on, dude," he said, "let's mount up. We got a long van ride ahead of us."

The two climbed into the van.

It was the last time Jeremiah would ever see Camp Laodicea. But it certainly wasn't the last time he would think about it.

||||||

Jeremiah and Dan had the typical camper's disease when they got back to Tulsa. And the name of that disease is Good Intentions.

They had every intention of keeping up with Matt. After all, he was only in Oklahoma City, a mere ninety miles down the turnpike. And yet—ninety miles might as well be a thousand when you're in your senior year, a distinction that applied to both Jeremiah and Dan.

Though they went to different schools—Jeremiah to the well-endowed public Union High School and Dan to the small private Victory Christian School—the pair was nearly inseparable. Sundays were for church (and football at Jeremiah's or Dan's house afterward). So were Sunday nights. Tuesday nights were for band rehearsal, which usually featured a lot of lounging around, chatting, jamming, and general tomfoolery until late into the evening.

Wednesday nights were for youth group, when the Teens Ablaze band would channel all their previous night's lounging around, chatting, jamming, and general tomfoolery into a loose mélange that resembled a praise-and-worship set. Fortunately, the members of the band were talented enough to stay on track in a listenable groove.

And oh yeah—the kids could worship to it, too.

There were regular youth group functions (pool parties, volleyball tournaments, laser tag, miniature golf, etc.) on almost every Friday or Saturday. And of course, there were plenty of movies to be attended, for what good is a teenager if he does not have an accurate critique of the latest display of flashing lights currently being shown at the cinema? And wasn't there some Sega Genesis hockey needing to be played somewhere?

After all the socializing came schoolwork. Jeremiah was perplexed by his schedule that fall, unsure whether to be happy or angry. He had a solid block of coast-able classes: Computer Application (typing, basically, except on a computer), Accounting (addition and subtraction—kids' stuff), then lunch, then he was an aide for his French teacher's French I class (grading papers, chatting with the cute sophomore girl who sat next to him), then French IV (he knew the basics of the language already; it was basically just memorizing new verbs).

Easy.

Except that easy day was bookended by horrific, horrific classes. He began the day with AP Calculus and ended it with AP English. And though he was good at those two subjects, he still hated their labor-intensive nature—there was homework aplenty, and not enough time during his fluff classes to do it.

All this to say: Jeremiah was a busy guy, and Dan's schedule was just as bad.

There just wasn't time to correspond with some kid a thousand miles down the turnpike.

CHAPTER FOUR

FATE BUYS A CD

And that's how Jeremiah completely forgot about Matthew Ripke until the following fall. Graduation had been fun, though Jeremiah had attended roughly five hundred thousand graduation-related events at church, school, and home. By the time graduation actually rolled around, he was a little partied out.

The notable thing about graduation, though, was the scholarship he received to attend Oral Roberts University, a private Christian university located right smack dab in the heart of south Tulsa, where Jeremiah already lived. He had applied for scholarships at other schools in the area and some state schools farther away, but Jeremiah's heart leapt at the scholarship he received from ORU for one simple reason: He did not want to leave Tulsa.

He was so involved in his church that he didn't want to go anywhere else—and, frankly, he liked living at home. He wasn't even going to live on campus—he would commute every day. It would be like he was still in high school! Just . . . harder.

Dan, on the other hand, had decided to join the ranks of the nine zillion people who attend The University of Oklahoma, a gi-normous state school in Norman. The intriguing thing was that Norman was only a few short miles from Oklahoma City, and so whenever Jeremiah and Dan spoke of Dan's impending departure for OU (why not U of O, or simply UO? Ask the University of Oregon), they thought fondly of Matt, and even hoped among themselves that Dan might run into him while living so near.

OU was renowned for its football-factory program; perhaps Matt would be one of the 90,000 fans in attendance seven times a year? Or perhaps Dan and Matt would run into each other at some hip, trendy something-or-other that college students did. Why, Matt might even attend OU himself, if he, like Jeremiah, wanted to stick close to home.

Why these thoughts never turned into an actual seeking-out of Matt to determine his plans, no one will ever know. Neither Jeremiah nor Dan ever thought of it.

| | | | | |

Jeremiah and Dan and their circle of youth group friends spent most of the summer together, hanging out at each other's houses, or going to movies, or eating out, or—well, that was pretty much all Tulsa had to offer the bright, upstanding Christian teen of the early '90s.

Dan's school started classes earlier than Jeremiah's, so on Dan's last night in Tulsa, the friends stayed up late, lying on the huge trampoline in Dan's backyard, staring at the stars and talking about college.

"You're so lucky," Jeremiah said.

"Why's that?"

"Going out of town with that full ride. That's pretty sweet."

Jeremiah heard the smile in Dan's voice. "It ain't bad. I still have to work on campus, though."

"I guess."

"Gotta do something to afford books and all that," Dan said.

"You have to buy your own books? They don't just give them to you?"

"No way, man," Dan said. "You gotta buy everything. Books. Parking sticker. All that kind of stuff."

Jeremiah stared at the moon as a wispy cirrus cloud passed in front of it. "What about all those late-night study sessions with, like, coffee and pizza and stuff?"

Dan chuckled. "I'm pretty sure I'm on the hook for that, too."

Jeremiah's entire concept of college life came from movies and television, and he'd pretty much chucked all the parts that dealt with bad-boy fraternity behavior. This left him with strong notions of all-nighters, stuck-up professors, and their occasional hearts-on-their-sleeve counterparts who went to extraordinarily dramatic lengths to teach poetry or some other artistic subject to a bunch of dullards.

"So if Robin Williams tells me to rip the introduction out of my textbook, I gotta pay for that?"

Dan turned his head to look at Jeremiah. "Dude, that was prep school, not college."

Jeremiah shook his head. "All the college stuff looks free in the movies."

"It isn't."

"Well, I guess since you're taking off tomorrow, I'm gonna have to find something to do," Jeremiah said, crossing his arms, mentally connecting stars like a dot-to-dot, trying to find new constellations. "Probably need to get a job."

"It's about time, you slacker."

Jeremiah thought he might have found a constellation he would call the Big Mac. "But what should I do? I don't want to work in the burgeoning supermarket or fast-food fields."

"My mom and dad always tell me to do what I love. That's why I'm going to major in music."

"Hmm . . ." If only that one star wasn't so out of place, Jeremiah would've found the Mug. "I guess that means I need to play bass somewhere. Maybe for my dad?"

"You aren't old enough to play in bars, bro."

"Yeah." Just discovered: The Pudgy Abraham Lincoln Head. Jeremiah should be writing these down.

"You like Christian music," Dan said. "Why don't you go apply at the Armory?"

Jeremiah forgot all about his dot-to-dot game and sat bolt upright, which is much harder to do on a trampoline than it sounds. "That's a great idea!"

||||||

The Armory was the Christian bookstore down the street from Jeremiah's house, a place he had frequented since he was a little boy. Tucked away in the corner of one of Tulsa's many strip malls, it was actually a fairly gargantuan place: 19,000 square feet of nothing but Christian products. Bibles, books, Bible reference books, books about the Bible, Precious Moments figurines, Christian art, Christian jewelry, Christian apparel—if it was a retail product and it could have the word "Christian" as an adjective, it was probably available at the Armory.

But Jeremiah didn't care about any of that stuff (although he did love to walk into the Bible section, open up a Dake's Annotated with a genuine leather cover, and take a big whiff). No, as soon as he was done satiating his olfactory glands' craving for tanned cowhide, he would make a beeline for the ultimate section: music.

For it was here, amidst the tapes and CDs, that Jeremiah felt at home. Having a music-infused lineage, Jeremiah felt as though he shared a bond with these artists who had all achieved the notable success of actually being *paid* to record their music. Their stuff was good enough to turn a profit!

It was here that Jeremiah had discovered the music that had set him free as a lad in the '80s: heavy rock 'n' roll that wasn't about drugs or chicks or warriors of the night or any of the nonsense that plagued the hairsprayed, guitar-lick-driven music scene of the time. Instead, Jeremiah found bands like Krystian, Rokken, and Sacred Soldier—bands who weren't afraid to wrangle on the spandex, bust out the Aqua Net, accessorize heavily, and rock for the Rock.

A few years later, around the dawn of the '90s, when the rest of the music world had moved on from its infatuation with eye-linered, bad-boy rock stars and begun idolizing eye-linered, bad-boy pop stars, Jeremiah had also grown weary of the falsetto wailing and anthemic group vocals and began to yearn for rock music that knocked away pretense and just plain *rocked*.

He found it in the listening section of the music department of the Armory in early '91. The listening section was his favorite place. He loved to try out new stuff, to listen to something just because he had never heard it before. He had no expectations, no reason to be disappointed. The music was simply unique to his ear, and he had a wide palate of appreciation—mainly because he was still too young to know good music from bad.

The listening section also provided a certain risky, gambling type of atmosphere. A tape rack was mounted on the wall, one of those wooden, fiber-board numbers with individual slots for cassettes to slide into. Customers were free to select a tape and listen to it at one of the three machines provided, deciding whether they liked it before they bought the real thing. It was the Armory's way of protecting themselves from returned product—after all, you never knew *what* was going to offend some Christians. Better to be safe and let the customer listen first; then the store clerks could argue with customers about an album's Christian merits *before* the person bought it—the arguments seemed to carry more weight when the customer wasn't also demanding a refund.

The listening section was also smack against Jeremiah's other favorite part of the Armory: the Christian T-shirt department, a little cul-de-sac of racks that featured all the latest Christian T-shirts, as well as a hand-lettered banner above them encouraging shoppers to "Wear You're Witness!"

Jeremiah had caught the grammar error around the time he was in the fourth grade.

It was never fixed.

Regardless, Jeremiah still loved the rack at the listening station because it never looked the same way twice. Sometimes it would have new tapes in it for him to check out; other times it would be the same selection as last time, just rearranged one at a time by hundreds of customers over the past few weeks since Jeremiah had last been there.

The summer before his sophomore year, Jeremiah had noticed in the tape rack a tape he hadn't seen before. The cover featured a blue, swirling vortex of some sort of wispy gas—smoke, or clouds, or something—and at the center was a riveted steel cross.

The band was Cross-Eyed. This was their debut album, *Funnel Vision*.

Though the cassette players at the Armory were perennially plagued with crummy headphones that would play out of only one side, Jeremiah was still moved by the initial crunch of the guitar, the depth and immediacy of the bass. It sounded more raw than anything he had ever heard.

And then—the singing. It wasn't the wailing falsetto he was used to. He—he couldn't describe it. In later years, he would say that the voice was "earthier" and "authentic," but at the time, it just blew his mind.

Cross-Eyed scratched Jeremiah's musical itch, and, as the first song ended, he let the tape play on to the second song. And then the third. And the fourth.

He was snapped out of his reverie by a tap on his shoulder. Dad.

"Jeremiah," he said, "what are you doing? I've been looking all over for you."

Jeremiah knew this wasn't exactly the truth, because Dad always found him in the same place.

"I've been right here, Dad."

"Well, I'm done looking around," he said, snatching the headphones from Jeremiah's head and laying them on top of the well-used cassette player. "Let's go."

Jeremiah hopped up from the stool he'd been sitting on, raced toward a nearby shelf, and seized a *Funnel Vision* cassette bearing a large, yellow, sunburst-edged sticker shouting a sale price of $6.99. He showed it to his father. "I'm gonna get this."

"Do you have any money?"

"I'll pay you back."

His dad shook his head. "I don't think so." He took the tape from Jeremiah and set it down on a nearby shelf. "I'm not shelling out for another tape. You have more than you listen to as it is."

Jeremiah picked the tape back up. "It's on sale, Dad. That isn't going to last forever." He showed his father the sticker. "And my tapes take up way less room than all your records."

Jeremiah's dad pondered it for a second, looking back and forth between Jeremiah and the tape. Finally, he took the tape from him and used the corner of it to point mock-threateningly at his son's chest.

"Fine, I'll get it. But you're mowing the lawn the second we get home."

Jeremiah beamed. "Great! That'll give me a chance to listen to it on my Walkman."

His father headed toward the register. "Oh, like you won't put it in your Walkman the second we get to the car."

Jeremiah smiled and hurried after him.

His dad was right, too. He would have that tape unwrapped before they got out of the store.

||||||

The morning after Dan suggested it, Jeremiah headed over to the Armory, filled out the requisite form, and asked to speak to the manager, Betty, with whom he was already on a first-name basis.

Betty strolled up to the registers, her late-middle-age self topped by a large round head of blonde hair and built upon a foundation of black orthopedic shoes, with a plain brown dress in between. "Hi, Jeremiah," she said, holding out her hand in greeting. "Let me see that." She pointed at his application form. She donned a pair of ornate glasses hanging by a beaded chain around her neck and took a cursory glance at it. "Going to ORU?" she said.

"Yes, ma'am."

"I saw your dad the other day," she said, without looking up from the form. "He played a concert at Rick's."

Jeremiah's attention began to wander. He looked longingly toward the music department. "Yeah, he plays a lot."

“He’s very talented. My husband just adored him.”

Jeremiah wondered if he would be allowed to take home the demos overnight, listen to them in his car or something, if he got the job. “Mm-hmm.”

Betty put down the application, took off her glasses, and looked at Jeremiah. “Well, our immediate need is at the cash register.”

That wasn’t optimal. “Oh yeah?”

“Yes,” she said. “But you do get a . . .” And then she said three magical words.

Twenty Percent Discount.

“I’ll take it!”

Jeremiah began his job the next day. The register system took a bit of getting used to (the lack of a backspace key on the register frustrated him — if he entered a price wrong, he had to hit clear and start over), so his line frequently backed up.

He was just packing one customer’s purchases into a plastic bag when he spotted something moving. He glanced down and saw that the object was a CD, spinning across the counter, coming to rest right in front of him. The cover was an aerial view of a helicopter with the rotors replaced by a riveted-steel cross. It was the newest Cross-Eyed album, *Rotormouth*, their third album in as many years (*Eyes on the Prize* had been released on the heels of *Funnel Vision*). It had come out the previous Tuesday, and Jeremiah already had most of it memorized.

He took in all this information in an instant, all while hearing a familiar voice speak to him.

“I hear it rocks,” the voice said.

Jeremiah looked up to see Matt Ripke, standing in line, money in hand.

He smiled. Matt smiled back.

Jeremiah immediately took Matt’s hand in that strictly guy, fist-clamp way, like they were about to arm-wrestle. He pulled him in for a quick half-hug and clap on the back. "Dude! What are you doing here?"

Matt clapped him back. "I'm just getting ready for school, dude."

"Really? What're you doing in Tulsa to get ready for OU?"

Matt let out a bewildered but easygoing grunt. "OU? What makes you think I'm going there?"

Jeremiah remembered that there was a CD purchase transaction to make and started punching the appropriate keys to make it happen. "Oh, Dan and I figured you'd go there, since you live in OKC."

Matt laid his money on the counter. "Nah, man. My dad wanted me to go to ORU. He went there, so I got a good scholarship."

Jeremiah froze just as he punched the "AT/TL" button (the one that made the cash drawer pop open after tallying a sale). The drawer sprang open and smacked him in the upper thigh. He turned slowly to look at Matt. "Seriously?"

Matt nodded.

Jeremiah broke into a wide grin. "Me, too, man!"

"No way!"

Jeremiah kept grinning as he nodded his head. "Yeah, dude. Yeah."

The linguistic conference was interrupted by a pleasant, heavily made-up woman standing in line behind Matt. She didn't say anything, but began edging her shopping cart closer to Matt to the point of touching him (yes, the Armory was large enough to merit shopping carts—a true anomaly in most Christian bookstores). She leaned well over the cart and began emptying its contents onto Jeremiah's counter. Matt scooted down the counter. "So, you living on campus or what?" he asked.

Jeremiah shook his head as he began ringing up the pushy-yet-pleasant woman's purchases (a parade of Christian self-help books and a brick of Chick tracts). "Nah, I'm staying home for now. I have a scholarship, but it's not huge, so I figured I could save some money."

"That's cool. I'm in EMR."

Jeremiah knew each of those letters, but had no meaning of them in that order. Should he know what EMR meant? Was he already behind the curve in his collegiate years, though they had not officially started yet? Should he ask Matt for clarification, or would that not be cool?

"Oh, my husband lived in EMR when he went to school there," the pushy-yet-pleasant woman said. "That's the best dorm on campus."

Okay, that answers *that* question.

"That's what I hear," Matt said to her, smiling. "My dad gave me the rundown."

Jeremiah finished ringing up the woman's purchases. "$67.42," he announced. She fumbled in her purse.

"What are you doing in Tulsa already?" he asked Matt. "School doesn't start for another couple weeks."

Matt shrugged his shoulders. "Yeah, I know, but OKC was getting boring, so I came up early to learn the campus a little, find my way around. Maybe find a good church."

Jeremiah accepted the woman's debit card and slid it through the machine next to the cash register. "You should come out to my church," Jeremiah said. "We're actually starting a new college-and-career ministry because so many of us that were in the youth group aren't in youth group anymore."

Matt held his CD to his mouth in contemplation while Jeremiah started bagging the pushy-yet-pleasant woman's purchases. "Yeah, man. I think I will," he said.

Jeremiah looked at Matt as he handed the woman her bag of books. "Cool."

"Thank you," said the woman, heading toward the door.

"You're welcome," said Jeremiah.

Matt gestured after the woman with his thumb. "I should probably get going, too."

"Right on."

"What time you get off? You wanna hang out after work or something?"

"Sure thing, man," Jeremiah said, nodding. "I get out of here at eight."

"Cool," Matt said as he unwrapped his CD. "I'll swing by around then." He offered the wrap to Jeremiah.

"Right on," Jeremiah said as he took the wrap from Matt and discarded it in the wastepaper basket underneath the counter.

Matt gestured toward the door again, this time with the CD. "All right, I'm out. See you at eight!"

CHAPTER FIVE

JEREMIAH CUTS A RUG—IN THE SHAPE OF A GIRL

Jeremiah didn't understand exactly why the Armory was open until eight in the evening. From what he could tell, business didn't exactly boom from about six thirty on. He counted the number of customers he checked out over the last half-hour of his shift, and even counting the little girl who bought a pack of Breath of Heaven mints ("Free from Sinnamon" flavor) after her mom went through the line, he was at precisely seven.

Seven customers.

It would've been okay if he could have stayed in the music department, among the tapes and CDs he adored, but he was stranded at the register with no reprieve. He couldn't desert his post; that would've been unthinkable to an upstanding young man like himself.

Well, at least until he'd been working there a little longer.

Time marched on at its usual precise rate, despite Jeremiah's dragging feelings, and at 7:55, Matt marched through the door, just as promised.

"Dude, that CD *does* rock." Matt said, striding in and hopping up to sit down on Jeremiah's counter in one smooth move.

"I know," Jeremiah said.

"I've already listened to it three times."

"I think I listened to it, like, five or six times the first day I bought it."

Matt clucked his tongue. "Day ain't over yet, bro."

Jeremiah chuckled as he pulled a big, blue bag made of heavy vinyl out from under his register. "Sit tight for a second. I gotta do some stuff to close up."

Moments later, the pair of teenagers stood on the sidewalk in front of the strip mall.

"Your car or mine?" Jeremiah said.

"Let's take mine," Matt said, gesturing toward the only car parked near the store.

"A Camaro, huh?" Jeremiah said.

"Yep."

Jeremiah bent to look in the window. The car was maroon, complete with gray leather interior, a half-yellow/half-white graduation tassel dangling from the rearview mirror, a kickin' CD player, and a black metal grille in the back window.

"Graduation present," Matt said. "I don't really like it, but . . . hey, free car, you know?"

He gestured for Jeremiah to get in, which Jeremiah did, swinging open the heavy door, one of only two on the '94 Camaro. He plopped into the deep bucket seat, swung the door shut, and found himself ensconced in fine, American-made luxury.

Matt started the car, the engine roaring to life a split-second before his kickin' CD player did. The new Cross-Eyed blared from the speakers in pristine tones, the bass grooves assaulting Jeremiah's chest like a heart attack, or one of those goopy movie aliens.

"'Molasses for the Masses,'" Jeremiah said, hollering over the din of the perfectly reproduced rock anthem. "I love this song."

"Yeah, it's cool," Matt hollered back. "Is it about the media?"

"Something like that."

"Cool."

The two sat there, taking in the music for a minute or two before Matt turned the stereo down and said, "So where we headed, homey?"

"Man, I don't know."

"Well, I don't either. I'm new around here, remember?"

Jeremiah thought for a moment before actually snapping his fingers at the bright idea that popped into his head. "I know! There's this Christian dance club right out by the school."

"Christian dance club?"

"Yeah, it's pretty cool."

Matt let out a slight chuckle from the side of his mouth. "Man, we don't have anything like that in OKC."

"Welcome to Tulsa," Jeremiah said. "There's a Christian everything. If you don't want to go to that dance club, there's a church over on 21st that shows Christian movies every Friday night. It's only two bucks." He narrowed his eyes. "Of course, they only show those end-times movies from the '70s. Every week it's some variation on someone getting left behind." He paused, then grinned. "There's a better chance of girls at the dance club."

Matt nodded. "Dance club it is."

| | | | | |

Club David was in full swing when Jeremiah and Matt arrived. Yet another Christian service business tucked into a corner of a

Tulsa strip mall, Club David was a seemingly happening place, even though it was a barely renovated version of the instructional dance studio that had occupied the space six months earlier. The floor-to-ceiling mirrors along the far wall were still in place, but most of the flooring in the one-room cotillion now had gray industrial carpet.

The owners of Club David strove for an authentic club atmosphere, with patchy lighting illuminating the non-dance-floor areas and a fruit salad of intelligent lighting illuminating the wooden dance floor, a slightly raised parquet number that occupied a fifteen-by-fifteen foot corner of the club. There were colors everywhere, all roving and moving in time with the pounding beat of Zippo, one of the handful or so of Christian "dance" acts with CDs out at the time. Jeremiah had checked them out once; they were far from rocking, but he dug the animalistic nature of the music.

Of course, since he had never been in an authentic club, Jeremiah could only assume that this was a relatively smart copy of it, just without the cigarette smoke and alcohol he figured pervaded those places. But if the setup was similar to a secular club, the clientele was not, mainly because there was hardly any clientele there. A quick glance around the room (which didn't take long) noted only the DJ in his raised booth next to the dance floor, a trio of what looked like junior-high boys huddled around one of the small café tables that lined the near wall, a guy in his mid-thirties with a shock of spiky hair and an Adidas track suit of indeterminate color (Red? Dark blue? Black? It was hard to tell in the dim light) pacing back and forth between the DJ booth and the dance floor, his head cocked to one angle as though he was listening intently to the music, and . . .

Two girls.

Who looked to be about the same age as Jeremiah and Matt.

Score.

Jeremiah turned toward Matt, who was already looking directly at the girls. "Nice place," Matt said.

"You ever been dancing before?" Jeremiah said over the pulsing of the music.

"No. You?"

"A couple times. I suck, but it's fun."

Matt turned to look at him. "Well, let's hit it, then."

A few steps brought them to the dance floor, but before they actually stepped up to the parquet, they were met by the man in the track suit, who had his hand extended for a shake.

"Muh mee mee meh meh!" he said as he shook Matt's hand, then Jeremiah's. Jeremiah couldn't understand a word of it over the ear-splitting levels of Zippo now assaulting him.

Apparently Matt couldn't either. "What?" he yelled.

Track Suit Man leaned closer to them. "Good! Evening! Gentlemen!" He gave them a broad smile and then held up his hand, four fingers extended upward. "Cover charge!"

Ah. Jeremiah fished in his pockets and brought out a five-dollar bill, and saw Matt do the same. They each handed their cash over to the man, who in turn fished in *his* pockets to produce a damp, wadded single for each of them. "Have fun!" he said, patting Jeremiah on the shoulder.

Matt and Jeremiah stepped up onto the floor, where the girls had retreated to the far corner. They were both cute, but in different ways. One was a tallish, round-faced blonde with shoulder-length hair, horn-rimmed glasses, and the modest, denim-driven attire of a good Christian girl. The other was a shorter brunette, more bookish, with sharp features, huge eyes, and a largely thrift-store-based wardrobe. They weren't exactly dancing as much as swaying, the brunette air-drumming to the beat, rapping her hands on her thighs in time with the music, tapping her heel on the floor in sync with the bass drum on the soundtrack. Other than that, the two of them were whispering into each other's ears, and giggling.

Oh, and they were stealing glances at the boys.

Jeremiah's heart went crazy. He liked girls, but he hated it when they whispered about him. He hated it even more when they giggled. He always assumed they were giggling in an "Ohmigosh, who does he think he's kidding?" sort of way, like they saw through his façade of coolness into the nerd he knew he really was. Jeremiah began to slow his walk, thinking maybe this wasn't the best time to meet new friends.

But Matt continued undaunted, forcing Jeremiah to keep up. The last thing he wanted was to be stranded on the floor without any friends at all. He may have *felt* like a loser, but he didn't want to *look* like one.

The Zippo song came to its pounding conclusion and the DJ skillfully cross-faded to a synthetically peppy, high-BPM number from a group Jeremiah recognized as Tribe of Benjamin.

Matt offered a casual wave to the girls as he nodded his head to the beat. He began to step in time to the music, gyrating his shoulders slightly and resembling, to a degree, a Rock 'Em Sock 'Em Robot. He maneuvered himself toward the girls, who, having retreated as far into the corner as they could, smiled. The dark-haired one waved back and, seemingly, decided to take Matt up on whatever nonverbal offer he had just extended.

Jeremiah didn't understand girls at all.

Matt and the dark-haired girl began conversing as well as they could. Jeremiah could hear the sharp intonations of voices raised over Tribe of Benjamin, but he couldn't make out what they were saying to each other. He hung back for a minute more, then decided to throw caution to the wind and at least attempt to move to the music.

It was a pitiful display. Rhythmic though he was, Jeremiah was completely out of his element. If he was onstage, with a bass wrapped around his neck, a drummer at his side, playing a song he knew, he could come uncoiled with the best of them. But here, under scrutiny by attractive members of the opposite sex, in his work clothes, with a style of music he wasn't used to—it was tough.

Still, he decided to give it a whirl and opened up with a few mild breakdancing moves he'd had tucked in his back pocket since fourth grade. First came the wave, then a bit of moonwalk, though that was a challenge, what with the grip of his rubber-soled sneakers on the floor. Before he knew it, he was standing very near the blonde girl. Whether he'd maneuvered to her, or she'd maneuvered to him, or they'd maneuvered to each other, he couldn't tell.

She bobbed her head and nodded at him . . . approvingly? Could this be possible? A girl, looking at him with approval? And since he was on the dance floor, his normal tense hiccup behavior around girls was gone, already removed by the liquidity of his limbs. He felt like a new him.

He nodded back and leaned in to speak. "Hi!"

She smiled.

She smiled!

"Hi!" she said back, her husky voice barely intelligible over the steady jackhammer of Tribe of Benjamin.

Okay, so Jeremiah had made initial contact, and now he wasn't sure where to go. It wasn't like they could have a decent, get-to-know-you conversation there on the dance floor.

"I'm Jeremiah!"

"Amanda!" she said, extending her hand princess-style (palm down, as if Jeremiah was a Knight of the Realm who was expected to revel in the honor of kissing her signet ring).

As there was no signet ring to kiss, Jeremiah simply slipped his hand into hers, tilted upward ninety degrees, and gave it a little shake. Just the skin-on-skin contact alone was worth his four bucks. If he was suddenly dragged out of Club David by Track Suit Man, he would have considered it an evening well spent.

He then realized he was still holding her hand. He gave a shy smile, which she returned, and then let go.

Um. Okay. What now?

He checked Matt, who was having a laughing fit with the other girl. She was leaning well into him, her hand on his shoulder, her other hand covering her mouth as she laughed. The intelligent lights played off her long, straight hair and made her look almost saintly.

Jeremiah turned his attention back to Amanda, who was standing underneath a yellow-gelled light that gave her blonde hair a halo, a downright angelic glow. It also reflected in her glasses whenever her head bobbed up, giving her two mini-suns for eyes with every beat of the music.

The lights swung away from direct, overhead illumination, and a second beam shone on her from a distance, casting her jean jacket in a warm red glow. Something glistened from the lapel and caught Jeremiah's eye. He leaned in for a closer look.

It was a pin. In the shape of a riveted steel cross.

He pointed, making sure to keep his hand a good distance from her whole upper-body area. "Cross-Eyed?" he said, raising his eyebrows high to make sure she understood that it was a question.

Her eyes lit up (well, as near as he could tell: The intellibeams had swung upward and were now making her eyes minisuns again), and she nodded furiously. "Yeah!"

Rock on.

CHAPTER SIX

PRODUCTIVE SHENANIGANS

The four of them headed to a nearby IHOP half an hour later, tired of the relentless beating their eardrums were taking and of the hoarseness creeping into each of their voices from shouted conversations. Also, Track Suit Man was his own brand of creepy, hanging around by the DJ booth, just watching them.

So IHOP it was, the perfect place for a late-night conversation amongst four like-minded almost-adults. On the way over, the boys in their Camaro had followed the girls in the brunette's Honda Civic. The restaurant was less than a mile away, but there was a stoplight involved, and Matt had comically pulled up next to them at the stoplight, as if engaging them in a drag race.

When they were even with the Civic, Matt revved the engine, then looked over. His face changed from prankish to astonished. Jeremiah looked to see what the deal was, but couldn't figure it out. Amanda was making a screwy face at them, and the other girl was acting like she didn't know they were there, tapping her hands on the steering wheel.

Matt quickly killed the CD player and used the switch on the driver's side door to roll down Jeremiah's window. Thanks to his dad's record collection, Jeremiah recognized the muffled strains of Tower of Power's "Squib Cakes" emanating from the Civic, clearly taxing its stereophonic capacity.

"Dude," Matt said. "She's air-drumming again."

"Yeah. So?"

"Nothing. Just . . . interesting, is all."

Amanda tapped the brunette on the arm and pointed at the boys; Jeremiah made out that she was telling the brunette to roll down the window. The brunette still stared stoically ahead, tapping on the steering wheel, a slight smile beginning to form on the side of her mouth.

Suddenly, the Civic roared away. Jeremiah and Matt looked up and realized that the light was now green. Matt stepped on it, but the IHOP was just a few hundred feet past the light, and the girls were already halfway there.

The race was over before it began, and Matt had to laughingly admit defeat as he whipped the Camaro into the IHOP parking lot. "Oh, man. That was awesome." He grabbed a spot next to the Civic just as the girls were getting out of the car.

The boys exited their vehicle, both laughing. "You got me," Matt said to the brunette.

Amanda was giggling too. She walked around and gave Jeremiah a playful poke in the ribs. "Our plan worked perfect, didn't it, Liz?"

Liz smiled. "Like clockwork." She stood still for just a moment, then forcefully punched Matt in the bicep. "Gotcha!"

Matt leapt backward, stumbling into the door of his car. "Ow!"

Liz and Amanda doubled over in laughter. "Sorry," Liz

said. "I've been wanting to do that ever since I saw you guys walk into the club."

Matt rubbed his arm, his face an even mix of bewilderment, good humor, and awe. "Why?"

"Why not?"

Amanda grabbed Jeremiah's arm and pulled him toward the door. "Come on, guys, let's go inside. I'm starving."

Liz feigned another punch, and Matt took a quick step back. Liz laughed again. "Oh my gosh, I'm so sorry," she said. "Now you're never going to trust me."

He chuckled. "You're crazy."

"Nah, just delirious. Come on, hoss."

The four of them walked into the restaurant and found no hostess on duty.

Uh-oh. Jeremiah was a little uncertain of the seating arrangements here. What was appropriate? Table or booth? And who should he sit next to? Matt? Amanda? Having not done anything like this before, he was unsure of the proper etiquette, and he felt the tense hiccup returning.

A solution popped into his brain. "I have to use the restroom," he said. It was true—plus this way he could excuse himself, let the three of them sort it out, and they would never know that he had no idea what he was doing.

"Yeah, me too," Amanda said.

Aw, man. Guess it was up to Matt and Liz to figure it out.

Jeremiah made his way toward the restroom, Amanda following closely. He looked at her over his shoulder. He had never really been into glasses-wearing girls, but those horn rims had a strange allure. They complemented her hair, which, now that he was under the thousand suns cast by the modern fluorescent lightbulb, he could see wasn't so much true blonde as "dirty" blonde, as the terminology goes.

She flashed him a smile, and it looked really good on her.

"You following me?" he said.

She narrowed her eyes comically. "Yes. I'm your *stalker*." She said the word "stalker" in a faux-menacing whisper, and raised her hands like claws. Her voice had that slight twang possessed by roughly half the population of Tulsa.

Fortunately, the IHOP was even more free of clientele than Club David had been. They had the place to themselves, which was all the rationale Jeremiah needed to tip over a nearby chair, blocking Amanda's way. "Get away from me, stalker!" he yelled.

She let out a shriek of laughter. "If I can't have you, no one will!" She hopped over the chair and ran toward him.

He booked it. The bathroom door was close, but she was a faster runner than he'd expected, and she caught up to him just before he reached the door. He turned quickly and put his hand up. She pulled to a halt, almost smashing into him. Her hair swung forward, brushing against his chin. It smelled of apples. Delicious apples. "Sorry," he said. "No stalkers allowed in here."

She snapped her fingers in the "aw shucks" maneuver. "Man."

"Company policy."

"Well, I don't want to go in there anyway," she said, jokingly indignant. She spun on her heel and went noisily into the ladies' room. "See you in a minute," she said without looking back.

When he came out of the men's room, Jeremiah scoped out the seating arrangements. There was a booth involved, and Matt and Liz were sitting together on one side. Amanda had beaten him out of the restroom and was sitting by herself on the other side. She motioned him over. "Jeremiah!" she said, waving her arms in wild windmills. "We're over here! Saved you a seat."

Matt and Liz were already deep into a quiet conversation. Amanda rolled her eyes and pointed at them.

Jeremiah plopped down in the booth next to Amanda. "What's up?"

She shook her head. "Oh, Liz is already having the God conversation with your friend."

Liz stopped talking and looked at Amanda. "What's wrong with that? God's the biggest part of my life."

"Nothing's wrong with it, Lizzie," Amanda said. "But there *are* other things in this world to talk about."

Matt interjected. "I like talking about God. I can't think of anything else I'd rather talk about."

Amanda laughed. "Well, you guys are a great match, then."

Matt smiled.

"Amanda!" Liz said, looking embarrassed, staring daggers at her friend. The two girls succumbed to a sudden giggling fit.

Matt gave Jeremiah a sly thumbs-up. "I'm liking Tulsa right about now, bro," he said.

Amanda's giggling stopped long enough for her to say, "You aren't from Tulsa?"

Matt shook his head. "Nope. OKC. I came up to go to ORU."

Amanda nodded. "Ah, a good Christian boy."

Matt leaned toward her. "Yeah. Aren't you a good Christian girl?"

Amanda laughed. "Yes, I am," she said, making a crisscross motion across herself. "Cross my heart. In fact, if I could, I would go to ORU this year myself, but I can't afford it and I don't want to take out a loan."

"Well, that's cool."

Jeremiah looked at her. "What are you going to do for school, then? TCC?" TCC meaning Tulsa Community College, where many of Jeremiah's friends intended to carry on their higher learning until they, too, could afford pricier universities.

"No," Liz said, "Amanda's going to move up to full-time at the ol' Cracker Barrel so she can save up for school."

"Thanks, Lizzie," Amanda said in a voice that meant the exact opposite.

Liz gave her a button-cute smile. "You're welcome!" She turned to Jeremiah. "She wants to do college on her own terms. It's one of the things I admire about her."

Jeremiah gave a quick sideways glance at Amanda, whose turn it was now to look embarrassed and stare daggers at her friend. Jeremiah refocused on Liz. "What about you? Good Christian girl—you must be going to ORU like me and Matt, huh?"

Liz set her jaw and gave him a stern look. "Just because I'm a Christian, that doesn't mean I have to go to God Central for an education."

Jeremiah put his hands up in mock surrender. "Sorry!"

She laughed, then reached across the table and knocked his hands down. "For your information, I'm going to that OSU satellite campus downtown."

Matt snorted in disgust. "Uh-oh," he said. "Oklahoma State? You're going to be a Cowboy?"

Liz backhanded him across the shoulder. "What's wrong with that?"

"I'm an OKC boy. Soonerland. We can't be friends—it'd be bedlam."

Jeremiah nodded. "My best friend Dan actually just left to go to OU, so I have to support the guys on this one."

"Whatever," Liz said. She stuck her tongue out at him.

Amanda started looking around. "Where's our waitress, anyway?"

||||||

Jeremiah fought off sleep on the ride back to his car, still in the Armory's parking lot. They'd spent a good three hours at IHOP, and now it was past midnight, around the time Jeremiah usually went to bed. Still, the giddiness from his evening with Amanda (and those other two people) kept him awake. "Man, that was fun," he said.

Matt seemed distracted. He grunted under his breath. "Huh?"

"That was fun," Jeremiah said, leaning forward. "Getting to know those girls. Don't you think?"

Matt didn't answer for a moment, then turned to look at Jeremiah with dead seriousness. "You still play?" he said.

If Matt could hear Jeremiah's thoughts, he would've heard the non-word "Buh?" But Jeremiah simply said, "Um, yeah."

"Hmm."

"What?"

"Jeremiah," Matt said, sounding a lot like a youth pastor, "how's your walk with God?"

"What?"

"I have something important to tell you, but I need to know how your walk with God is."

Jeremiah considered the question. "It's good, I guess," he said. "I go to church. Pray. Read my Bible. You know, all the big ones." This was true, to a degree, but Jeremiah was addressing the letter of the question and not the spirit, and he knew it. His walk with God, to continue using the Christianese that

Jeremiah had become accustomed to growing up in the church, was less of a walk and more of a luxurious recline on a poolside deck chair. Jeremiah followed all the rules, kept his nose clean, and talked a good game, but that's as far as it went.

But his response was good enough for Matt, who was now smiling at him. "That's awesome, man."

"Why, what's up?"

Matt kept his eye on the road, removing a hand from the steering wheel to briefly grasp Jeremiah's shoulder. "Dude, I think God's doing something here."

"What do you mean?"

"I can't really explain it," Matt said. "Just . . . while I was driving up here with all my stuff, God gave me this . . . vision."

"Really?"

"Yeah. It was like a movie, playing on my windshield."

"Cool."

"Yeah."

Matt got lost in thought again, and Jeremiah noticed an almost surreal glow to his face. It wasn't an actual, physical light, but more of the way Matt was carrying himself, as if he'd been to the Mount of Transfiguration recently.

"So what was the vision, Matt?"

"I saw myself in a band. I couldn't see the rest of the members of the band, but I knew it was supposed to be a three-piece, with me singing and playing guitar. Then a bass player and a drummer."

This sounded cool. Now that Jeremiah wasn't in youth group anymore, he had been wondering how exactly he would keep playing. Was this his chance? "That's cool, Matt."

"Yeah," Matt said. "So then, the next day I go to a Christian bookstore to buy the new Cross-Eyed, and you're there, and I remembered that you played, so that sounds like God to me."

Jeremiah shrugged, trying to cover his excitement. He couldn't believe this. Matt Ripke was an amazing performer, and he was asking Jeremiah to be in a band with him? He would've leapt at the chance, vision or no vision. "Man, that would be rad," he said.

Matt smiled at him. "Yeah, it would." He gave another youth-pastor look, one of those looks that goes way beyond the personal eye boundary. "You want to know something weird, though? In my vision, I couldn't tell who the drummer was, but I knew it was a girl."

Jeremiah chuckled. "Yeah, that is weird."

Matt chuckled back. "Yeah." He turned his attention back to the road, then back again to Jeremiah. "Wanna know something weirder?"

"Of course."

"Liz plays drums."

CHAPTER SEVEN

PRAYING ABOUT IT

"How do you know that?" Jeremiah asked, astonished.

"I asked her," Matt said.

"Why? What made you think she would be a drummer?"

"I kept seeing her air-drumming."

"When did you find this out?"

"When you and Amanda were having your little action movie on the way to the bathroom."

"Hey—what do you think of her?"

"Liz? She's cool."

Jeremiah smacked him in the arm. "Come on, man," he said.

Matt howled in protest. "Hey, ease up!" he said. "I've taken enough hits to that arm tonight." He held up his hand as if to playfully backhand Jeremiah. "Anyway, yeah, Liz seems cool."

"Cool."

The two drove for a while without speaking, the crunchy sounds of *Rotormouth* the only sound.

"So you really had a vision?" Jeremiah said.

"Yeah."

"About a band?"

"Yeah."

"What kind of music?"

Matt shifted in his seat. "I don't really know. I was playing guitar. Electric. So I guess it has to be rock 'n' roll."

"Wait a second," Jeremiah said. "You don't play guitar."

"What?" Matt said, looking confused.

For a reason unknown to him, Jeremiah started riffling his fingers through the graduation tassel hanging from the rearview mirror. "Yeah, when we saw you at camp last summer, you only sang. You didn't play."

Matt laughed. "Dude," he said between chuckles, "I've been playing longer than that guitar player in the Shekinah Fire band."

Jeremiah let his hand drop. "Why didn't you play in that band, then?"

"They didn't need a guitar player, they needed a singer."

Jeremiah considered this. "I guess that makes sense," he finally said. "Rock on."

"Rock on indeed, my friend."

They pulled into the parking lot of the Armory, and Jeremiah pointed toward his white Chevy Corsica, the only car left in the lot. Matt pulled up next to it, and Jeremiah got out, then leaned his head back into the car. "So when do we start, man?"

"Let me pray about it," Matt said. "I just want God's hand on this, you know? I want to make sure Liz is the right fit. You pray about it, too."

"Okay."

"And then if we agree, we go talk to her."

"Okay."

"Okay."

Jeremiah bobbed his head for awhile, probably because it was spinning with all this new info. "Take it easy," he finally said as he closed the door.

Matt gave him a wave and sped off to wherever he was going. Jeremiah fiddled with his key ring, absentmindedly finding his car key. He got into the car, closed the door, and sat for a minute, thinking over what had just happened.

One: He had met an awesome girl who seemed to be interested in him, which automatically made her the record-setter for that particular category.

Two: He had been invited to be in a band with the most talented performer he knew. Except his dad. His dad was awesome.

It was a banner evening, full of events that had him positively buzzing.

But a girl drummer? Was such a thing even possible?

Still, it was Matt's vision. Well, God's vision, given to Matt.

Which—what did that mean? Did God really do that? Give people visions? Jeremiah had read about that stuff in the Bible, and he'd heard of that sort of thing happening, but he'd never had it happen to him.

He'd never started a band before, either.

And what did he really know about Matt, anyway? He was a cool guy, that's for sure. And he had a great gift onstage. And he seemed to be really concerned with doing God's will, so surely that had to mean something.

Jeremiah started the car and pulled out of the parking lot.

Matt had said to pray about it. This intrigued Jeremiah, because he heard people say that *often*. "I'll pray about it" or "Let me pray about that" or "I'll be praying for you, brother/sister." These were common phrases around his church. But as far as he could tell, they didn't mean anything. It didn't really seem like something most people followed through on; it was more just something they said.

Still, he'd never been directed to "pray about" something like this before. He hadn't prayed about joining the Teens Ablaze band. He hadn't prayed about going to ORU instead of OU with Dan. He hadn't prayed about getting his job at the Armory.

What if his whole life was screwed up because he *hadn't* been "praying about it"? He'd just done what seemed natural; what if God had been trying to tell him to do something different, and he just hadn't been paying attention?

Was he totally off-track right now?

He had stopped paying attention to his driving and realized he was now in his neighborhood. And if he didn't swerve immediately, he would run down a big, nasty possum crossing the street.

He swerved. The possum survived unscathed.

Was that a sign from God? Swerve? Your life's off-track, Jeremiah?

This was so confusing.

| | | | | |

When Jeremiah got home, he headed immediately for the shower, then bed. His fatigue had caught up with him, and he was ready for some shuteye.

When he lay down, he closed his eyes to say his regular evening prayers, which were usually some variation on "God, bless everyone I know and help me to live for you." That was the gist, anyway; they were often dragged out to list names and such.

After he'd said that much, Jeremiah hesitated for a moment, then tacked on, "And Lord, if it's your will for me and Liz to be in Matt's band, um, make it happen."

Somehow, that didn't seem quite right. But it was all he knew to say.

CHAPTER EIGHT

CHRISTMAS COMES EARLY TO JEREMIAH AND MATT

The next morning, Jeremiah was absentmindedly minding his Armory register, half helping customers and half wondering about the band, when Betty rushed up. "Jeremiah, we need your help unloading the truck," she said. "I'll cover your register for you."

"What's up?"

"It's the first week of Christmas stock."

Jeremiah furrowed a brow. "But it's August."

"I know," Betty said, rolling her eyes and exhaling sharply. "We get it early around here. And there'll be more."

So Jeremiah spent most of the day handling Christmas stock. The Armory had a centrally located warehouse that served all the Armory outlets in Oklahoma (there were six), shipping all the product in big green plastic tubs, and the truck that had just arrived was full of those tubs. Jeremiah's job was to open a tub, determine what department in the store it went to, then take it there.

Tub after tub, Jeremiah was blown away by the variety of goods. Christmas books. Christmas CDs and tapes. Christmas videos. Christmas sweatshirts. There was a whole tub of lapel pins that said "Jesus Is the Reason for the Season." There was another whole tub of cheap plastic snow globes featuring the Nativity inside. He got a chuckle out of those, imagining snow covering the mostly arid Bethlehem. Who would need a star to herald the arrival of the Messiah? The unseasonable and foreign wintry mix would have been herald enough.

The snow globes went for ninety-nine cents. The pins, $1.99.

Jeremiah was knee-deep in boxed Christmas greeting cards when he heard a knock on the swinging stockroom doors. He couldn't figure out why any of his coworkers would knock instead of just walking in.

"Uh—come in?" he said.

One of the doors swung inward a little, and Matt's head poked into the room. "Hey, man," his head said as the rest of him walked into the room.

Jeremiah was grateful for a break from the cognitive dissonance of Christmas in August. "Hey, what're you doing?"

Matt stepped toward Jeremiah, weaving through the multiple green tubs strewn over the stockroom's concrete floor. "Just trying to find you, man. You pray about Liz?"

"Yeah." It *was* the truth. He *had* prayed. Once. Should he have prayed more? Would God have heard him better if he had prayed more? He didn't have time to existentialize any further, because Matt interrupted.

"Me too," he said. "I think she's the one, man."

Whew. At least Matt had heard from God. "Great!"

"Is that what God told you, too?"

Jeremiah just nodded. "Mm . . . hmm."

Matt clapped his hands together. "Man, this is awesome! God's really bringing this whole thing together."

Jeremiah hesitated. Though he had been raised in church and understood Christianese, he always had a difficult time forcing his tongue to speak it. "Amen," he said.

Matt laughed. "You said it, brother." He looked around. "So, when do you want to talk to Liz? Tonight?"

"Uh, sure," Jeremiah said. "Sounds great."

"Great. I'll call her," Matt said, looking around some more. "Is there a phone back here I can use?"

| | | | | |

There was no phone in the stockroom, so Jeremiah sent Matt up to the register to make the call. Jeremiah stayed behind to sort Christmas cards, so he didn't know exactly how Matt presented the whole join-our-new-band concept to Liz.

The sudden banging open of the swinging doors, followed by the bounding of Matt into the stockroom, followed by a loud, excited whoop from Matt's mouth led Jeremiah to believe that it had gone well.

"She said she'd love it! At least get together and jam."

"Rock on!"

"Yeah, man," Matt said with a beaming smile. "This is great!"

Jeremiah leaned against a stack of tubs as tall as he was. "Think she's any good?"

"Of course she is. Why else would God put her in our band, dude?"

Jeremiah nodded. Of course, of course.

"Well," Matt said, folding his arms, "can you get together tonight and jam?"

"Sure," Jeremiah said. "I get off at 5:30. But where?"

"Don't know yet."

"I have a key to my church," Jeremiah said. "It's Saturday night—there won't be anything going on in the youth room, so we can go there."

Matt actually jumped in the air. "Awesome! That'll be perfect! I'll go call her back."

"There's a drum kit and everything," Jeremiah said. "She just needs to bring some sticks."

"Rock on," Matt said as he walked out, the door bursting onto the sales floor in front of him.

"Hey, Matt!"

Matt swung himself back before the doors could shut again. "Yo?"

"Um, could you let her know that, uh, Amanda can come if she wants?"

Matt gave a wry smile. "I already did, bro."

CHAPTER NINE

GOD KNOWS WHAT HE'S DOING, MAN

Jeremiah rolled into the parking lot of Crow Creek Christian Chapel around 6:00, finishing the last bite of an Arby's roast beef sandwich at the same time. There was an Arby's in the parking lot of the strip mall where the Armory was located, which meant Jeremiah ate a lot of Arby's dinners.

Crow Creek Christian Chapel, which Jeremiah's dad affectionately called "C4" ("It's only a matter of time before we blow up Tulsa!" he often said, with a half-mocking grin), was in Tulsa's Brookside district, an area of mostly businesses butting up to Peoria Avenue. The church, a brownstone behemoth that stuck out among the many bars and restaurants that dotted the Brookside landscape, had been erected in the late '60s, and no renovations had been done since.

Matt rolled into the parking lot just after Jeremiah. He bounced out of his car. "Man, this is *awesome*!" he said. He stretched out his arms. "Look where we are. It's like we're coming out here to play a show."

Jeremiah smiled as he snagged his bass from the trunk of his Corsica. "Well, we kind of are. For ourselves. And Amanda, I guess."

"True, bro." Matt opened the trunk of his Camaro and pulled out a guitar case and a backpack. "There's a guitar rig inside, right?"

Jeremiah nodded. "It ain't much, but it's there." He tipped his head toward the building. "Let's go inside and get set up."

Jeremiah let them in with the key he'd conveniently borrowed from his dad when he sped home after work to grab his bass. He flipped on the lights and led the way to the Teens Ablaze youth room, where he'd spent so many nights in rehearsal throughout high school.

The youth room itself looked a little kidsy to him now. Odd that just a few months earlier, it had felt like home. Now, the posters of different Christian rock bands on the walls looked childish. Except, of course, for the Cross-Eyed poster along the back wall. And that Zippo one was kind of cool.

Jeremiah led Matt up the aisle through the folding metal chairs to the stage, a shallow, carpeted platform about two feet high. A battered acrylic podium stood in the center; band equipment lined the back wall. From left to right: a dusty set of black Tama drums with cymbals in a state of tarnishing, surrounded by an equally dusty acrylic drum shield; a small but heavy Crate bass amp nicknamed "Widowmaker"; a guitar stand missing half the rubber sleeve, making for a dreadful clinking sound whenever it was used; a modest Fender Twin guitar amp, dustier than the drum kit; and a Yamaha DX-7 keyboard on a metal keyboard stand. Plus a couple of microphones on stands.

The boys set their respective cases down on the platform while Jeremiah pointed out the guitar amp. "There's your rig. Like I said, not much."

"It'll be fine," Matt said. "Even if it doesn't sound the best, it's all music to God's ears, right?"

Jeremiah was already moving toward the sound booth in the back corner of the room. "Right," he said.

"What's right?" said a female voice with a slight twang.

Jeremiah whipped his head toward the door, then did his best to act super-cool and not at all like a giddy schoolboy whose current big crush had just walked into the room. "Hey, Amanda!" he said, a little too enthusiastically. "Matt was just saying how all music is music to God's ears, whether it's coming from a good amp or not."

Amanda smiled at Jeremiah. "I know," she said. "I heard."

"Don't be such a punk," Liz said, walking into the room carrying a stick bag. "Hi, Jeremiah."

"Hey, Liz."

"Liz! Hey!" Matt said. He ran over to greet her. "Welcome, welcome. I'm glad you're here," he gave her non-stick-bag-holding hand a vigorous shake. "I'm excited, man."

"I can tell," she said with a wink.

Matt gave Amanda a wave. "Hi, Amanda. Glad you could make it."

"Are you kidding me?" she said, sitting down in one of the metal chairs. "This is music history in the making. I wouldn't miss this for the world." She flipped her hair back, "Besides, I picked up an extra shift today, so I'm ready for *anything* that doesn't involve breakfast food."

"So . . . no IHOP after rehearsal, then?" Jeremiah said.

The look Amanda gave Jeremiah could wilt entire ecosystems.

"I'll just go turn on the sound system." Jeremiah hurried to the back and flipped the switches that brought the sound system to life. He didn't know how it all worked, especially with the rat's nest of cables both in the sound booth and onstage; he only knew what buttons to push to make the sound come out of the speakers.

Meanwhile, Liz was situating herself behind the drums and Matt was unbuckling his guitar case to reveal a gold-top Epiphone Les Paul.

Jeremiah let out a whistle as he made the trek from the sound booth back to the stage. "Nice axe."

"Thanks," Matt said. "Not as good as the real thing, but it does the trick."

"What's the real thing?" Amanda asked.

Matt held the guitar up for her to see. "This is a cheaper version of a Gibson Les Paul."

Amanda made a matter-of-fact face. "Well, once you get your big fat rock 'n' roll check for being so great, you guys can all buy new guitars. The real things." She gestured with her hands toward the drums. "Except you, Lizzie. You'll have to buy drums."

Liz did the old comedy drum accent (buh-dump, BAH). Somehow, it sounded ironic.

While Matt unloaded a few effects pedals from his backpack, Jeremiah opened up his bass case and brought out the tree trunk. He swung the strap over his shoulder and anchored himself for the long night ahead, ready to plug it in and play.

Liz kept clicking the hi-hat shut and testing the bass drum pedal. "This kick doesn't sound half bad," she said. She gave the snare a couple of good whacks with a stick she'd produced from her bag. "This has a pretty good sound, too."

"Thanks," Jeremiah said. "I had nothing to do with any of it."

She laughed.

Matt was busy futzing with pedals, taking them out of their respective boxes and connecting them all with little cables. He had a series of Boss pedals, the standard stuff: overdrive, distortion, delay, tremolo. There was a wah involved, too.

Several minutes later, Matt had everything ironed out and plugged in correctly. He hit a couple of chords, adjusted some knobs on his pedals, hit a couple more chords, adjusted some knobs on the amp, hit a couple more chords, adjusted a knob on his guitar, hit a couple more chords, and finally seemed satisfied with the result.

"All right. Let's rock," Matt said.

"What do you want to play?" Jeremiah said, after riffing for a few seconds.

Matt played a short chord progression. "I don't know. I got some stuff I've written. We can try that?"

"Yeah," said Jeremiah, not really wanting to begin life as a potential band by playing something two-thirds of them had never heard before. "Or maybe we could start with some praise-and-worship stuff?"

Matt hit a quick chord. "That's an idea."

Liz spoke up. "How about a couple of Cross-Eyed songs? You guys know that stuff inside and out, right?"

Jeremiah pointed at her. "That's a great idea."

"Yes!" Matt said. "Let's do it."

Matt stomped on a few of his pedals, played a couple of chords, knelt to twiddle some knobs as the last chord died down, played another chord, twiddled another knob, then stood as the sound faded. "Let's pray real quick, before we get started," he said, bowing his head. The other three followed suit. "Lord, please bless this time we have together. Bless us as we play. Help us to worship you, even here and now. We love you. Amen."

He took a deep breath, then launched into the intro of "Kill Me" note-for-note, twelve bars of riffing, played perfectly.

Halfway through, Jeremiah turned to Liz. "This is 'Kill Me,' the song he's playing," he said. "You know it?"

She twirled her stick at him, offering a cocky smirk. "I got it."

Liz proved it by hitting her opening drum fill exactly as it was on the album. Startled, Jeremiah missed the first couple notes of his part.

Liz didn't, though. She was flat-out laying down the groove, and Jeremiah's heart was skipping a beat. She was dead on, exactly how the song sounded on the album. Jeremiah was now certain Matt *had* heard from God about her.

The Teens Ablaze band had never jammed on Cross-Eyed before, so while Jeremiah knew all the Cross-Eyed songs by heart, including the new ones, he'd only ever played along with the CDs at home.

Now, here he was, jamming this awesome song with a couple of new musicians—and sounding downright professional.

Jeremiah hadn't thought to set up a microphone for Matt's vocals, for some reason, but the lack of a mic didn't seem to bother Matt. He started belting the song at the top of his lungs, barely audible above the rest of the cranked music.

Out of the corner of his eye, Jeremiah saw Amanda get up and hurry to the stage. She grabbed a microphone and stand from the edge of the stage, and set it in front of Matt. She jogged back to the sound booth, and, a few seconds later, Matt's voice came roaring through the speakers.

Amanda sported a very proud grin.

And she had every right to be proud, because, while the jam had sounded fine as an instrumental, Matt's voice made it sound magical. His vocal tone was both refined and gritty, soaring, yet artfully restrained.

It was, Jeremiah decided, a thing of beauty.

The song ended on a big down chord, which the three of them all hit at once, with Matt going a little overboard as they held out the chord.

Amanda applauded. "Woo! You guys are great. Sign me up for the fan club!"

Jeremiah looked back and forth between Matt and Liz. "What'd you guys think?"

Liz nodded her head, clearly a little surprised. "That was fun. And good."

Matt showed more teeth in his smile than Jeremiah had ever seen on any human being. "All I got to say is: God knows what he's doing, man."

CHAPTER TEN

HELP COMES FROM A VIDEO GAME

The next few weeks flew by, and Jeremiah pretty much forgot about college. He went, but he didn't pay much attention. After work at the Armory, he devoted all his spare time to playing music with Matt and Liz.

Oh. And hanging out with Amanda.

That was probably the brightest spot. Yes, he was glad he had some new friends in his bandmates, but Amanda was just this super cool girl that he had a lot of fun with. She always rode to rehearsal with Liz, but often, Jeremiah would take her home afterward, sometimes stopping off at the Braum's by her apartment to share a banana split, or just hitting the park and going for a little walk.

If someone asked Jeremiah if he and Amanda were dating, he never felt secure enough to say yes. He considered their relationship friendly, though he wished beyond hope that it could be more. All the signs and signals said that Amanda liked him as more than a friend and wanted to move the relationship up a notch, but he couldn't be sure. It's so hard to interpret the signs and signals when you're the one getting them; much easier to do from outside the relationship.

So, to sum up: just friends, thank you.

Meanwhile, Matt and Liz were as inseparable as conjoined twins fused at the elbow. The two of them were always together, always laughing, always talking about God or music or both. Usually God. Jeremiah had no idea how they managed to find so much to talk about when it came to the Big Guy.

He had tried to have a God conversation with Amanda one time, but it hadn't really gone very far.

"Do you think God really brought the band together?" he said.

Amanda shrugged her shoulders. "I don't know. You guys sound good, so . . . yeah?"

That was about it.

They had a much better time discussing their upbringings, Tulsa, their respective high schools (while Jeremiah had gone to Union, Amanda had gone to Jenks, making them bitter rivals scholastically—their relationship was the high-school equivalent of Matt and Liz's OU vs. OSU bedlam), life at Cracker Barrel or the Armory, and general chitchat about movies and music. Turns out Amanda had been at the same Cross-Eyed show Jeremiah had attended, but on the opposite side of the auditorium.

And then there was the rehearsing. They started off playing mostly Cross-Eyed songs, but soon moved into working up some of Matt's originals, which Jeremiah thoroughly embraced. He was really liking the music they were making, and Matt was a keen lyricist. He pulled almost all his themes from the Bible, drawing on obscure passages or some of the rampant poetic imagery to create something entirely unique.

Jeremiah's current favorite song of Matt's was "Coaltongue," about the prophet Isaiah. Matt had to show Jeremiah the passage in the Old Testament to prove that it existed. Another favorite was "Ham-Fisted," which Matt had explained had something to do with Moses and how he couldn't speak well, but the symbolism was lost on Jeremiah.

As for sound, the more they rehearsed, the further they got from copying Cross-Eyed directly. Liz wasn't so much a rock drummer, as Jeremiah had supposed, as a very confident, loud funk drummer. He found himself grooving more and more each time they got together to play, and it was showing up in his bass lines. There was overall more motion, more syncopation and space in what he was doing. He was leaving breathing room, not playing constantly anymore. It was liberating.

Matt, though, was a man possessed. Well—possessed by God, if such a thing could happen. He smiled through every rehearsal, sometimes laughing to himself if a song sounded particularly good. And he played like a maniac. He dove into his guitar-playing role, playing so hard and furious that he sometimes wound up with a bloody finger or two.

One day after rehearsal, a few weeks into their time together as a band, Matt made an announcement while they were packing up their gear. "ORU has a Battle of the Bands coming up in a couple of months," he said. "I signed us up for it."

"Sweet!" Jeremiah said.

"Cool," Liz said.

"But," Matt said, pointing his finger for emphasis, "this does present us with a slight problem. We don't have a name."

Ah, yes. The name problem. This had been bugging Jeremiah for a couple of weeks, but he never brought it up because he wanted to have a few suggestions ready to go when he did. This had led him to keep a spare scrap of paper in his pocket to jot down anything that came to mind, which had led to him leaving the spare scrap of paper in his pocket, which had led to it getting washed, which had led to a lecture from his dad and a near revocation of the dad/laundry privilege.

When it came to names, he had bupkes.

Matt had apparently fared better as he produced a notepad from his guitar case. "Let me run these by you."

Jeremiah and Liz took seats in the metal folding chairs, next to Amanda.

"Okay," Matt began. "Now, I really think our name needs to have meaning, and I think it needs to come from the Bible. But it also needs to be edgy and describe our music. So with that in mind," he consulted his list, "how about Talking Donkey?"

Liz snorted with laughter.

Jeremiah wanted to, but refrained.

"What?" Matt said, and he wasn't kidding around.

"Matt, that's a little ridiculous," Liz said. "And if you really wanted to be edgy, you'd call it Balaam's Ass."

"I don't think there's a need for that kind of language," Matt mumbled, looking at his list once more. "Well, how about Third Heaven?"

That sounded fine to Jeremiah.

"Too ethereal," Liz said. "People hear 'heaven' and think of harps and lyres."

"Okay," Matt said, scanning his list some more, "I guess that rules out Seraphim."

"I think there's already a band called that," Jeremiah said.

Matt stared at his list. Jeremiah began to wonder how many names were on there. More specifically, he began to wonder how many names had to do with heaven, since Matt seemed to be mentally skipping quite a few entries. Finally: "How about Winnowing Fork?" he said.

"Is that in the Bible?" Jeremiah asked.

Liz turned to look at him. "Yeah, Jesus talks about using a winnowing fork to separate Christians from non-Christians." She looked back at Matt. "That's not bad, but I don't see the connection to our music."

"Like, we weed out the bad music and just play only good stuff," he said. "Christian stuff."

"Huh."

Amanda chimed in. "What else you got?"

"Well, I just have one more."

"Lay it on us."

Matt folded his paper, and Jeremiah could tell he was a little embarrassed at the name he was about to say. "SoldierSaint. All one word."

Jeremiah, Liz, and Amanda all gave him blank looks.

Matt hung his head. "You guys are right. They all suck."

Liz hopped up to console him, taking his hand and patting it. "Matt, they're a good start," she said. "But we'll know the right name when we hear it." She turned to Jeremiah. "Let's all start thinking of names like Matt did, and start writing them down."

Amanda clapped with glee in her seat. "Oh, can I do this, too?" she asked.

Liz smiled at her. "Of course."

"Yea!"

"And then," Liz continued, "we'll all tell each other our suggestions after our next practice. Okay?"

Jeremiah and Amanda grunted their assent.

"Okay, Matt?" Liz said, squeezing his hand.

He smiled. "Sounds good."

"Great!" Liz said. "What do you guys want to do now?"

||||||

It was Jeremiah who thought of going to the arcade. His rationale: He hadn't been there in forever, and he wanted to play some pinball. He loved pinball. Especially the machines that had those ramps and chutes and metal tubes crisscrossing each other.

A few short miles in a piled-in car later, the four of them were piling out at Fun House, a large arcade at the end of yet another strip mall that it shared with one of Tulsa's many movie theaters.

A clown logo greeted them as they walked in, Jeremiah heading for the change machine and plugging it with a twenty-dollar bill. The resulting outpouring of quarters filled both of his hands and one of the pockets of his jeans.

In the meantime, the others had scoped out the place and found a few games. Jeremiah approached them with all the quarters and said, "Games on me."

There was much cheering and congratulating as Jeremiah handed out some of his booty. He didn't know exactly why he had decided to be so generous with his hard-earned cash, but it just seemed like the right thing to do. Maybe in the back of his mind, he was trying to impress Amanda.

But before he could get too full of himself, Amanda dragged him over to Streetfighter: Championship Edition, announcing along the way, "Thanks for paying for me to kick your butt."

"Oh, whatever," Jeremiah said. "I'll be that guy with the long arms and you won't even touch me."

"Oh my gosh, it's on."

They reached the game and realized that Matt and Liz had followed them over.

"Hey, we got next game," Matt said.

"Sure thing," Jeremiah said.

He popped in two quarters and the two of them started the game.

It was a bloodbath from the beginning. Jeremiah couldn't figure out how to make his guy do his long-arms thing, so he kept getting pounded. Amanda definitely had a take-no-prisoners attitude toward video games. She had a girl player, and she kept punching Jeremiah's guy in his nose-ring-enhanced face.

Jeremiah was wincing visibly as his avatar got pummeled. "Hey," he said. "Ease up!"

"No way!"

"Come on, Jeremiah!" Matt said. "It's up-up-down-A-B!"

Liz smacked Matt on the shoulder. "No cheating!"

Jeremiah kept pushing buttons as fast and as furiously as he could, but it wasn't doing him any good. His guy's little bar of life was shrinking, and there was nothing he could do to get back at Amanda. She was brutal. "Come on, Amanda," he said. "Let me catch my breath at least."

"No way!"

He stole a glance at her and saw the determination on her face, her nose wrinkled so cutely, a grin spreading into the corner of her mouth. Truth be told, he didn't mind getting beaten, if she was the one doing it.

"Amanda, I already ate," he said as she pounded the crap out of him. "I don't need a knuckle sandwich."

"Too bad, buddy," she said, laughing. "I'm force-feeding you this one. And I packed a bag of chips and a Capri Sun to go with it."

"Whoa!" Liz said, her voice taking on a tone that had a twinge of destiny.

"What?" Jeremiah and Amanda said at the same time.

"Jeremiah, I think you just named our band," she said.

All three non-Liz heads spun to look at her.

"What?" Matt said.

"Knuckle Sandwich," Liz said. "It's perfect. Our music is hard-hitting. And as for Matt's desire to have our name mean something from the Bible, well, Paul calls the Bible 'solid food' somewhere in there."

"Knuckle Sandwich," Matt said, trying the words on. "I like it."

"My name is Jeremiah Springfield, and I play bass for Knuckle Sandwich, and you're listening to KROS, today's best Christian rock," Jeremiah said. "Yeah, that works great."

"It's awesome," Amanda said. "I mean, I know I'm not in the band, so whatever, but I like it, too."

Matt gave Liz a sidearm shoulder hug. "Way to go, Miss Creativity," he said. "I knew if we just gave this thing to God, it would come back around."

"So I guess that settles it," Jeremiah said. "We're Knuckle Sandwich."

"Yep!" Liz said. And then she punched Matt in the bicep.

"Ow!" Matt said, rubbing his arm yet again. He turned to Liz. "Okay, we're not going to call ourselves that if you're going to hit me every time someone says it."

She didn't just laugh; she cackled. "Sorry!"

A kid about twelve approached them, pointing at Streetfighter. "Hey," he said, "if you guys aren't going to play, could you let me in?"

Jeremiah and Amanda turned to look at the game. They had both stopped playing when Liz mentioned the band name, and now the game was almost over; Jeremiah's guy was pounding the stuffing out of Amanda's girl.

"What in the world?" Amanda said.

Jeremiah inspected the control panel—his "A" button had gotten stuck, making his character punch nonstop. Amanda's character's life bar disappeared, and the words "Game Over" appeared on the screen.

He'd won without doing a thing.

CHAPTER ELEVEN

THE BATTLE OF THE BANDS

The highlight of the next couple of months: Matt wrote two more songs, bringing his total to seven. Jeremiah really dug "Break the Tablets," which had a sort of reggae backbeat on top of this huge, chunky riff Matt played off the cuff one day. The other song, "Golden Calf," was a slower number, and one that would almost work as a praise-and-worship tune. The lyrics went:

I may be confused,
But I don't know how
Your chosen people
Got wrapped up in a cow.
Am I like that?
I wonder if my love is real,
Or if I go back and forth
Like the people of Israel.

O Lord,
This is my battle.

O Lord,
  I'm not serving cattle.
O Lord,
  Break me in half.
O Lord,
  Melt me like the golden calf.

On the relationship front, things were still playfully platonic between Jeremiah and Amanda, though Jeremiah was definitely beginning to feel vibes from her that he hadn't felt before.

Still, she confused him. For example: They were standing in a lengthy line to catch *Addams Family Values* at the Park Lane Twin one night when Jeremiah said, "Man, there are a lot of people here. This might take awhile."

"Well, I can't wait forever, *Jeremiah*."

They saw *My Life* instead, while he tried to figure out what she'd really meant.

As for the music: The band turned a corner shortly before Halloween during a rehearsal.

"Guys," Matt said as he finished setting up his pedals, "I know this sounds stupid, but I really feel like God gave me this chord progression last night." He strapped on his axe, tuned his top string down to a D, floored his volume pedal, and ripped into a choppy, spacious riff that immediately set Jeremiah's head to bobbing.

Matt paused for a moment. "Then this is the chorus," he said, launching into a more staccato version of the verse riff. Jeremiah angled himself to catch a peek at the neck of Matt's guitar to see where Matt's fingers were landing.

He had it after a few bars and began playing along. Liz kicked into a stellar beat at almost the exact same time, accenting the riff in all the right places, bringing out its rhythmic elements.

And then it struck Jeremiah—he was throwing his accents in at the same places as Liz.

He whirled around to face her, intently looking at the front bass drum head, watching it ripple in time with her kicks. It lined up perfectly with the plucking of his fingers.

Jeremiah couldn't tell if he was copying Liz or if she was copying him. Or if they were copying each other. He was dimly aware of Matt hollering "Verse!"

He obeyed, and so did Liz, each of them giving a little fill during the down space between the chorus and verse. And each of their fills complemented the other one.

Whether Jeremiah was anticipating Liz's tendencies as a player or whether she was anticipating his, he didn't know. All he knew: They were meshing together, and it was working.

"Owwwwwwwww!" Matt screamed into the microphone. "Woooooooooooo!"

Jeremiah turned around. The first thing he noticed was Matt's strumming arm going up and down like a piston as he down-picked every chord. His head was limp, tilting slightly backward and to the left, his eyes closed.

Suddenly, Matt snapped his head forward, his eyes remaining glued shut. "Chorus!"

Liz and Jeremiah followed him.

"God . . . only . . . knows!" Matt sang, his voice strong and confident. "God . . . only . . . knows!" He belted it to the back row of the Teens Ablaze room. Sweat began to trickle down his furrowed eyebrows.

"Where are those? With no clothes? With pierced nose? Those who go? When life slows?" He was on the verge of screaming now, his head twitching back and forth to punctuate each questioning lyric. "God! Only! Knoooooooooooooowwwwwws!"

Jeremiah shot a questioning glance at Liz. "What's he doing?" he mouthed. Liz, in perfect time, managed a shrug of her shoulders. "Is this new?" Jeremiah mouthed again. Liz just nodded, again in time.

During the course of this exchange, Matt had sung more impromptu lyrics and was back to screaming "God only knows" at the top of his lungs. He finished off with an especially long and intense "*knoooooooooooooooooooooooooowwwwwws!*" holding it out as he rocked back on his heels, away from the microphone, looking as if he were attempting to bend backward at the waist. He went into a momentary free fall, then kicked his right leg back to catch himself, almost immediately sloshing forward until he was almost bent double.

And the whole time, he never stopped jamming on the riff. The riff, it seemed, had to go on, no matter what rock 'n' roll gymnastics Matt performed.

Jeremiah followed Matt's lead, his neck turning to gel. Extremely soulful, hard-rockin' gel. His head bobbed this way and that, his body bouncing slightly to the rhythm he and Liz were laying down.

Liz began to get funkier, to emphasize the backbeat a little more. Jeremiah went along, adding a few notes to his lines, adding some accents that hadn't been there before. She matched them.

And Matt just played, hanging down like an unpinned scarecrow.

With a massive jerk, Matt whipped himself upright once again. He began strumming hard down chords at the beginning of each measure, holding up a raised fist in between each strum. Jeremiah got the distinct feeling that Matt was bringing the song to a close.

Matt hit one more down chord and held his hand outward, palm down, as if to quiet Jeremiah and Liz. Both of them had instinctively played hard downbeats with Matt's down chords, Liz punctuating them with cymbal crashes. At the last one, Liz gave a cymbal crash and let it ring, Jeremiah following suit with his final note.

Eyes still closed, Matt leaned forward as the song died down, bumping his chin into the microphone. "God only knows!" he screamed one more time, giving his guitar a staccato strum, then muting it immediately, the musical exclamation mark to match his vocal one.

Matt stood there for a moment, breathing deeply in, then out.

Jeremiah felt like he needed to crank the A/C in the room.

Matt broke into a wide smile as he opened his eyes. "That, my friends," he said, "was *so freaking anointed*."

Jeremiah smiled and nodded, turning to Liz. She twirled a drumstick and said, "That was pretty nice." She looked at Matt. "You were having, like, an experience there, huh?"

He said nothing. Just kept smiling. He looked down at his guitar and played a couple of chords, softly. He muted his guitar with his hand, then looked back up at the two of them, a smirk on his face. "There's no way we can't win that Battle of the Bands."

"Definitely," Jeremiah said.

"We sound good," Liz said, "but I don't think we'll win."

Jeremiah whipped his head around. "What?" He looked back at Matt, who simply had his head cocked to one side.

"Why do you say that, Liz?" Matt said.

"We sound good, but judges don't judge only on whether you sound good," Liz said, setting her drumsticks on her snare drum and folding her arms. "We're a bunch of freshmen—and

I don't even go to your school. They'll give it to a band with more seniority."

"I guess we'll see," Matt said. "We'll see."

"Yeah, we will," said a voice from the back of the room. "I think it was good, if anybody's wondering."

Jeremiah had forgotten Amanda was there.

| | | | | |

The night before the show, the band decided to get a little extra practice on just the songs they were going to do. But first they had to decide what exactly those songs would be.

"I think we should do 'Coaltongue,' definitely," Jeremiah said in the midst of the debate. "We should open with it—it's our hardest rocker."

"I agree," Liz said.

"But we only get two songs," Matt said, a little huffiness in his voice. "And I definitely want to do 'Golden Calf' and 'God Only Knows.'"

"Matt," Liz said, "is that because those are our two newest songs, or is it because you think those represent us best as a band?"

"Both," Matt said. "'Coaltongue' is a good song, but I'm just starting to get tired of it."

"Dude," Jeremiah said, "no one's heard any of these songs, except us and Amanda. Just 'cause you're tired of it doesn't mean it's no good."

Matt shook his head. "Whatever, man. Just forget it. We'll do 'Coaltongue' and whatever else you want to do."

Jeremiah could tell Matt was feeling miffed. "Matt, we don't have to do 'Coaltongue' if you don't want to. I just think it's one of the best songs we have."

Liz chimed in. "Yeah, it is. I mean, you wrote it, so it has to be decent, right?"

Matt looked up at her with a slight sparkle in his eyes.

"So, why don't we do that one and," Liz continued, "let's see, 'God Only Knows.' Two different songs that still have our own sound to them."

Matt pouted a little longer, but finally gave his guitar a strum and said, "Okay." He gave another, more confident strum. "Yeah, that'll be good." Strum. "Cool." A pause, while he mulled something over in his mind. "Let's get to it."

||||||

The Battle of the Bands competition arrived less than twenty-four hours later, and it's safe to say that every member of Knuckle Sandwich, including their unofficial roadie (Amanda couldn't be official until they actually went on the road), was equal parts nervous and confident.

Jeremiah certainly was. He vacillated between galling confidence and sheer panic almost minute-by-minute, telling himself that they were going to rock ORU harder than it had ever been rocked before, then following that by telling himself ORU was going to witness a band train wreck like it had never witnessed before, then following *that* by telling himself that train wrecks were all in his head and that he knew they were going to rock.

Wash, rinse, repeat.

He couldn't pay attention in class all day long, and he barely ate anything for lack of tasting it. Finally, it was time for the big event, which was to take place in ORU's Mabee Center, Tulsa's only large concert venue. If a big-name act came to Tulsa (and all the Christian ones did), they played for the 10,000-plus mustard-colored seats at Mabee Center.

"Ten thousand seats," Jeremiah had said in one of his regular evening phone conversations with Amanda the night before. "That's insane."

"It's a lot of seats," she said.

"Will they all fill up, you think? I mean, ORU doesn't have anywhere close to that many students."

"I dunno."

Jeremiah's nervousness calmed when he walked into the auditorium and saw that about 8,000 of the seats were blocked off by two large curtains. A good two-thirds of the oval arena was cut off, leaving the middle third of seating available. There was no stage; instead, the bands were performing on the arena floor.

Still, looking around, there were a lot of seats up there. Way more than there were in the Teens Ablaze room, or in the Tabernacle at Camp Laodicea. Jeremiah stood on the floor, bass case in hand, gazing up at the rising seats, all the way into the balcony.

Yipes!

The floor itself was a beehive of activity as the different bands filtered in. A proscenium had been erected on the arena floor, which Jeremiah walked through to the backstage area. Where was everyone else? Jeremiah was apparently the only member of Knuckle Sandwich there.

A jolly-looking college student with a black dress shirt, jeans, and two-days' worth of stubble approached him. "Hi, I'm Mark, I'll be emceeing the event. Which band are you in?"

"Knuckle Sandwich."

Mark smiled. "Great name," he said, laying his hand on Jeremiah's shoulder. "I'll have mine with mayo!" He laughed at his own joke, then mimed spreading something on his closed fist and punching himself in the face. "Ouch!" he said, laughing some more. "That'd hurt. And be messy!"

"Um. Yeah."

Mark spoke with the smoothness of a Vegas entertainer. "I'm just messing with you—what's your name?"

"Jeremiah."

"I'm just messing with you, Jeremiah," Mark continued slickly. "It's just what I do. Part of the emcee life, as they say."

"Yeah," Jeremiah said, nodding. "Hey, do you know when we play?"

"I do," Mark said, fiddling with his pockets. "Let me just see here." He produced a folded piece of paper from his back pocket, unfolded it, and studied it. "I have you guys playing tenth."

"Cool. Out of how many?"

"Ten."

"Great."

Mark gave Jeremiah a chipper smile, then motioned toward some of the other people in the backstage area. "Jeremiah, I gotta go make sure this confetti cannon is all loaded and ready to go, so . . . good luck out there. Hope you brought some chips!"

He gave a wave, laughed some more, and wandered off.

"What was that about?"

Jeremiah turned. Matt was approaching from the backstage entrance, carrying his guitar case and backpack.

"That was the emcee," Jeremiah said when Matt got a little closer. "He likes our name."

"Well, he should. It's awesome."

Jeremiah nodded. "We play last, by the way."

Matt whistled. "That's pretty sweet. It's like we're the headliner."

"Yeah, I don't know how that all worked out."

"Hey, boys."

Liz was coming through the backstage curtain, carrying her familiar stick bag.

"Where's Amanda?" Jeremiah said.

"Hi, Jeremiah," Liz said. "So nice to see you, too. Amanda's working tonight."

"I thought she got out of it."

"Yeah, her replacement got sick. Sorry."

Jeremiah sighed heavily. "It's okay." He looked around for somewhere to set his bass down. He was suddenly tired of carrying it.

Liz looked around the backstage area. "We should probably find out when we're going to sound check."

Fortunately, a stagehand was nearby, identifiable by his clipboard and headset walkie-talkie. Liz waved him over, and he complied. "When do we check?" she asked.

"What band are you?"

"Knuckle Sandwich."

The stagehand smiled as he consulted his clipboard. "Cool name."

Jeremiah actually looked at the floor in a cartoonish display of bashfulness. He hadn't intended it to be cartoonish; it just came out that way.

The stagehand found what he was looking for on his clipboard. "We're checking in reverse, so since you guys play last, you check first," he said. "That means you check in"—he consulted his watch—"twenty minutes."

An icy river made its way down Jeremiah's spine. "But we haven't even loaded all our gear in."

"You got your instruments?"

They nodded.

"That's all you need," the stagehand said, pointing toward the proscenium. "We have a bunch of universal gear up there."

"Oh," Matt said. "Okay."

"Let's check it out," Liz said.

They were pleased by what they found.

"A DW kit!" Liz said. "Awesome."

"That's a Marshall half-stack," Matt said, approaching the guitar amp. "That's gonna sound sweet."

Jeremiah nearly wet himself when he saw the bass rig procured for him: an Ampeg amp with a speaker cabinet almost as tall as him.

Clearly, they were going to rock even better than they had imagined.

The guys quickly got out their guitars to try out the equipment, Jeremiah plugging into his amp with all the reverence of an Old Testament priest. He couldn't believe he was about to play through such superior equipment. He wished he had a different bass—playing his T-40 through that cabinet was, to him, like having the biggest big-screen TV in town and a crummy, foil-lined antenna. Sure you could watch the QUAILS Awards for Outstanding Christian Music (Quality, Uniqueness, And Individualism with a Loving Spirit) on a screen bigger than Montana, but what good was that when the picture was grainy and full of ghost images, with the occasional hitch in the horizontal hold?

Even so, when Jeremiah got up the nerve to pluck a string, he felt like he had just discovered plutonium. By accident. Actually, truth be told, he felt like Lance Stanley, bass player for Cross-Eyed, though the depth and richness of the amp wasn't liquefying his intestines just yet. They were just rather gelatinous.

The rest of sound check went fine, with a few of the other bands paying attention to them as they ran through "Coaltongue." Jeremiah tried not to focus on them, instead concentrating on locking in with Liz. The stage setup here was much bigger than he was used to. The cramped Teens Ablaze stage forced him to sync up with whoever was on drums. Here, with room to spread out, he found himself disliking the fifteen feet or so between him and the kit.

He struggled through the rest of the sound check, feeling like he was off his game. When they were finished, he went backstage.

"Dude, you okay?" Matt said.

"What? Why?" Jeremiah had been hoping his lack of game was all in his head.

"You just sounded kinda off. Get with the program, homey."

"Yeah, I was— " Jeremiah said, stammering. "I was, just, I don't know. Like you said—something's off."

"Well, figure it out before we go up there," Matt said, annoyed. "This is a big deal—it's our first show. I don't want to start off on the wrong foot."

"Neither do I, Matt."

"Good." Matt picked up his backpack. "I'm going to go change my strings and pray. See you in a bit."

"Yeah."

Jeremiah put his bass in the case, clasped it, and sat down on the floor to think. Was he just not made to play bass on the big stage? Was he choking? Was he destined to play for bands like Teens Ablaze for the rest of his life? And was that a bad thing?

"What's wrong, Jeremiah? You okay?" came a voice.

Jeremiah looked up to see Liz standing over him.

"Yeah, I'm fine," he said. "Just a little—I don't know. Something's off to me."

Liz plopped down on the floor next to Jeremiah. "Yeah, it sounded kinda wiggly out there."

"Wiggly?"

She moved her hands back and forth, like they were fish swimming upstream. "Yeah, wiggly. Like, not solid." She stopped moving her hands and held them parallel to each other, perfectly straight. "Like that."

"I get it," Jeremiah said. "What can we do, though? It's just in my head, I think."

"Nah, you were just too far away."

"Well, I was trying to focus on playing."

Liz let out a slight guffaw. "No, really—you were too far away. You're used to playing on that tiny stage at Teens Ablaze, right? And now you're, like, halfway across the stage from me. Just move closer when we play tonight and you'll be fine."

"Seriously?"

Liz nodded. "Just try it out," she said. "You'll see."

||||||

Jeremiah fought back a vomitous feeling the rest of the night, a feeling that grew progressively worse with each band that played. Band after band took the stage, played their two songs, and got off. Some of them were pretty good. There was a punk band of upperclassmen called Shetland Barbecue, and even though both their songs sounded the same, they were enjoyable. There was a rap act called Royal-T that had played with a live band—Liz really dug them.

There were also some bands that Jeremiah just didn't get. One band called Sturm und Drang just seemed to make a lot of noise with guitar feedback and their many spring-coil reverb pedals. And Scarlet Crimson, while having a cool name, was just too . . . acoustic.

After each band finished their set, they'd come backstage to receive accolades from the other bands, usually in the form of handshakes. Phrases like "Good job" and "You guys rocked it" were being handed out like candy.

Soon, the vomitous feeling rose even higher as Matt approached them, his Les Paul hanging over his shoulder. "Hey, I think we should pray," he said.

"Okay," Jeremiah said.

"Sure," Liz said.

Matt held out his hands in the standard "let us join hands" maneuver practiced in every prayer circle Jeremiah had ever been involved in. Jeremiah and Liz obliged as Matt began to bow his head and speak. "Lord, please help us to honor you as we play. Help us play to the best of our ability, and if it's your will, help us to win. Give us favor with the judges; help them to see how much we rock."

From the wings, Jeremiah heard Mark's voice: "Ladies and gentlemen, I hope you brought some Doritos and a pickle spear, because it's my honor to present to you, for the first time ever: KNUCKLE SANDWICH!"

The audience clapped with gusto, but Matt kept his head bowed. "Thanks, God, for this opportunity. Amen." He jerked his head up and looked at Jeremiah and Liz. "Let's rock, guys."

He slung his guitar over his head into playing position and rushed onstage, one hand holding the Les Paul by the neck, near the body, and the other hand raised up in the air in a big fist. Liz crept straight from backstage into her little drum cove, sticks in hand. Jeremiah snatched his bass from the case nearby and threw it over his shoulder as he went onstage, striding along the back of the stage, giving a token wave to the applauding crowd as he made his way to the bass rig.

He plugged in, turned up the volume on his bass, and gave the strings a gentle pluck. Still bowel-shaking.

He turned to watch Liz as she set the tempo for "Coaltongue," but before she did, she motioned him to come closer, with a smile. He read her lips: "Come on. Let's rock."

Jeremiah stayed rooted for a moment while Liz clicked off the song with her sticks. He came in slightly behind the beat and immediately began to panic. He flitted a glance at Liz, who looked at him with reassurance, laying down the beat and jerking her head as if to say, "Get over here now, moron."

He took a few steps until he was right next to the drums, maybe only a foot away. Ah. Much better. He bobbed and weaved and tightened up with the groove Liz was laying down. He was now able to dig his mammoth sound.

There's a word in the music world for that incredible time when a band sounds as perfect as it can. That word is "pocket." The phrase usually used is, "That sounds so pocket." Or something along those lines.

Knuckle Sandwich was so pocket they could open their own pants factory.

Matt was going crazy, hopping all around the place, screaming into his microphone, bending over to rock during the instrumental part of the bridge, and just generally creating a one-man pandemonium.

They had the audience in the palms of their hands, just one song in.

"God Only Knows" went about the same way, and Jeremiah was able to settle down enough to look into the crowd. He saw a lot of heads bobbing in time with the music. And that freaked him out.

Those people out there—all 2,000 of them—were listening to music that he had helped create . . . and they *liked* it. This wasn't just his own spin on existing praise-and-worship tunes; this was original material.

They hit the last downbeat, Liz crashing out her cymbals as they held the note. Matt did a few pick slides down the neck of his guitar, turned toward Jeremiah and Liz, smiled huge, then jumped up in the air, his guitar raised. They ended the note at the precise moment that he landed on his knees. Then, a split-second of silence.

Followed by an eruption of applause. Cheers. Whistles. Jeremiah looked out and saw people standing up. Standing up! A standing ovation! For his band! He was positive that he wore the stupidest grin ever worn on a human being before.

"Give it up for Jesus!" Matt said. "He gets the glory!" He gave a big wave and headed toward the back of the stage.

"Hey-oh!" Mark the emcee said, strolling onto the stage with his wireless microphone. "One more time for Knuckle Sandwich, everyone! Talk about *hit* songs, people! Ouch! I think I lost a tooth on that last one!"

The audience kept applauding as Jeremiah unplugged his bass and joined Matt and Liz as they exited the stage. Matt smacked him on the back.

"That was *awesome*, bro! Did you feel God moving?"

"Yes," Jeremiah said as they hit the backstage area.

"Dude, whatever you did to play so great . . . never stop, okay?"

Jeremiah smiled and looked at Liz. She smiled back and gave him a thumbs-up. "Okay," Jeremiah said.

Matt clapped him on the back once again, then disappeared into a crowd of people from other bands, all handing out those candy phrases.

CHAPTER TWELVE

CONFIRMATION COMES IN THIRD

Jeremiah just looked at it. There, on the table, the fluorescent lights of IHOP causing its shiny, gold, plastic lyre to gleam.

"Third place," he said. "I didn't even think they had a third-place trophy."

Liz, sharing the bench on the other side of the booth with Matt, picked up the bauble by its wooden base and weighed it in her hands. "Well, this thing isn't going to fool anyone into believing that's real wood," she said. "Or gold. It's light as a plastic feather."

Matt snatched the trophy away from her. "Hey, it's something," he said, holding it aloft in the light, slowly twisting it back and forth in the harsh beams. "It's a symbol of our success. We rocked it out there tonight, and this harp is proof."

"I think that's a lyre, actually," Jeremiah said.

"Whatever," Matt said. "The first-place trophy had a harp."

"Yes, it did."

"That's the one we should've won," Matt said, setting the trophy back down on the table next to his rapidly chilling cup of coffee. "We were way better than Scarlet Crimson or Shetland Barbecue. I mean, those guys were okay, but not as good as us."

Liz pointed her forefinger into Matt's arm like a fencing foil going for the kill. "I told you: upperclassmen."

Matt shrugged off her finger and looked at her with a smirk. "How'd you get so smart?"

"Lucky guess."

Jeremiah patted his pockets, feeling around for spare change. He had none. "Either of you guys have a quarter? I wanna call Amanda."

"Sure thing, homey," Matt said, reaching into his pocket and producing the coin. He flipped it to Jeremiah, who snatched it out of the air like a magician catching a bullet.

"Thanks," Jeremiah said, sliding out of the booth and heading to the pay phone over by the restrooms. He made his way through the mostly empty tables, past a handful of sweatshirt-wearing ORU students in a corner booth talking loudly about their upcoming humanities exam, and to the phone, slipping the quarter into the slot and lifting the receiver.

He dialed her number. The phone rang once.

Twice.

"Come on, pick up," he said under his breath.

Three times.

Four times.

Click. For a second, Jeremiah's heart leapt at the sound of the phone being answered. It only lasted a second, though. Liz's pre-recorded voice came warbling through the handset.

"Hey, you've reached the fabulous apartment of Liz and Amanda. We're probably braiding each other's hair or talking about boys or something, so leave a message and we'll giggle back to you."

Beep.

"Uh, hey, Amanda. It's Jeremiah. I, uh, figured you'd be back by now, but I guess you're still at work. Um. We won!" That didn't sound quite right. "Well, we didn't *win* win, but we got third place, and Liz says that's really good for freshmen, so that's pretty cool, huh?" Asking questions on an answering machine = bad idea. "Well, *I* think it's cool anyway. So. There you go." Wrap it up, Jeremiah. "I'll call you later to tell you all about it. Okay?" Question again. Come on. "Okay. Um. Bye."

He hung up the receiver, feeling pretty dorky right about then.

Still: *third-place* dorky.

Jeremiah made his way back to the booth, only to see Matt and Liz sliding themselves out of their seat, Matt picking up the trophy with one hand and throwing a few bills down on the table with the other.

"Hey, we're gonna go to a midnight movie," Matt said, "Wanna come?"

"Aw, man," Jeremiah said. "Yes, I do want to come, but I can't. I have to work tomorrow morning." He pointed his thumb toward the door. "I should probably get going."

"All right, man," Matt said, clapping him on the shoulder. "You did good tonight. Sounded awesome."

"Yeah," said Liz, giving him a perky thumbs-up. "I think it was that bass rig. I know I played better because of those drums."

Jeremiah just nodded. That bass rig had been the sweetest rig he'd ever played through.

||||||

Jeremiah hit the shower as soon as he got home, changed into some sweats and a T-shirt, and decided his brain was going a little too crazy to go to sleep right away. Instead, he headed to the living room and flopped onto the just-out-of-fashion couch to watch that night's syndicated episode of *Cheers*.

No sooner had Sam fought with Diane than Jeremiah heard the jingle of keys outside the front door, then the door opening with a squeak and closing with a muffled thud. Jeremiah knew from the noise and the sudden fragrance of secondhand smoke that his dad was home.

"Hey, Jeremiah," Dad said as he toted his guitar case into the living room and set it down with all the other guitar cases, stands, amps, microphones, microphone stands, speakers, and other musical equipment that littered the space. "How'd it go tonight?"

Jeremiah muted the TV, silencing the bar patrons' cheer of "Norm" around the beginning of the "R" sound. "It went good. We got third."

Jeremiah's dad plopped himself down on the couch next to Jeremiah. "Really?"

Jeremiah smiled and nodded.

His dad gave him a thwack on the closest knee. "Awesome!" His face lit up like the back of a forty-five-watt tube amp. "Third place is really good for a bunch of freshmen like you guys!"

"That's what Liz said."

His dad's mouth tightened and went over to one side. He gave his head a quick shake. "I wish I could've been there, son."

Jeremiah elbowed his dad in the arm. "It's okay, Dad," he said. "I know you had a gig." He turned in his seat to face his dad. "How'd it go?"

His dad waved off the question with a broad arm movement. "Oh, you know. Same set, different day." He turned to face Jeremiah. "I'm sure your evening was much more exciting. Tell me all about it."

"Well, it was just cool. I got to play on this sweet bass rig they had set up."

His dad's eyebrows shot up. "What was it?"

"Ampeg head and cabinet."

"What size cabinet?"

"I think it was a two-twenty."

His dad let out a low whistle, then chuckled. "I bet you sounded like a titan, huh?"

Jeremiah gave a chuckle of his own. "Yeah, it was nice." He glanced at the ceiling for a moment, gathering his thoughts. "You know, I felt like I played better just because I was playing on that amp."

"Good gear'll do that for you," his dad said, pointing across the living room to his guitar. "So, did Matt and Liz do good, too?"

"Yeah," Jeremiah said, laughing again. "Matt went a little nuts. He was crazy." He waggled his arms around in a simulation of Matt's antics. "All over the place."

"That's kind of his style, though. Right?"

"Definitely."

"And so you guys got third!" His dad laid a hand on Jeremiah's shoulder. "I'm really proud of you, son."

Jeremiah looked into his dad's eyes and saw pride. "Thanks, Pop."

Jeremiah's dad took his hand down, and the two of them turned back to the muted TV, sharing a satisfied silence. There was a commercial for some spindly exercise device.

After a few moments, Jeremiah piped up. "Dad, did I ever tell you that Matt had a vision from God about our band?"

"No, I don't think so."

Jeremiah turned back toward his dad. "Yeah, he did. He thought I was supposed to be in it. And Liz."

"Yeah?"

"Yeah," Jeremiah said. He scratched his neck. "Do you think that, maybe winning third place means something? Like, that Matt really heard from God?"

Jeremiah's dad looked him dead in the eyes. "I think it means you guys are talented enough to win. And as long as you're making music for God, inside?" He tapped Jeremiah softly on the chest. "From in here? You're doing the right thing."

"Is that what you do, Dad?"

His dad smiled. "You bet, kiddo. It's the best thing in the world." His smile faded slightly. "Still, I wish I could've been there. I really want to hear you guys."

"You will, Dad."

||||||

That night, Jeremiah lay in bed, his head spinning. Third place meant something. It meant that there was potential in this band. That maybe Matt's vision from God really did include him. Tonight's show was about more than just playing—for Jeremiah, it was confirmation that his life was on the right track.

He said a short prayer. "God, whatever you're doing? Never stop, okay?"

CHAPTER THIRTEEN

AN HONEST-TO-GOODNESS, FOR-REAL, OFFICIAL DATE

"OH MY GOSH!" Amanda screamed, causing crazy distortion in the earpiece of Jeremiah's phone. "That is so cool that you guys placed! I'm so mad I missed it!"

Jeremiah was about to head into work, but he'd called Amanda first to make sure she'd gotten his message.

"Yeah, I was kinda bummed you missed it, too."

"I am so sorry, Jeremiah. I was feeling sick, so I came home early from work and went right to bed," she said. "YOU GOT THIRD!"

"So, I guess you're feeling better, then?"

"Yeah, I just had a stomach thing, I think."

"Oh, good."

"OH MY GOSH, JEREMIAH!" Amanda said. "I can't believe this!" She had settled down a bit. Instead of crazy distortion, now it was slightly more sane distortion. "I *have* to make this up to you. This was, like, your biggest night ever and I wasn't even there!"

"Oh, you don't have to— "

"Yes, I do!" Amanda said. "I'm going to take you out tonight."

Whoa! Would it count as a date if Jeremiah didn't do the asking?

"Uh . . ." Jeremiah didn't know what to say. He'd been thinking of asking Amanda on an official date but didn't want to screw up their friendship. So why was her demand of a date right now throwing him for a loop? And if he didn't say something soon, would it hurt her feelings and make her think that he wasn't turning backflips in his stomach right now?

"Unless you . . . don't want to?" Amanda said, sounding crestfallen. There was no distortion in Jeremiah's ear this time; in fact, he could barely hear her.

"NO!" Jeremiah said, maybe a little too loudly. "I mean, YES!" Dangit! What did he mean? "Yes, I'd love for you. To make it up to me. Tonight. And take me out. To the Cracker Barrel. Or wherever."

Amanda had started laughing somewhere in the middle of all that. "Do you work today?" she said.

"Yeah. I get off at 5:30."

"Okay. Why don't you come meet me at my house after you get off?"

"Sounds good," Jeremiah said. "Hey, what about Matt and Liz? Wanna invite them to come along?"

"Oh, I think they already have plans."

"Okay," Jeremiah said. "Rock on. I guess I'll see you around 5:30."

||||||

For some reason, even though Jeremiah couldn't think of anything he would rather do than go out with Amanda, he felt nothing but apprehension about that night's festivities, and his apprehension did nothing but build as the day wore on. He was flubbing up at the register, keying in incorrect prices, scanning the wrong items, and generally just making a mess of it.

He thought about it and couldn't fathom where his apprehension was coming from. He eventually settled on this: He was both nervous and upset with himself for not having read the now-obvious signs and asking Amanda out a long time ago. His apprehension came not from her, but from himself.

Another thing bothering him: He'd never been on a proper date. What should he do? How was this going to be different from the times they'd hung out together? Or would it? Should he act differently? Would she?

So many questions. He began to wish for 5:30 just so he could get some answers.

After clocking out, he hopped into his Corsica and headed toward the apartment Amanda and Liz shared. A few minutes later, he was there, knocking on the door.

Which Amanda threw open, greeting him with a "JEREMIAH!" Jeremiah immediately noticed three things:

1. Amanda's slight southern twang was more pronounced when she hollered his name. It came out "Jair-uh-MAH-yuh." He'd never noticed this before.
2. The apartment smelled like someone had been doing some home cooking, though he couldn't place the exact fragrance. He could tell bacon was involved.
3. Amanda was radiant, her hair pulled back in a classy ponytail, a hint of makeup, a modest-yet-flattering party dress. It wasn't anything fancy, but it was definitely a step up from her usual jeans-plus outfits (jeans plus T-shirt, jeans plus sweatshirt, jeans plus sweater, etc.).

Jeremiah glanced down at his own work clothes and suddenly felt highly underdressed.

"Well, don't just stand there, Jeremiah, come on in, you big rock star!" Amanda was beaming, and it threw Jeremiah off a bit.

"Okay," he said, stepping over the threshold, instantly surrounded by that bacony aroma. It matched the dim, cozy atmosphere automatically created by the apartment's lack of square footage and appropriate lighting.

"You know your way around," Amanda said, closing the door, then slipping past Jeremiah into the kitchen.

"Well, yeah, since there's hardly any 'around' here," Jeremiah said. The apartment was a trifle small, and the girls had packed it with overstuffed furniture along the living room's three white walls, saving space only for a small television (with antenna), a halogen floor lamp, and a decent-sized CD rack packed with CDs.

Jeremiah followed Amanda, making a U-turn at the dining room to reach the very tiny, very yellow kitchen.

"Something smells good, Amanda."

"Oh, thank you," she said. "I don't know how to cook much other than a big country breakfast, so I made you one."

Jeremiah's eyebrows shot up. "For dinner?"

"Yeah!"

"Are you going to eat, too?"

"Of course, silly!" she said, smacking him on the arm with a fish-themed oven mitt.

Jeremiah smiled. "Great." He had never had breakfast for dinner, but now that it was being offered, he decided it was possibly the best idea he'd ever heard.

He looked around the kitchen and saw pancakes, scrambled eggs, the afore-smelled bacon, and orange juice. Oddly enough, it sounded like just the thing to satisfy Jeremiah after his long, apprehension-filled day at work.

Amanda heaped healthy helpings of the breakfast bonanza onto a couple of paper plates, taxing their capacity, then gestured toward the dining-room table with a nod of her head. "Sit down, sir. Dinner is served."

||||||

"This is really good," Jeremiah said for about the fourteenth time.

"Thank you," Amanda said, almost blushing. "Like I said, I don't do much, but I can do this."

"Well, I'll take it."

She giggled.

"So, what's happening after dinner?"

Amanda giggled again. "Nothing much. I just hope you brought your dancing shoes."

Jeremiah looked down at his sneakers with a wry grin. "Um, since these are my only shoes, I guess they'll have to be my dancing shoes," he said. "Are we going to Club David?"

She smiled and nodded vigorously, her eyebrows almost touching the ceiling. "Yeah, I thought it would be fun," she said. "You know. For old times' sake."

"Old times," Jeremiah said. "Yeah, we sure have had some old times, these past, what, like, three months?"

She giggled again. "Something like that." She pointed at his plate. "You done yet?"

Jeremiah looked at his plate with a slight pang of regret that he was full. "I think so. I mean, it's so good I could keep on eating it, but," he patted his stomach, "I don't think I need to."

Amanda flashed him a cute, wrinkled-nose smile. "Well, nobody *needs* to, but that shouldn't stop you."

Jeremiah waved a hand at her. "No, thanks. I'm good." He handed her his plate, which she promptly threw in the trash. "And I'm eager to go hit that dance floor. For old times' sake."

She giggled again. "You're going to have to change clothes, mister."

||||||

They drove to Jeremiah's house so he could dash in and change. As she came in with him, he realized that she'd never been to his house before. Never met his dad.

"Sorry for the mess," he said, pointing out the gear in the living room. "Just a couple of bachelors living here."

"No big deal," she said. "Where's your dad?"

"He has a gig tonight." Jeremiah hit the stairs. "I'll be down in a sec," he said, taking them two at a time.

Truth be told, he was a little relieved his dad wasn't home. He wasn't sure how to introduce Amanda. Was she his . . . girlfriend?

Now he was all mixed up. It certainly seemed like they were on a date, and boys and girls don't go on dates unless they're boyfriend and girlfriend. Right? Still, there was no formal commitment yet, no Declaration of Dependence signed by either of them, swearing they each needed the other in order to live.

But perhaps there would be, later tonight. Jeremiah felt something in his bones tell him that, while Amanda had made the first semi-move, it was up to him to seal the deal. Which would require a little bravery on his part, because . . . well . . . what if he was *wrong*?

In his room, he leapt into a pair of nice jeans and a black dress shirt, the closest approximation he could find to Amanda's informal formal wear. He hadn't been kidding about his sneakers being his only shoes, so he slipped those back on and headed back down the stairs, mulling his current quandary:

How could he advance their relationship without killing their friendship?

It was up to him; he would find a way.

CHAPTER FOURTEEN

DANCE-FLOOR FIREWORKS

"You live in a nice house," Amanda said as they drove to Club David.

"Thanks," Jeremiah said. "I guess it is kind of nice, for what it is. I don't even think about it anymore. I guess I've lived there so long I kind of take it for granted."

"Yeah," Amanda said softly. She waited there a moment, then brightened and continued. "Do you have any brothers or sisters?"

"Nope," Jeremiah said. "Just me and my dad."

"That's sad."

"I kind of like it," he said, hitting the "track forward" button on the CD player. "Well, I'm used to it, anyway."

"I still think it's sad," Amanda said, her head tilted as she twisted her ponytail around her index finger. "Where's your mother?"

"Don't know," Jeremiah said with an absence of hurt. "She got sick of the musician's-wife life pretty early on. Took off with some, I don't know, stockbroker or something."

"That's awful."

Jeremiah shrugged his shoulders underneath his seatbelt. "It's the truth."

"Well, it's still awful."

"We do fine," Jeremiah said as he whipped the Corsica into the tiny Club David parking lot. There were a few other vehicles there, but not many. "We're here."

Amanda leapt out of the car and ran around to the driver's side, almost pulling Jeremiah out. She was so excited that he began to suspect a surprise party or something inside.

But when they went through the doors, Club David looked about as deserted as it had the last time Jeremiah had come, which had been when he and Matt had met Amanda and Liz and his whole life had changed. The floor was literally empty, though a few patrons milled about on its outskirts.

Track Suit Man was still there, still track-suited up. Jeremiah was ready for him this time, though, and had a ten-dollar bill already in his hand. He offered it to Track Suit Man, who grinned and handed him back a pair of singles.

Meanwhile, Amanda had skipped over to the DJ booth and was carrying on a conversation with the DJ, standing on her tiptoes to see over the high wall. He wore a pair of headphones, one ear exposed, listening to Amanda, who was gesturing madly toward Jeremiah. The DJ nodded and began to flip through a massive CD folder.

Jeremiah approached Amanda, which didn't take long, given the diminutive size of the club. He pointed up toward the DJ booth. "What was that about?"

Amanda smiled mischievously. "Just making a small request," she said. She grabbed his hand and steered him to the dance floor. "Come on!"

They hit the floor as the current song, which Jeremiah didn't recognize, faded out and Tribe of Benjamin faded in.

That was strange. Jeremiah knew there wasn't a giant selection of Christian dance music, but what were the odds of the same song playing as the last time he was here?

Wait a minute. Amanda requested this.

"What's going on?" he said. Fortunately, the volume in Club David wasn't as crushingly oppressive as last time, and he didn't have to shout to be heard.

"Whatever do you mean?" Amanda said with mock innocence.

"This is the same song we danced to last time we were here. When I met you."

"Oh, is it? I hadn't noticed." She giggled again. "Okay, Jeremiah—don't pretend you don't know."

"Know what?"

"What today is!"

"Saturday?"

She clubbed him on the arm. "No!"

"Well, actually it is, but I guess that's not the answer you were looking for?"

"No," she said, laughing. "As of today, we've known each other for *exactly* three months!"

She said it with such satisfaction and joy, as if she was talking about—well, Jeremiah hesitated to even think it—an anniversary.

Oh, what the heck. "Like an anniversary?" he said.

He'd never seen her smile so big. "Now you're getting it."

And it was at this point that Jeremiah took the biggest step he'd ever taken in his entire life. It all came together for him, and in a massive brain wave, he saw exactly how to proceed.

The two of them had been semi-bobbing to the music, but Jeremiah stopped. He stood stone still, delicately reached out and grabbed Amanda's shoulders, and held her steady, looking into her eyes.

"Amanda, I'm going to ask you something, and I want you to be honest with me, okay?" he said. "No matter what you think I want to hear."

Her eyes grew wide and expectant. "Okay," she said.

"Do you ever see us becoming more than just friends?"

There was a reason he phrased it like that. The hoped-for answer was a delighted "yes," after which there would be much hugging and smiling and relief on his part. But. The flip-side of the question offered him a tactful way out if he was somehow misreading all these signals from Amanda. If she said "no," he could play it off. "Oh, good, because I was starting to think that you liked me, and I just wanted to establish that we're just friends and nothing more." Or something like that. It would come to him.

He wouldn't mean it, but at least he wouldn't be rejected and humiliated. Well, not publicly anyway.

So, there the question hung. "More than just friends." Amanda hesitated for a moment, considering the words. Jeremiah panicked in this moment, sure she would come back with a negative answer.

Or not. "Yes!" she said. He could see the fire in her eyes, despite the reflections of the intelligent lighting in her glasses.

So he kissed her.

Fireworks went off inside his body—his brain, his heart, his stomach. Other areas. Time stopped. Then went backward. Then fast-forwarded into the future a hundred thousand years, then reversed again to the present. Lights went crazy around them. The beat pulsated. Their bodies sighed and leaned into each other. She felt warm.

It wasn't a long kiss, really, but it felt like an eternity to Jeremiah, mainly for one reason.

"That was my first kiss," he said, looking into Amanda's enormous eyes. "Was it okay?"

She nodded, smiled, closed her eyes, and kissed him.

More of that time warp stuff. Fireworks. Crazy lights.

"So that's a yes, then?"

| | | | | |

The two of them danced much more closely to each other than they had last time they were at Club David. Biologically, Jeremiah was freaking out. His body didn't know how to react to a female of the species taking a physical interest in him. They kept themselves clean, to be sure. Left room for the Holy Spirit, as the old youth-group admonition went. But still, come on, this was a woman, and she was very near him, and she *liked* him, and she had *kissed* him, and how was he supposed to deal with that? Huh?

He pulled back and looked in her eyes, the lights low enough to cause no reflection in her glasses. Some words appeared from the mists of his memory.

Time doth transfix the flourish set on youth, And
delves the parallels in beauty's brow,
Feeds on the rarities of nature's truth,
And nothing stands but for his scythe to mow;
And yet to times in hope my verse shall stand;
Praising thy worth, despite his cruel hand.

She scrunched her nose. "What's that?"

Jeremiah let out a laugh. "Shakespeare. One of his sonnets."

"Wow," she said. "He likes words."

She put her head on his chest and hugged him close. Jeremiah figured she wasn't really wanting to talk much.

After twenty minutes or so, the two of them took a break, strolling off the dance floor holding hands (just that touch alone, with the fingers interlocked, was driving Jeremiah's body crazy). On a whim, Jeremiah pulled Amanda over to the DJ booth and caught the DJ's attention.

"Hey, man, you got any Cross-Eyed up there?" he said.

The DJ nodded. "Yeah, I think so."

"Can you play it?"

The DJ looked around the room. Jeremiah turned and did the same. The place was more deserted than the surface of Mars. He turned his attention back to the DJ, who nodded at him.

"I think I can swing it," the DJ said.

"Thanks, bro."

"Not a problem, dude." The DJ suddenly took his headphones completely off and pointed at Jeremiah. "Wait a second, man—I *thought* I recognized you! You're in that rock band from last night!"

Jeremiah was simultaneously taken aback and deliriously pleased. Amanda was too, apparently—she squeezed his hand with glee.

"Yeah, man. That's . . . right."

"Dude, you guys rocked."

"Thanks, man. Thanks."

"When are you playing next? 'Cause I wanna come check you out again. And some of my friends, too."

Jeremiah shrugged. "I don't know. We haven't really gotten that far."

The DJ threw his hands in the air. "Dude!" he said. "You can totally play here!"

Jeremiah looked at Amanda quickly, who gave him that look people give when they think, "Well, isn't that interesting? Tell me more, sir!"

He looked back at the DJ. "Tell me more."

CHAPTER FIFTEEN

AN HONEST-TO-GOODNESS, FOR-REAL, OFFICIAL SHOW

"You got us an actual show? Like, a real show, where we play more than two songs?" Jeremiah wasn't sure, but it looked as though Matt was vibrating with excitement over the prospect of playing at Club David.

"Yeah," Jeremiah said, plugging his T-40 into the old reliable C4 youth room amplifier. It had been all Jeremiah could do to keep this tidbit of info to himself over the past two days—he had to deliver it in person.

"Will there be any other bands?" Liz asked.

"Only if we want there to be," Jeremiah said. "But we'll be the main act."

"Get out!" Matt said. "Seriously?"

Jeremiah nodded and cast a quick glance at Amanda, who was sitting on the metal folding chairs, smiling and taking in the scene.

"Yeah, the DJ there freaked out when he realized who I was," Jeremiah said. "He was at the Battle of the Bands, loved us, told all his friends about us. He's sure he can get quite a few people there."

"No way!" Matt said.

"That's what he said."

"Nuh-uh! That's awesome," Matt said. He looked heavenward. "God is so awesome, you guys."

"So when is it?" Liz said.

"Two weeks from last Saturday."

"Well," Liz said, unzipping her stick bag. "We better practice, then."

| | | | | |

Jeremiah was so busy with school, work, and his new girlfriend, as well as all the rehearsing Matt insisted on, that he scarcely had time to think about the show. He knew it wouldn't be as big a deal as the Battle of the Bands had been, but even though that had taken place on a big stage, there had been a little comfort in knowing they only had to play two songs.

Now they were playing every single one of their songs, as well as a cover of Cross-Eyed's version of "His Eye Is on the Sparrow," which sounded decidedly different from the traditional hymn.

So, two days before the show, the band (and Amanda) gathered at the C4 youth room to rehearse every song in their arsenal, again. Matt bopped into the youth room with the energy of a five-year-old. "Guys, I have an awesome surprise for you!" he said.

"What is it?" Jeremiah said.

"You'll see." He reached the stage and began unpacking his guitar and pedals. "Come on, let's get set up."

A few minutes later everyone was ready to go.

"Let's run through something," Matt said. "How about 'Break the Tablets'?"

He didn't wait for a response, cranking into the song's intro immediately. Liz and Jeremiah joined in. This was a newer song, and Jeremiah was happy to play it. He had worked hard to create a melodic bass line that counterbalanced the melody; it was the first time he'd ever experimented with something like that, and he felt the experiment had been a success.

Three and a half minutes later, the song was over.

"All right," Matt said. "Now that we're warmed up, check this out." He clicked off his distortion pedal and clicked on his tremolo. He began picking out a mournful chord progression that reminded Jeremiah of an old hymn, though he couldn't place which one.

"Have you ever felt so sad?" Matt sang, eyes closed, voice slightly raspy. "Have you ever felt so bad? Have you ever felt like / you could never ever feel glad?"

He stepped back from the microphone and picked through some more chords, his eyes still closed, his shoulders rocking slowly to the metronome in his head.

"There is a mystery / To all this history / To why you feel ill at ease," Matt sang again, this time powerfully, a bit of spittle flying from his mouth on the word *feel.* "I'll show you how / I'll show you now / How to fit the puzzle peace," he sang, easing up on his picking to let the last note ring out. "Puzzle . . . peeeeeaa aace." He picked up the progression again, but opened his eyes and looked at Jeremiah and Liz.

"I was praying with my guitar the other night and this song came to me," he said. "What do you think?"

Jeremiah didn't know what he thought about it.

Liz piped up. "Do you mean 'puzzle piece' like an actual piece of a puzzle, or do you mean 'peace' like 'peace on earth'?"

"Peace on earth."

"Huh."

Matt kept playing the chord progression, which was growing on Jeremiah.

"It's a little slow," he said, "but I kinda dig it."

Matt closed his eyes and grooved on the progression for a couple of seconds, then leaned into the microphone. "I wanna play it at Club David."

"That's an idea," Jeremiah said, "although it's a little late, don't you think?"

"No way," Liz said, setting her drumsticks down on her snare drum. "Bad idea."

Matt stopped playing and opened his eyes at the same time. "Are you saying 'no way' to me or Jeremiah?"

Liz placed her hands on her knees and leaned forward. "You," she said. "Matt, just because you have this song, that doesn't mean we have to do it the second you write it."

Matt threw down his guitar pick in disgust. "Come on, Liz—you know it's not like that."

"Matt, come on. Be reasonable, here."

"I'm not being reasonable?" Matt said, the huffiness apparent in his voice.

"You're wanting to play a song live that we just heard for the first time."

"But it's a song that God gave me. It's freshly anointed; that's why God gave it to me right before the show," Matt said. He was on the verge of whining.

"Okay," Liz said in a soothing tone. "But it isn't ready. We can't work it up in two days."

"Whatever." Matt fished another pick out of his case and started to strum the intro to "God Only Knows." He closed his eyes, released a heavy sigh, and said, "Let's just go over something else."

"Matt . . ." Liz said.

"Liz, come on. Be *reasonable*."

Liz rolled her eyes.

"Okay," Jeremiah said. "Let's do 'God Only Knows' for a little while."

"Fine with me," Matt said, continuing to play the intro.

Liz gave a four-count click, and she and Jeremiah came in and played the rest of the song with Matt.

The rest of the practice went without a hitch. By the end, Liz and Matt were back to their normal selves, and Jeremiah figured they'd made up in their own nonverbal way. The two of them spent so much time together that it seemed like they conversed by telepathy. And though they hadn't officially christened themselves a couple like Jeremiah and Amanda had, they certainly weren't fooling anyone as to their relationship status.

On the day of the show, Jeremiah fought the same nerves he'd fought about the Battle of the Bands. He fought them while he worked that day. He fought them while they loaded in their equipment at the club. He fought them while they ate dinner. He fought them as he sat at a café table with Amanda for a half hour, waiting for showtime to arrive.

"Is your dad coming?" Amanda said. At least that's what Jeremiah thought she said—he was concentrating on all the people streaming into the club. He figured there had to be at least fifty, and that was about forty-five more than he'd ever seen in Club David.

"What's that?" Jeremiah said, just for confirmation.

"Is your dad coming?"

He turned toward her. "No, he has a gig tonight. Again."

She reached out and took his hand in hers. "Aw, Jeremiah. I'm sorry."

He placed his other hand on top of the rapidly growing hand-pile in the center of the table. "It's okay. I understand. He'll get to a show someday."

Probably seventy-five, actually. That's a lot of people.

Matt and Liz approached. Matt knelt next to Jeremiah, placing a hand on his shoulder. "How're you feeling, hoss?"

Jeremiah nodded. "Good."

"Great," Matt said, glancing at his watch. "Hey, we got about five minutes; let's pray real quick and then we'll go on."

"Sure thing."

The foursome all bowed their heads where they were. Jeremiah and Amanda were still joined at the hand.

"God, you're awesome," Matt said, eyebrows furrowed with sincerity. "Thanks for this show. Thanks for blessing us with musical talent, and for giving us a way to give it back to you. Please help us to play well, to be tight, and to rock this place hard. Amen."

"Amen," the other three said, almost simultaneously.

They all took a second to look at each other.

"Let's rock," Matt said, grabbing Liz's hand and heading to the dance floor, which, just for that evening, was doubling as a stage. Jeremiah gave Amanda a quick peck and followed.

The assembled throng began to scream and cheer as Knuckle Sandwich took the stage. Jeremiah even detected a hearty male voice screaming the word "Awesome."

"Good evening," Matt said into the microphone. "We're Knuckle Sandwich. How you guys doing tonight?"

Cheers galore.

"Anyone here ready to rock for the Rock?"

Screams aplenty.

"Well, let's get to it, then!"

And with that, the band busted into "Ham-Fisted," and there was no turning back.

The small dance floor was a perfect fit for Jeremiah's newfound comfort zone with Liz, and he felt good about the initial groove. He moved within a foot of Liz again and latched on to her for the whole show. Together, they laid down a thick foundation that gave Matt plenty of solidity to go off.

And go off he did. He dipped, he soared, he engaged the crowd. He sweated all over them. He got so lost in "God Only Knows" that he started reeling back and forth, eyes closed, playing the riff as hard as he could. He almost knocked someone in the teeth with the headstock of his Les Paul.

The remaining songs on the set list dwindled until they got to the final two. They finished "Golden Calf," which left "Coaltongue"—the song that had brought down the house at ORU—to be the big, showstopping finale. They had rehearsed a smooth transition between the two songs, where one would end, then, as Jeremiah sustained the last note, Matt would come in softly with a clean-tone intro. It sounded sweet when they rehearsed it.

This time? Sour. Jeremiah held the note like he was supposed to, but Matt never came in with his intro. Jeremiah flashed a nervous look at Liz, who muttered under her breath, "Oh, great."

Assuming the end of the song, the crowd began to cheer, but Matt held up a hand to silence them. He strummed chords seemingly at random.

"You know," he said to the audience, "a lot of times, God's ways seem . . . strange to us. Sometimes, he goes against our plans." He turned to look at Jeremiah and Liz. "Even when we don't understand it, he gives us a feeling where we know we're doing the right thing by following him." Then he looked back at the audience. "This is a new one. It's called 'Puzzle Peace.'"

Jeremiah looked blankly at Liz, leaning close to her ear. "What do we do?" he said quietly.

"Follow him, I guess."

Jeremiah feverishly tried to remember how the song went. It started on E, he knew that. But after that, he was shaky. He moved away from Liz to try to get a view of the neck of Matt's guitar, hoping to get an inkling of the progression.

He fumbled his way through the song, while Matt gave it his all. Jeremiah finally got a handle on the gist of the song, but being so far away from Liz, and concentrating too much on the notes instead of the groove caused him to feel less than enthused about his playing.

The song went into the bridge, which forced Jeremiah once more to pay attention to Matt's hands. Matt always wrote tricky bridges that didn't sound quite right until you got used to them. Jeremiah muddled through until Matt finally got back to the chorus, where Jeremiah knew his way around. He strolled back over to Liz and finished the last two choruses strong.

"Someone needed that song tonight!" Matt said into the microphone. "We weren't gonna play it, but someone needed it." He turned around to Jeremiah and Liz. "Someone needed it, guys," he said, almost apologetically, as if he'd been forced to play it against his will.

He turned back to the microphone. "This is our last song. It's about desperately wanting to be free from sin. This is 'Coaltongue.'"

The rest of the show, all one song of it, went great. Jeremiah and Liz were back in fine form, and Matt once again became the insane performer he was.

The song ended, and more cheers and screams erupted from the crowd. Matt yelled "Thank you, Tulsa!" into his microphone and then stepped away to face Jeremiah and Liz. "Awesome show, guys. Awesome. Thanks for following me."

Jeremiah shrugged. "Sure."

The three of them stepped off the stage and back toward the café table, where Amanda had remained seated throughout the show.

Liz grabbed Matt by his shirtsleeve and pulled him into the corner. "Matthew, if you pull something like that again, you're going to be playing it solo."

"Liz, I— "

"No!" she said, taking a breath to regain control of her voice. "You can't just do stuff like that," she said. "We're all in this band together, right?"

Matt looked from left to right. "Yeah."

"Okay," she said. "So act like it. All right?"

He nodded.

Then she gave him a hug. A big one.

"You did great tonight, Matt," she said, "even if you are sweaty."

CHAPTER SIXTEEN

ADVENTURES IN PROFESSIONAL REPRESENTATION

After the crowd at Club David had dispersed (but not before asking about the next show, and where they could buy a CD of those songs, and were there any T-shirts available?), the members of Knuckle Sandwich packed up their gear. Jeremiah had pulled his Corsica around to the back door and was trying to remember how he had gotten the Teens Ablaze drum kit in there when he looked toward the stage and saw an African-American man talking to Matt.

Jeremiah wandered closer. He was far from racist, but there was a bit of cognitive dissonance happening for him right now. Sure, there were African-Americans who liked rock music, but they generally dressed the part, whereas this guy was more buttoned-down, in a three-piece suit, looking like a businessman with a fade haircut and a highly trimmed goatee. He was not a rocker. So why was he talking to Matt?

Matt saw him coming. "Ahh, here's Jeremiah," he said. "Jeremiah, this is Michael Weathers."

Michael extended his hand. "It's a pleasure, Mr. Springfield," he said.

Jeremiah shook the guy's hand, turning to look at Matt and hoping that "Who the heck is this guy?" was coming across in his eyes.

Matt answered Jeremiah's look. "Michael is a talent agent, Jeremiah. He manages musical acts."

"It's true, Mr. Springfield," Michael said with a million-dollar smile. "Right now I'm managing a hip-hop artist and an R&B group, and I've been looking for a good old-fashioned rock 'n' roll band to add to my repertoire."

"Really," Jeremiah said.

"Yes, sir."

"What artists do you represent right now?"

"Well, Demon Wrecka is a very talented, up-and-coming rapper who reminds the Body of Christ about their authority over the devil. And the R&B group is three very talented young men who call themselves Fresh Oil."

"Fresh Oil?"

"Yes. I got the name off a construction sign in my neighborhood, if you can believe that. They had just put down some new asphalt and they put that sign up. And I thought that would be a wonderful way of reminding the Body about how the Holy Spirit brings the oil of joy in a fresh way."

Jeremiah thought it over a minute. "Cool."

Liz had ambled over by now. "I actually heard Fresh Oil down at Greenwood a couple of Sundays ago. They're really funky."

Michael looked confused but retained his smile (it looked like about $750,000 now). "Girl, you were in a black church?"

Liz smiled now. "Actually, I go to Greenwood every Sunday. I like the music."

Michael's smiled leapt to a million and change. He clapped Jeremiah on the back. "Well, now I *know* this was meant to be."

| | | | | |

IHOP again. Jeremiah, Amanda, Matt, Liz, and Michael were all crowded into a corner booth, each working on a different stack of pancakes, except Michael, who was sticking with coffee.

"Man, that show made me hungry," Jeremiah said.

"Well, eat as much as you want," Michael said. "It's on me tonight, gang."

"Fanx," Matt said through a mouthful of pancakes and/or sausage. Jeremiah couldn't tell for sure.

"Yes, thank you," Liz said, her mouth free of breakfast-food impediments.

The group chewed for a bit. Michael took a sip from his cup.

"So, what do you have in mind for Knuckle Sandwich?" Matt said after he had swallowed.

"I feel like Knuckle Sandwich can remind the Body of the freedom they have in Christ," Michael said. "You have a lot to offer the Body, and I want to help you get your message out."

"That's nice of you," Liz said. "But how exactly do you plan to do that?"

Michael laughed, a deep, rich laugh that was deeper and richer than the cup of coffee he was two-thirds of the way through. "You sound like you have a good head on your shoulders, Liz," he said, putting his hands up in mock surrender. "I assure you, I am not out to exploit your artistry. That's why I don't ask for any money up front."

"That's good," Jeremiah said, turning to Amanda. She just nodded slightly, raising her eyebrows.

"Way I see it," Michael said, "if you don't get paid, I shouldn't either."

Liz tapped her fork on her plate, looking down at her pancake in contemplation. "Yeah, that makes sense."

Matt polished off his tall stack, set his fork down, and leaned forward. "So, what do you have in mind?"

Michael leaned in on his elbows. "Well, for starters, I want to get you guys onstage as much as possible. Starting next week."

Jeremiah and Liz stopped chewing.

"Now, don't think I'm putting you out on the road or anything. I'm just talking about a few shows here and there to remind the Body of your presence. I can get you in at a Christian place in Muskogee that would welcome you with open arms."

"Sounds good," Matt said.

"But," Michael said, "we can't book many shows without a demo, so that's my main priority."

"You want to record us?" Liz said.

"Like, *record* record?" Amanda said.

Michael gave his hugely expensive smile and nodded. "I have an associate who owns a Christian recording studio. Tongues of Fire. Fresh Oil recorded their demo there. Engineered and mixed all nineteen tracks on Demon Wrecka's full-length album there, too." He began to pat the pockets of his overcoat. "I think I have a CD here."

He reached into a pocket and produced a shrink-wrapped CD that featured a camouflage cover with the words "Demon Wrecka" printed in a stylized font reminiscent of military stenciling. He placed it on the table and slid it in the general direction of Matt and Liz. "You guys can have that."

| | | | | |

“How was the Demon Wrecka CD?” Jeremiah asked Matt and Liz at rehearsal the next day. “Did you guys listen to it?”

“Dude, it was awesome,” Matt said.

“Awesomely square,” Liz said, shaking her head. “It’s not funky enough.” She began to take a pair of sticks out of her stick bag. “And I don’t think it’s possible to ‘take out demons wit’ a spiritual gat.’ What does that even mean?”

“Like, prayer is your weapon against the enemy, Liz,” Matt said.

“Okay, so explain that whole song about, what, assassinating demons?”

“‘X-ecuta?’ ”

“Yeah, that one.”

Matt thought for a moment. “I don’t think I can.”

Liz laughed. “See!”

Jeremiah decided to jump in and end the madness. “Well, regardless of the style, does it sound good? Like, do the Tongues of Fire guys know what they’re doing?”

Matt and Liz agreed that they did, and that was the end of that.

A week later, Knuckle Sandwich found themselves piling all their gear—well, Teens Ablaze’s gear—into Michael’s almost-nice ’87 Grand Caravan, after which they found themselves piling themselves into the limited remaining space—made all the more limited by Amanda tagging along—and pointing the hood ornament toward Muskogee.

They listened to Demon Wrecka on the way there—Michael always listened only to his own artists. “That’s why I had to sign someone else—give me some new music to listen to!” he joked. Liz finally begged to listen to Fresh Oil, even though they only had rough mixes—their demo wasn’t done yet.

Jeremiah agreed with Liz, though. He’d rather listen to Fresh

Oil. They were funky, and though he'd never really been exposed to high levels of funkiness before, he was starting to like it.

When the van reached Muskogee proper, Michael consulted a map several times and made his way along side streets until he came to a building that looked like a gas station.

"This is it!" Michael said.

The reason the building looked like a gas station is because it had once been a gas station. It had been modestly renovated into something else, though the telltale rain-roof cover thing that all gas stations have over their pumps remained. The multitude of windows had been filled (on the inside) with purple paisley and gingham curtains on gilded rods, and the two big glass doors had golden curtains hanging in them.

Along the parking lot, next to the roadway, there was a large sign, the kind with the lighted arrow on top and the setup that allowed the sign's owner to place letters within it to make a message. It read:

JOSHUA'S SUPPER CLUB
NUCKLE SANWICH 2NITE!

"Wow," Jeremiah said.

Matt let out a low whistle.

"Oh. My. Gosh," Amanda said.

"Michael?" Liz said. "Are we the entertainment or the special?"

Michael laughed. "Liz, that's what I love about you. You always say what you mean!" He turned off the van. "Come on, let's go inside."

They piled out of the van and headed in, where the view did not improve much. Whoever had done the remodeling had decided that faux wood paneling and fake ivy were definitely the way to go. It was apparently a Christian-themed restaurant of some sort, as all the square, plain tables were adorned with laminated placemats touting the Jesus Always Network, a cable channel that showed nothing but religious programming twenty-four hours a day.

The place was completely empty, save for the proprietor, a round, gleeful woman who approximated a dumpling in a white apron. She gave them a cheerful wave and walked over to them.

"Hi, I'm Bernice, owner of Joshua's," she said in a thick southern accent. "Welcome, all y'all. Come on in."

Jeremiah wondered why he would need to be told to come in, seeing as how they were already in, but he said nothing.

He felt a squeeze on his arm. It was Amanda, who was looking at a menu.

"Oh my gosh, Jeremiah," she said. "All the dishes have Bible names."

Jeremiah leaned in for a closer inspection. Some of the selections included:

"Cain and Abel" (lamb with seasonal vegetables)

"Quail in the Wilderness" (which, according to the listing underneath, was chicken fingers and tater tots)

"Jacob's Birthright Stew"

"Turkey a la King of Kings"

To drink: "Milk of the Word" or "Wailing and Gnashing of Tea" or "Bloody Mary Magdalene (Virgin)," which seemed to Jeremiah to be way too confusing.

And for dessert, "White as Snow Cones" or "Forbidden Fruit Salad."

After he and Amanda perused the menu for a bit, he looked at her with disbelief. "Sounds tasty," he said.

"Jeremiah, did you see that every meal is served with 'Showbread?'"

Jeremiah stifled a laugh. "No. No, I didn't."

Bernice crashed their little party. "Y'all gonna play me some rock 'n' roll tonight?"

Michael had been looking around, eyeing the place warily. His smile was down to five hundred grand, easy. "Yes, ma'am. And all your customers."

She gave a cackle. "Well, we'll see who comes in. I only let Christians in here, you know. I had some sinners comin' in here th'other day, and I said to 'em, I said, 'Hey, there's tons o' places 'round here you sinners can go—this is the only place in all Muskogee what's for Christians and Christians only.' They done hightailed it right outta here."

Bernice said this almost proudly, as if she had done a good thing.

"Seriously?" Liz said. "You don't let non-Christians in here?"

"Yes'm!" It was unmistakable—Bernice *was* proud of it.

Liz cleared her throat. "Well, it sounds like . . . well, Bernice, do you think Jesus would really like that? Doesn't he love those people, too?"

"Well, they weren't payin' customers anyways," Bernice said, shuffling off to the back and, presumably, the kitchen. She gestured in the direction of a raised area in the corner of the restaurant. "There's where y'all can set up. Just move them tables out the way."

Bernice never came out of the kitchen again.

| | | | | |

After they had loaded in all their gear, set up, and done a quick sound check, the band decided it was time to eat. Michael disappeared into the back for a while, and Jeremiah showed Matt and Liz the menu, to their amazement.

Michael reappeared with no smile. He looked like zero dollars.

"Well, listen up, guys," he said. "I talked to Bernice, and she feels like, since she's paying you a hundred dollars to play tonight, you should buy your own food."

Having grown up the son of a gigging musician, Jeremiah knew without a doubt that, regardless of all the Christians-only stuff Bernice had talked about, *this* was really wrong. You bring in a band to play? You take care of them. That was, like, rule number one. Jeremiah had known that by the time he was four.

"Dude, that's not right," he said.

Michael looked apologetic. He shook his head. "I know, Jeremiah, I know. But there's nothing I can do." He handed them a twenty-dollar bill. "Look, my advice? Go down to Subway and get a six-inch for three bucks. This place is too expensive and—" he lowered his voice—"not that good, from what I can tell."

"Then what?" Liz said.

"Then come back here, play your show, let me collect your check, and we'll head home."

To no one's surprise, at showtime, their audience consisted of Michael and Amanda.

"This sucks," Liz said.

"Hey," Matt said. "If we do what we're here to do, and we do it to the best of our ability, then even though no one's watching, we're still honoring God."

To this, Michael added, "Just think of it as a paid rehearsal."

"Let's just play," Jeremiah said, taking a step toward the stage.

"Yeah," Matt said, about to follow him.

"Aren't we gonna pray?" Liz said, staying put.

Matt and Jeremiah stopped. "Sure," Matt said, turning back toward the group, Jeremiah following his lead.

They joined hands, bowed their heads, and Matt began his prayer: "God, please help us as we play. Bless our time. Amen."

It was an auspicious beginning to what wound up being an entertaining evening. Jeremiah and Liz cut loose on a funk jam halfway through the set that had Michael doing a little dance on top of a Jesus Always Network placemat.

Matt tried to improvise a new song on the spot, but realized halfway through that it sounded exactly like the theme song to *Sesame Street.*

All told, they had a good time, collected their check, and headed home.

After gas, they made $70, minus Michael's commission, which, after splitting three ways, gave Jeremiah $18 for the night's work.

Turns out it was the most satisfying paycheck he'd ever gotten.

CHAPTER SEVENTEEN

SOMEWHERE IN THE NEIGHBORHOOD OF A DEMO

Winter break came sooner than any of them expected, and it was a good thing, too, because Jeremiah was having a hard time focusing on his classes, what with his musical career taking off.

After the semi-nightmare at Joshua's, the band played Club David a couple more times and even got invited to play a "fifth quarter"—a post-football-game party—for Jeremiah's former high school. And everywhere they played, they fired up the crowd and tightened up their performance.

Michael had scheduled some time at Tongues of Fire so the band could record during winter break from ORU. Fortunately, Liz's winter break coincided with ORU's, so Michael set up their session for the third week in December, giving them plenty of time to record and then head off to wherever to celebrate the holidays.

There was, naturally, some consternation over which songs should be on the demo. Jeremiah had expected this. Matt wanted to record *all* their songs, his rationale being that, the more songs on the record, the more they could charge for it when they sold it at their shows.

Jeremiah thought that Matt *really* just wanted to record all the songs because he liked them all and couldn't stand choosing only four.

"Why do we need to do four songs?" Liz said. "Three sounds better to me. Less is more."

"*Three*?" Matt said, aghast. "For crying out loud, Liz, why don't we just not do any at all?"

"Oh my gosh, don't be so dramatic," Liz said.

"I just can't believe you're only wanting to do three."

"How many are we supposed to do?" Jeremiah asked. "Shouldn't we talk to Michael about this? Wouldn't he know?"

Matt and Liz were both silent.

They consulted Michael a couple of days later and found out that the demo was indeed to be only *three* songs, contrary to their original belief. Matt was livid, until Michael pointed out to him that this demo wasn't the apex of his career; it was the tool they were going to use to get someone *else* to pay for their record.

"Matt, we can do all your songs, if you want," Michael said, "but that's studio time *you're* paying for. Might as well do three and let someone else pay for that studio time. In a better studio."

It made sense to Jeremiah, and apparently to Matt, too, because he didn't say anything else about it.

Since Michael was the manager, the group deferred to his wisdom on song selection. "Coaltongue" would be the first track, followed by "Golden Calf," and then "Puzzle Peace," which they had now worked up into a full arrangement.

So, armed with their track listing, Knuckle Sandwich met up at Michael's house on the morning of the first day of recording to follow him to the studio, because, as he put it, "It's a little hard to find."

Jeremiah was glad that Amanda was there in the Corsica with him as they followed Michael's Grand Caravan through the streets of Tulsa. It was a semi-overcast day, chilly, gray, and, like the cold, a dread was creeping into his pores. Whatever he played today—whatever he recorded—was on tape for all time. If he made a mistake live, it was no big deal, because as soon as he made it, it was done. There was no going back to that moment in time.

But now, if he made a mistake, everyone could listen to it. Again and again. It could be put on a continuous loop to be mocked and ridiculed for eternity. Maybe he wasn't cut out for recording; maybe he was a live-only musician.

He looked at Amanda, cute underneath her fuzzy stocking cap, staring out the window. He began to feel his dread ebb away. She believed in him. They were always together, and, if Jeremiah had to venture a guess, he'd say they were in love. Or, if not "Love," at least "Serious Like."

Amanda glanced at him, embarrassed. "What are you looking at?"

Jeremiah smiled. "You."

She smiled back. "Why?"

"You just . . ." He looked back at the road. "I'm kinda nervous about this, and looking at you makes me feel better."

She melted onto his shoulder. "Aw," she said, "that's so sweet."

"It's true."

She took one his hands from the steering wheel and held it in her own. "Well, I'll be right here with you the whole time. I got the whole week off."

Jeremiah yanked his hand out of hers with glee. "Serious?"

She nodded.

"Awesome." He pulled up to a stoplight, turned his head, and looked her in the eyes. "Thank you."

She took his hand back. "You're welcome."

They pulled onto a side street off 71st, the main road. They were in a residential neighborhood now. Perhaps there was a commercial zone somewhere on the other side, and this was a shortcut.

He was even more baffled when Michael's minivan came to a stop in front of a duplex, and he motioned Jeremiah to pull into the driveway. Jeremiah did, killed the car, and got out.

As Michael was getting out of his van, Jeremiah hotfooted it to him and asked. "Is this it?"

Michael nodded. "Oh, yeah. Tongues of Fire Productions, right inside there. Well, the right one, anyway. That left one is occupied, but the woman who lives there is at work right now, so we won't bother her."

It was a largely sandstone, symmetrical, two-story edifice with two front doors on either side of one shared garage, and one driveway. It was certainly not what Jeremiah had been expecting. "We're going to record in someone's *house*?"

Michael laughed and clapped Jeremiah on the back. "Jeremiah, you'd be surprised how many of the records you listen to are recorded in someone's house. It doesn't matter. It all sounds the same, wherever you track it. What matters is the excellence of the equipment and the skill of the engineer."

Matt and Liz had pulled in behind Jeremiah and were now getting out.

"This is it?" Matt said to Michael.

"Yes, sir," Michael said.

"But it's someone's house."

Michael laughed again. "You boys all sound the same!" He turned to Liz. "What about you? You going to say this is someone's house?"

Liz smiled. "I was actually thinking along the lines of,

'Someone actually lives there?'"

Michael laughed again. "Y'all heard Demon Wrecka's album, right? Doesn't it sound good?"

They nodded.

Michael pointed to the duplex. "Right here, baby," he said. "Now, let's go in and get started."

CHAPTER EIGHTEEN

BURNING IT UP AT TONGUES OF FIRE

Recording turned out to be much less exciting, at first, than Jeremiah had expected. Liz set up her drums, and then they all spent the rest of the morning watching Chris, the engineer, set up microphones all around the drums. He carefully pointed one microphone at each drum, then had Liz sit down and play each drum repetitively while he fiddled with different knobs on the huge mixing board.

Here was the set-up: The duplex was a two-story number, with the living room and kitchen on the first floor. There was a set of stairs next to the front door that led up to the second floor, where there was a master bedroom on the right, a little landing that overlooked the living room, and another bedroom and bathroom on the left.

Chris had his mixing board and all his equipment set up in the master bedroom, so he had Liz set up her drums on the landing, since they wouldn't fit in the master bedroom and he didn't have long enough cables to set them up in the other bedroom.

After lunch, Chris was still testing the drums, EQing and tweaking and doing all the things engineers do that ordinary people don't understand. Jeremiah just thought it was boring.

Besides, he had much more interesting things to do downstairs, namely, sharing a large papasan chair with Amanda. He was also ostensibly chatting with Matt about the finals they'd taken the previous week—how rough the oral comm exam had been. Or maybe that was mass media and communication. Something like that. Jeremiah was having a hard time engaging with Matt fully, what with the effect on him of the closeness of Amanda's body.

So Amanda wound up doing most of the talking, with Jeremiah thinking more about how fast his heart was racing, and how shallow his breathing was, and whether there was sweat on his forehead, because there sure was sweat on his palms, and about the biological urges emanating from down below, and how was he going to record with this whole distraction going on?

Not that he minded, of course.

| | | | | |

At long last, they were ready to begin tracking "Coaltongue." Jeremiah didn't even need to set up his amp—he was going to plug directly into the sound board. Chris had Matt set up his amp in the other bedroom, though he would play on the landing next to Liz.

Jeremiah had figured that recording would be just like it was in movies, on TV shows, and in music videos: everyone playing and singing at the same time, into those big microphones with the weird circle of what looked like a piece of pantyhose in front of them. He was perplexed when he saw no such microphones set up on the drums or in front of Matt's amp, and even more perplexed when there was no microphone for Matt to sing into.

"Where's Matt's mic?" Jeremiah asked Chris.

Chris sort of chuckled. "Uh, dude—can't track vocals out here. Too loud."

"Well, how am I going to sing?" Matt asked.

"You'll do that later. It's not like we have to get everything at once."

"We don't?" Jeremiah said.

Chris laughed again, "Nah, dude. There's tons of tracks; we'll go back and get the vox."

"Oh."

"Yeah," Chris said like a wise sage, "I don't usually like to track all the instruments at once, but we're a little crunched for time, so we're doing you guys together. Usually I do 'em one at a time." He stacked his hands on top of one another. "Build it. Layers."

Jeremiah nodded as if he understood. He didn't.

Chris headed into the master bedroom, then turned around. "One thing, dudes—and lady," he nodded to Liz, who nodded back. "Uh, I only have two sets of headphones, so one of you is going to have to go without."

"Oh," Liz said. "I can do it, I guess."

Chris waved her off. "Nah, you have to have 'em to listen to the click. I was talking to one of these two."

Jeremiah looked at Matt, who looked right back at him. Jeremiah hoped he would be allowed to have the headphones, what with him needing to be locked in to Liz. Without them, he wouldn't hear anything he was playing—just the loud banging and crashing of the drums. It would be like playing by Braille.

By the look in Matt's eyes, Jeremiah knew it was a lost cause.

"Bro, I think I got more goin' on here than you do," Matt said, gesturing to his guitar.

Jeremiah sighed. "You can have them."

Matt smiled. "Thanks, homey."

"Thanks, Jeremiah," Liz said, smiling at him. She was sitting down at her drum kit, twirling a drumstick in her right hand. "Just follow me and you'll be fine."

Jeremiah turned to Chris. "So, I won't be able to hear anything?"

Chris shook his head. "You'll hear the drums for sure, dude."

"But not what *I'm* playing, right?"

"Right."

"What if I screw up, though? Won't we have to keep playing the song until we all play it right?"

Chris did a double take. "You've never recorded before, have you?"

Jeremiah shook his head.

"Dude-man, we can fix all your mistakes, just you. It's easy." He gave Jeremiah a friendly pat on the shoulder. "Just loosen up. Feel it."

"All right."

And so Jeremiah's first recording session began with him deaf to every note he was playing. Liz clicked off "Coaltongue" and they began to play. Jeremiah concentrated as hard as he could with the clanging cymbals boring into his eardrums like an ice pick, but since he couldn't hear, he had no idea how good—or bad—he sounded.

He was standing by the landing, trying to sync up with Liz's drumming. He watched her face, her hands, her right foot on the drum pedal. He entered a zone. He was no longer just him; he was becoming one with Liz, the two of them playing in chorus together. His hands were moving in the same rhythm as hers, his fingers in the same rhythm as her foot. They were laying it down for all eternity.

When the song was over, he let out a deep breath he didn't realize he had been holding. He looked over the landing and saw Amanda, far below on the papasan chair, curled up, asleep.

||||||

Listening back to the song, Jeremiah was surprised at how good his part sounded. At how good the whole thing sounded. It was strange for him to hear his own playing coming out of those studio-quality speakers. He'd made very few mistakes, and as Chris had promised, they were easily fixed later by "punching in," which involved Jeremiah playing along with himself while Chris, at the appropriate moment, punched the "record" button on his huge ADAT tape deck.

Jeremiah had headphones for this part. They made it much easier.

By the end of the day, they had raw music tracks of all three songs.

"This is just the foundation," Michael said. "We'll add more texture tomorrow. After that, we'll move on to vocals, so take care of that voice, Matt."

Matt nodded.

Michael turned to Chris. "Could I get a CD of these tracks?"

Chris nodded. "Sure."

Whoa. A CD? Of their songs? Just like that? Jeremiah assumed that the recording process went thusly: Play a song until everyone makes it through without screwing up, then send the tape to the CD-making place, and then pick up your CDs when they were ready. He'd already had his bubble burst on the first part, but surely there was no way for Chris to make a CD of what they had *just* recorded.

Turns out there was. Chris reached into his desk, removed a white jewel case with the Hewlett-Packard logo on it, and held it up to Michael. "These are, like, four bucks each, so I can only do one today."

"That's fine," Michael said. "I just want to get some ideas for tomorrow."

Chris unwrapped the CD and put it into a large computer. Several minutes of mouse clicking later, out it popped; Chris retrieved it and put it back in the case it came with, which he handed to Michael.

In the driveway, Jeremiah stopped Michael and pointed to the CD. "Can I see that?"

Michael smiled and handed it over.

Jeremiah popped open the lid. The disc looked like it was made of gold, with a plain white label on it. On the disc, Chris had written in Sharpie marker:

KNUCKLE
ROUGH

"This is really our songs?" Jeremiah said, looking at Michael in disbelief.

"Lemme see it, Jeremiah," Matt said, reaching for the disc.

Michael started laughing. "It's a little weird at first, isn't it?" He pointed to the CD. "That isn't going to be the last CD you see with your songs on it, though." He got serious, then looked at Liz, then Matt, then Jeremiah. "You guys are too good to stay on a CD-R."

"Thanks, Michael," Liz said.

"Can we listen to it real quick?" Matt said.

Michael laughed again. "Yeah, sure. Come on."

They all piled into Michael's van, right there in front of the house. Within a few seconds, "Coaltongue" was pouring out of the speakers, enveloping them in semi-rich sound. Jeremiah had never realized how much he liked this song; now, hearing it on its own, without playing it at the same time—it was really good. He'd heard it on the studio monitors, sure, but there was something different about listening to it in a car. He just listened to so much music in a car—hearing his own in a car was about as mindblowing as it got.

Matt was sitting in the passenger seat, listening intently, eyes closed. "I think I hear a solo here, Michael."

"That's what I was thinking," Michael said.

Jeremiah was sitting between Liz and Amanda in the backseat. Liz turned to him, hand held high. "High five, Jeremiah," she said. "We sound awesome."

Jeremiah gave her the requisite five. "Yeah, we rocked it."

"Way to go, partner."

Jeremiah turned to a beaming Amanda. She gave him a big, sidearm hug, whispering in his ear, "I'm proud of you, Jeremiah."

CHAPTER NINETEEN

RECORDING ENDS, OTHER THINGS BEGIN

The rest of the week flew by, and during that time, they added a few guitar solos, some percussion, and some tambourine on "Puzzle Peace." Chris came up with an idea for a keyboard part on that song—Matt was resistant at first, but after Chris played it for him, he liked it.

The band and Michael were gathered in the master bedroom when Chris turned in his swivel chair and looked at Matt. "You ready to record some vocals, dude?"

Matt nodded, as excited as a child who had just been told he could eat all his Halloween candy in one sitting.

"Well, let's pop open the vocal booth." Chris crossed the room in four steps and cracked open a door in the corner Jeremiah had never noticed before. "This is as pro as it gets," Chris said, breaking into a boyish grin.

Liz was the first to laugh. "Matt—you're going to sing in the shower!"

Jeremiah moved closer and saw that Chris had opened the door to the master bathroom. The walls had been covered in gray foam with all sorts of ridges and dips in it. In the middle was a tall microphone stand, and, finally, that big microphone with the weird circle of pantyhose.

"Hey, Chris," Jeremiah said, "what's that thing in front of the mic?"

"That's a pop filter, dude," Chris said. "Keeps your Ps from sounding too crazy."

Jeremiah nodded as if he understood. "Rock on."

But other than that nugget of information, Jeremiah didn't take much interest in the recording process once the instruments were done. Since there were no speakers on while Matt was recording—his microphone would pick up the music—it was kind of a kick to hear Matt wailing loudly by himself. However, soon that novelty wore off and became more of an annoyance. He and Amanda retired to their papasan chair; Liz hung out on the nearby couch.

"Man," Jeremiah said after seemingly the ten-thousandth time Matt had sung one line that he kept getting wrong, "he sings these songs great on stage all the time—why's it so different in the studio?"

"It just is," Liz said. "You know Matt—it has to be perfect. He's getting way too into this. It's all he talks about." She shifted forward into her seat to get into rant position. "I mean, last night, we went on our own little tour of Christmas lights in Maple Ridge, and he hardly paid attention. He was too busy listening to our CD." She put her hands to her mouth to make a megaphone. "I was like, 'Hello, romantic thing happening here with your dream girl! Care to pay attention?'"

"Ugh, that is *so* annoying," Amanda said. She gave Jeremiah a hug and snuggled into him. "Fortunately, I don't have that problem."

Jeremiah smiled. She always made him smile.

"You two are just a picture of . . ." Liz trailed off, clearly searching for the right words. "Disgusting."

Amanda laughed and threw a pillow at her roommate. Jeremiah took the opportunity to extricate his arm from the pile of persons he and Amanda had made. He consulted his watch. "This is taking forever."

"You can't rush perfection." Matt's voice descended from above.

They all twisted their heads to see Matt standing on the landing, overlooking them.

"Hey, Matt," Liz said. "Sounding good."

"Yeah." Matt disappeared from view, replaced by the sound of his clunking footsteps on the stairs. "I think I finally got it down," he said as he reappeared in the first-floor living room. "Not that any of you would know."

"What's that supposed to mean, exactly?" Liz said.

"Nothing," Matt said. "Just—you know what? It—it's . . . never mind."

"Okay," Jeremiah said.

"Yeah," Amanda said.

"Whatever," Liz said.

The four of them simply remained where they were, silent.

"Matthew, you are gifted at reminding the Body how much God loves them." Michael walked into the room, eating an apple. "We are getting some truly anointed vocals up there."

"Thanks, Michael," Matt said.

"I think we're done for the day," Michael said. "Rest your voice tonight; we'll finish them up tomorrow, then start mixing."

| | | | | |

In addition to their days, Jeremiah's and Amanda's nights and evenings that week had been spent entirely together, sometimes with Matt and Liz, sometimes not. Matt and Liz loved to go the movies, but Jeremiah and Amanda didn't always go with them, and when they didn't, they would usually wind up back at Amanda and Liz's apartment to hang out and do whatever.

Of course, young adults being young adults, "whatever" usually meant "make out feverishly until Liz came home."

Be that as it may, Jeremiah had been careful not to give in to what his youth pastor had always called "fleshly lusts."

On the occasion of the "vocals day," Jeremiah decided to take Amanda to Gold Coast, a trendy little coffee shop near C4 whose hipness quotient was so large that it almost felt intimidating just to walk through the door. A thick, cigarette-smoke haze lay murkily throughout, enveloping mostly college-age patrons with unwashed hair, wool sweaters, and (Jeremiah assumed) left-leaning political opinions. And Jeremiah's dad.

"Jeremiah!" His dad spied them seconds after they entered and immediately waved them over to the corner of the shop he was occupying, fiddling with the speaker cables of a small PA system.

"Who's that?" she asked as they maneuvered through the shop.

"Amanda," Jeremiah said, "this is my dad."

Jeremiah's dad extended his hand. "Bruce Springfield."

"Amanda Wayne—it's nice to meet you, sir. Jeremiah's told me so much about you."

Jeremiah's dad turned to him. "Well, that's nice to hear," he said, smiling. "Jeremiah, why are you telling this charming young woman so much about me?"

Jeremiah flashed a sheepish grin. "Well, we're sort of"— he flicked his eyes at Amanda—"she's my girlfriend."

Amanda punctuated Jeremiah's statement with a single, proud nod.

Dad's smile got bigger. "I had no idea!" he said to Jeremiah. He turned toward Amanda. "Jeremiah never told me he was, uh, romantically involved with someone. But then we hardly see each other these days. I guess our schedules aren't really conducive to a whole lot of chatting."

"Well, it's really nice to meet you anyway," Amanda said.

"Thank you," he said. "So, what are you kids doing out here?"

"Came to hear you play, Pop," Jeremiah said. "I'm ready to listen to some music other than our own."

Jeremiah's dad let out a bellowing laugh. "Recording driving you nuts?"

"Yes," both of them said at the same time.

"I've done my share," Jeremiah's dad said. "It isn't for everyone." He gestured toward the counter on the other side of the room. "Why don't you guys get a cup o' joe on me, then settle in. I have to finish hooking up these speakers and then I'm ready to go."

Dutifully, Jeremiah and Amanda headed to the counter. Having been a coffee drinker only since he entered college, Jeremiah was overawed by the different varieties available, as well as the wide array of foreign words written on the chalkboard behind the counter.

"What do you want?" The attendant was a wire-thin guy of indeterminate ethnicity, sporting what appeared to be a child-sized T-shirt advertising the Police's *Synchronicity* tour.

"I'll have a . . . coffee."

"Me too," Amanda said.

The guy grunted with derision. "That it?"

Jeremiah nodded. "It's on my dad." He used his thumb to indicate the dad in question.

"Sure thing."

The guy went to work while Jeremiah glanced at Amanda with wide eyes. "I didn't know what to order," he whispered in her ear. She giggled.

"Here you go, man." The attendant slid two enormous white cups filled with deep black liquid toward them. "Pair o' coffees. Enjoy."

The two of them picked up their scalding hot beverages and headed to a table close to the music, where Jeremiah's dad was strumming his mellow hollow-body guitar and saying "Check" into the microphone several times.

He gave the two of them a wink, then, without introduction, launched into "The Way You Look Tonight."

Jeremiah looked at Amanda, who smiled at him, then leaned on his shoulder.

What a perfect evening.

| | | | | |

The last half of Thursday and all day Friday were taken up with something Chris called "mixing," which Jeremiah had heard of before but had never understood. Michael explained that they had to "mix down" the recording, and that everything they had been listening to so far had been just "rough mixes." Jeremiah thought they sounded fine, but he deferred to the pros.

Mixing involved Chris listening to each individual track and turning all the little knobs on his mixing board, sometimes in infinitesimal increments. Jeremiah was thoroughly uninterested in the process and felt like it drained all the life out of the music. He enjoyed music for the spontaneity, for the feeling of playing it live, for the magic that happened in that moment. This was an analysis of that magic, and it drove him nuts.

“I’m mixing bored,” he said on Friday afternoon.

“No kidding,” Liz said. “Anyone know any jokes or anything?”

Jeremiah searched his brain. “I got one. How many drummers does it take to change a lightbulb?”

“Watch it,” Liz said.

“None. They’re all being replaced by machines.”

Amanda laughed while Liz socked Jeremiah on the thigh. “I think all this recording has driven you silly,” Amanda said.

“Yeah, the same thing happened to Matt, but in the opposite direction,” Liz said. She pointed upstairs, where they overheard Matt saying something about giving the kick more oomph.

He actually used the word “oomph.”

“Hey, guys!” Matt yelled out the door of the master bedroom. “Come up here for a sec!”

The three of them hesitated for a minute, each looking to the other one to be the first up the stairs.

“Come on! It’s important!” came the holler from above.

Without a word, the living-room trio hauled themselves out of their respective furniture and tromped up the stairs.

“What do you think of this hi-hat sound?” Matt asked when they all arrived. He looked at Chris. “Play it.”

Chris pushed a button and the now sickeningly familiar chorus of “Puzzle Peace” played through the speakers. Jeremiah did his best to focus on the hi-hat sound, but he was so burnt out on the whole concept that his attention began to wander. He became fascinated with an LED readout on the tape machine that showed the track time down to the hundredth of a second. It just went so fast.

The time counter stopped abruptly. Jeremiah snapped to, hearing Matt calling his name.

“Jeremiah. Dude. You gotta focus.”

"Sorry, Matt," Jeremiah said. "I just can't tell any difference between this one and the way it used to sound."

"Well, what about the shaker?"

"What about it?" Liz asked.

"Should it come in on beat one or beat three?"

"Does it matter?" Jeremiah said.

"Yes! This stuff is important!"

"Well, why don't you pray about it, Matthew? Let God guide you?" Liz said. Jeremiah wasn't sure, but he thought he detected a hint of sarcasm in her voice.

Matt said nothing with his mouth, but his eyes gave Liz an earful.

Jeremiah avoided the tension by trying to mathematically make the individual digits on the time counter equal "24."

Matt let out a long, deep breath that reminded Jeremiah of air escaping from a tire.

"Okay, Liz. Guys. Look, it's just . . . " Matt waved his arms around, attempting to conjure the appropriate words out of thin air. "Let's get it right. You know?"

3:31.06. Let's see. Three times zero equals zero. Plus three, plus one equals four. Times six equals twenty-four.

It was Liz's turn to exhale. "Yes, let's get it right," she said. "Let's get it perfect. Let's keep working and working and working until our brains have been liquefied. But for Pete's sake—let's be done with it soon."

Or: Six plus three plus zero equals nine. Minus one equals eight. Times three equals twenty-four.

"For crying out loud, Liz," Matt said. "Just . . ." Flustered, he let the word hang there.

Or: Three plus one equals four, times three equals twelve. Plus six equals eighteen. No, that one wouldn't work. Maybe there was a solution involving division?

"Jeremiah, you want to weigh in here?" Liz said.

"Hmm?" Surely there had to be a solution with division?

"Do you have anything to add to this conversation?"

Jeremiah turned his attention away from the time counter and toward Liz and Matt. "Maybe we should just take a little break. Go get something to eat? Get out of here for a bit?"

"Yeah, dude-man," Chris said. Jeremiah had forgotten he was there. "I think we're pretty much done, actually. That's a good idea. Get out of here, let me finish up here, and I'll have some CDs for you guys when you get back."

||||||

They piled into Jeremiah's Corsica, and Amanda suggested heading to a specialty pizza place called Hideaway. Matt sat in the back seat in silence, looking out the window most of the way there.

They shuffled into the restaurant and took a table near the back.

Liz leaned over to Matt and said softly, "It's good to see you sitting at something other than that mixing board."

Matt cracked a smile.

"Yeah, man," Jeremiah said. "At least here we can argue about toppings and not about whether the bass tone is round enough."

Matt laughed. "Hey, I take the band seriously, you guys."

Liz was filled with mock—or was it real?—indignation. "Oh, so Jeremiah and I don't?" she said.

Matt retreated. "No, no," he said, waving his hands in submission. "That's not what I meant."

"So what *did* you mean?"

Matt let out his leaky-tire exhale again. "I meant that I

take the band *too* seriously. And that I got obsessed with the recording."

Liz gave him a look that said, "Go on."

"And that you and Jeremiah—and Amanda—have a much better handle on life than I do. And that you're a better musician than me. And cuter. And . . ."

Liz put a hand up to stop his list. "That's enough, Matt. All is forgiven."

"And," Matt continued, "that I'm going to take you on that Christmas-light tour again, and I'll pay attention this time."

Jeremiah and Amanda laughed.

Liz pointed a finger at him. "A-ha! I *knew* you weren't all there with me."

Matt took her hand. "Well, baby," he said. "I promise to be there with you this time." He gave Liz a kiss. "We'll go tonight."

Amanda squeezed Jeremiah's hand, and he gave her a knowing look. Looks like they just got some free time at the apartment.

| | | | | |

"I got you a Christmas present," Amanda said.

"What?" Jeremiah said. "Why'd you do that?"

"Because it's what girls do."

"I didn't get you anything."

"Liar."

Jeremiah chuckled. Even in the dim, multicolored, twinkling light beaming from the apartment's pitiful living-room Christmas tree, he could see that Amanda was clearly enjoying this whole gift-giving/receiving moment entirely too much.

And it was true. He was a liar. He'd gotten her a little piece of Christian jewelry with his Armory discount: It was a cross pendant, fashioned out of nails. He'd even wrapped it himself, and it was currently in the glove compartment of his car, waiting for the perfect moment.

That moment, it seemed, was now.

"I'll be right back," he said, hoofing it to the car and back in record time. When he got back into the apartment, Amanda was sitting on the couch; in her lap was a rectangular box, beautifully wrapped. She held it out to him. "Here!" she said. "Open it!"

He sat down next to her and tore open the package.

"You know, Jeremiah," Amanda said as he dug into his present, "you're always wearing, like, work clothes, or school clothes. And when you aren't wearing those, you're wearing those Christian T-shirts all the time?"

Jeremiah had the box open. A nice-looking polo shirt.

"Yeah?" he said.

"Well," she said, reaching out to touch his arm reassuringly, "please don't take this the wrong way, but those Christian T-shirts were okay in high school. But you're in college now, and you need to dress like a college student." She took on a matter-of-fact tone. "I'm just trying to help."

Jeremiah removed the shirt from the package and unfolded it to have a look.

"I like it," he said. "I like it a lot." He flipped it over to look at the back. "Yeah, I think you're right. I've been wanting to make a change."

"Really?"

"Yeah."

She clapped. "Oh, yea!" she said, then pointed to the bathroom door. "Go try it on. Go try it on."

Jeremiah went into the bathroom, ditched his "Surf Waves of Gold. Surf Heaven" shirt (it had airbrush-looking art of a tropical island on it, and cursive writing that looked appropriately beach-like), and put on the smart polo he'd just received from his girlfriend. He looked at himself in the mirror. What a stud.

He strutted out of the bathroom, arms akimbo, then did a little runway turn in front of Amanda. "What do you think?" he said.

"Looks great!"

"I think so, too," he said. "I love it."

Amanda clapped again. "Okay, where's mine? Where's mine?"

Jeremiah retrieved the small package from his jeans and sat back down on the couch as he handed it to her. She had it open a moment later.

"Oh, my, this is sweet," she said. "I love it. Put it on me." She handed the box back to him, so he fished out the pendant, undid the clasp, and leaned forward to put it around her neck.

He stepped on some wrapping paper that had fallen on the floor, and when he leaned forward, he shifted his weight to be supported by that very foot. Unfortunately, wrapping paper on carpet is one of the slickest things known to man, so out from under him went his foot. He tumbled forward into Amanda, knocking her back into a prone position. He landed on top of her.

Jeremiah's internal biology went nuts. His brain drew a line of battle deep in his mental sand. Entrenched.

"Sorry about that," he said, unmoving.

Amanda smiled. "It's okay."

His biology ordered him to give her a kiss. His brain defied the order.

He kissed her. She kissed back.

His brain retreated slightly, then drew another battle line.

Don't cross this one.

"I, uh," Jeremiah said, stammering.

Amanda gazed into his eyes. "Mm-hmm?"

"Um, Amanda," he said. "Uh, should we . . ."

"Yeah, should we . . ."

"Get up?"

"Probably."

They both lay there, doing nothing.

Jeremiah's brain and his biology were at full-blown war. His brain had no more ground to give before it was rendered helpless, completely invaded.

This time, biology won the battle.

CHAPTER TWENTY

HURT WORSE THAN ANYTHING

The next morning, Jeremiah groggily noticed his alarm and, after punching the snooze button about three times, finally got out of bed. As he got up, last night's session with Amanda came flooding back, and he was instantly grateful for the half-second of his morning that he hadn't remembered the heavy guilt that had crept onto his heart last night.

He sat on the edge of his bed, head hanging. His chest felt heavy, as if tethered to the floor, and the tether was *just* too short, preventing him from standing up.

Yesterday, at this same time, he had been a virgin.

Today he wasn't.

So why did it bother him so much?

He ran through all the arguments his biology had used last night to convince his brain that it had been okay:

- Sex is a natural expression of love between two people.

- Sex is purely functional, and a great way to pass the time. There are no consequences beyond the moment, so you might as well go for it and live in the moment.
- Sex is inevitable; everyone else is doing it, so why shouldn't he?
- He was an adult now—in college—and sex is part of the college experience.
- God created the body; why was it wrong to give in to its desires?
- God created sex; why was it wrong to participate in it?

Last night, all those arguments and others had worked. In the heat of the moment, in the face of temptation, Jeremiah's brain had heard the rationale of his biology and lost the fight. Perhaps it had been too worn down from all the previous make-out sessions they'd had, when Jeremiah's body had started forming all those arguments.

Now, in the cold light of morning, Jeremiah saw through every one of those lame excuses to the bitter truth: They had messed up big time. He could tell from the way his heart felt. From the way his head hung. From the way shame had enveloped them both the second it was over. From the way he was, even now, still trying so hard to convince himself that it had been okay.

He had come to a realization: Everything he had told himself about sex last night had been bunk. And now fear had begun to set in. He felt connected to Amanda in a way he'd never felt connected to any human being, and just the thought of her opened up a torrent of shame and guilt.

It was that very connection—that deep bond that had formed last night—that convinced him they had gone against God. He'd heard a million sermons on the inappropriateness of premarital sex, but he had never *really* understood it until now. He and Amanda had bonded, and now he worried beyond worry that their relationship was going to fall apart. He could feel it in his bones: Something was going to happen that would wind up separating them.

And now, it was going to hurt worse than anything had ever hurt him.

He knew it.

He finally dragged himself off the mattress and sank into a kneeling position next to the bed. He clasped his hands together.

"God?" he said. "Um, I don't . . . know what to say, really." He gave a heavy sigh. "It's just—I just . . . I'm sorry. I know the Bible says not to do what I did last night, and I'm sorry. I'm sorry that I didn't believe what you said." His right eye started getting moist. "Please forgive me," he said, his voice cracking in a whisper. "Please, God."

And then the tears came.

||||||

"Hello?"

"Amanda?"

"Hey." Her voice was quiet. "What, uh, what are you . . . are you working today?"

"Yeah."

A pause.

"Um, Jeremiah?"

"Yeah?"

"I'm . . . sorry. About last . . ."

"No, I'm sorry. It was just . . ."

"Yeah."

Another pause.

"Amanda, maybe we should, uh, take some time . . ."

"Yeah, I was thinking that we, um . . ."

"Okay."

"Okay."

"Well, I'll . . . see you after Christmas?"

"Sure."

"Okay."

Another pause.

"Well, I guess I need to go to work."

"Okay, Jeremiah. Have a good day."

"You, too."

"Bye."

"Good-bye."

| | | | | |

Jeremiah spent Christmas in a very sullen state. His dad kept tiptoeing around him, and Jeremiah overheard snatches of phone conversations in which his dad speculated that Jeremiah must be having "girl trouble." He hadn't been home this much since he'd started dating Amanda.

His dad had tried to reach out to him as he sat alone in his room on Christmas Eve. "Jeremiah, you okay?"

Jeremiah just stared at the wall, wondering if he should tell his dad what had happened. Finally, he just shook his head.

His dad came in and sat on the edge of his bed. "What's wrong, son?"

Jeremiah stared. He should probably keep it to himself. He didn't want to disappoint his dad.

"Is it something to do with Amanda? You guys break up?"

Jeremiah turned to look at him. "We're just spending some time away right now."

"What happened?"

Here it was. The moment of truth. Let it all out—it'll feel great.

"We just . . ." Jeremiah said. He looked to the ceiling for inspiration. "We just needed to take a break."

Jeremiah's dad reached over and put his arm around him. "Relationships are tough, Jeremiah. You're going to have fights." He bent his head down and looked Jeremiah in the eye. "This'll get better, son. If you guys love each other, you'll work it out." He gave him a smile. "It's very mature of you to take some time off."

"Dad, I . . ." Jeremiah said, his voice trailing off.

His dad just nodded. "I'm proud of you, son." He gave Jeremiah a hug and got up. "I'll let you get some thinking done now." He walked to the door, then turned around in the doorway. "Jeremiah, if you want to talk about anything, I'm here for you. You know that, right?"

Jeremiah nodded slowly.

His dad smiled. "Okay," he said. "Merry Christmas, Jeremiah."

"Merry Christmas, Dad."

CHAPTER TWENTY-ONE

BIG THINGS IN STORE FOR '94

As winter break rolled on, Jeremiah started to feel a little better. The further away he got from that troubled evening, the less constricted and heavy his heart felt. Two days before New Year's Eve, he decided to give Amanda a call and see how she was feeling.

"Jeremiah!" She sounded totally back to normal and happy to hear his voice. Hearing her regular, up-tempo, enthusiastic voice instantly made Jeremiah feel much better himself.

"Hey," he said. "I just wanted to see how you were doing."

"I'm great," she said. "Great Christmas."

"Yeah?"

"Yeah," she said. "How about you?"

"Good, good."

Jeremiah was amazed to hear how natural Amanda sounded. He had expected some awkwardness, but she was remarkably calm and . . . herself.

"What are you doing New Year's Eve?" he asked.

"Nothing. Matt and Liz are going to a party, so I was thinking about going with them."

Matt and Liz. Jeremiah had been so consumed by shame that he hadn't thought about his friends. He suddenly felt like seeing them, like rejoining life, already in progress. "Can I come?" he said.

She squealed. "That would be awesome!"

"Great."

| | | | | |

When Matt found out that Jeremiah was coming to the party, he decided on the fly that Knuckle Sandwich should play, ushering in the new year onstage, where they belonged.

Of course, the party was at someone's house, so there would be no stage, but Jeremiah got the gist of it.

They showed up at the party about 8:00, which was happening in some random living room that Jeremiah had never been in. It was hosted by some friend of a friend of Matt's, someone who lived in his wing on campus. Although nearly everyone else at school had gone home for the holidays, Matt had decided to stay in Tulsa.

They set up in the living room, did a quick sound check, and then Jeremiah went off to find Amanda. He accomplished his mission when he cruised through the dining room to grab a soda and a plate of Lit'l Smokies. She was already there, talking to Matt's friend of a friend, the party's host.

He walked over to join in the conversation, and when he stepped up next to Amanda, she reached her arm around his waist and pulled him in close to her. He had been talking to her frequently over the past couple of days, but this was really the first time he'd had semi-intimate contact with her since the night he'd lost his virginity, and it raised a lot of negative feelings, just touching, side by side, even through a lot of bulky winter clothes.

Still, it felt nice.

He put his arm around her waist and gave her a squeeze. She kept talking.

They pretty much stayed like that until 11:30 or so, when Knuckle Sandwich took the "stage" to play their New Year's Eve set. Matt threw on his guitar and stepped up to the microphone and addressed the thirty or so revelers.

"Guys, I just wanna say," he said, "I've been praying a lot this week, and I really feel like God has big things in store for this band in 1994."

The people clapped. Jeremiah, still adjusting his bass, looked at Liz, who smiled at him and leaned forward in her drum throne.

"It's true," she said.

"So," Matt continued, "I just want to say thank you for sharing this moment with us. We're playing in a living room at the beginning of '94, and I have a feeling that, by the end of it, we'll be playing much bigger places!"

Everyone cheered and clapped while Matt played the intro to "Ham-Fisted." Jeremiah and Liz joined in, and the show was on.

It was nice to play again. Jeremiah hadn't realized how much he'd missed it. He put all his thoughts about Amanda out of his brain and focused on the music, on the creation of something, right there in the living room. He felt better than he had in weeks. Since the demo days.

He sold himself to the music. He didn't look at anything other than Liz and the drums. He didn't look at Matt, he didn't look at his own bass, he didn't look at the crowd, and he sure as heck didn't look at Amanda.

Beads of sweat began to form on his forehead. His perfectly coiffed hair began to lose its coif and spill down in front of his face, like a curtain between Liz and his eyes.

No bother. It was just him and the music.

Until midnight came. Matt kept looking at his watch after every song until they were three minutes until midnight. "Okay, people—1994's almost here!" he yelled into the microphone to much cheering from the crowd.

He turned to Jeremiah and Liz. "Hey, as soon as we hit midnight, let's play 'Golden Calf,' okay?"

Jeremiah nodded.

Liz pointed a drumstick at Matt. "*After* you kiss me, right?" she said.

Matt smiled. "Sure, baby. Sure." He looked back at his watch, "Two minutes, gang!"

Jeremiah didn't hear it. He had forgotten all about the traditional midnight kiss, mainly because he'd never had anyone to kiss at midnight on New Year's. What was this going to be like? Would he even want to kiss Amanda?

"One minute!"

Where was she? He didn't even see her in the crowd. Why was he so nervous? He'd kissed her a zillion times—what was one New Year's kiss going to do? It wasn't like they were going to have sex again right then and there. One kiss wouldn't hurt, right?

"Thirty seconds!"

It was just a kiss, nothing more. But if that was the case, why was he so nervous? His palms were sweating, and it wasn't from his bass playing. Was God trying to tell him something? His heart was racing.

"Ten! Nine! Eight! Seven!" Matt said.

The crowd joined in with him.

"Six! Five!"

Where was Amanda? Jeremiah scanned the crowd and didn't see her.

"Four! Three! Two!"

A dash of blonde hair came running through the crowd in his direction.

"ONE! HAPPY NEW YEAR!"

Jeremiah was assaulted by a beautiful blonde steamroller as Amanda plowed out of the crowd and straight into Jeremiah, wrapping her arms around his neck and giving him the strongest kiss she'd ever given him.

Fireworks.

Happy New Year, indeed.

When they were done kissing, Jeremiah noticed that they were the last to wrap it up. He assumed Matt and Liz had fulfilled their traditional duty, but he hadn't seen it happen. Matt was already back to the microphone and playing the intro to "Golden Calf."

Jeremiah dazedly let go of Amanda, licked his lips, and looked into her eyes, which were half-narrowed, a smile curling up at her lips. She looked like she had enjoyed her first act of 1994 as much as he had.

"Happy New Year, Jeremiah," she said.

Jeremiah said nothing. He just smiled at her, cranked up the volume knob on his bass, set his fingers, and played.

||||||

The drive home was uneventful. Jeremiah and Amanda had gone back to C4 to return all the equipment they'd borrowed for the show. (Liz still didn't have her own set of drums; Matt, however, had gotten a sweet Vox combo amp for Christmas.) Matt and Liz had volunteered to come, but Jeremiah had sent them on their merry way, telling them it was no bother and that he was happy to take care of the drums himself.

They'd unloaded the equipment with no problems, and now Jeremiah was driving Amanda back to her apartment. They pulled into the parking lot, and Jeremiah parked the car under a semi-private little grove of trees in the corner of the complex.

"Why are you parking here, Jeremiah?" Amanda said. "My apartment's farther in."

"I just want to talk for a second," he said.

"About what?"

"About our relationship," he said.

"What about it?"

"Well, I like you a lot, and I really want to keep seeing you," he said.

"But?"

He turned toward her. "But I don't think we should have sex again."

She sighed with relief. "Whew! I thought you were breaking up with me."

"No!" Boy, that came out a little stronger than he intended. He wasn't *desperate*, for crying out loud. "No, no. I don't want that. I just want to . . . slow down a little."

"Well, good. I think you're right."

They sat in silence.

She turned toward him. "Can we still kiss?"

He thought a moment. "Yeah, I don't see why not."

"Good," she said, closing her eyes and leaning in. She kissed him and he kissed her back.

They went like that for a little while, getting closer, more heated.

Jeremiah's brain and biology were at it again, and all the shame and guilt he had felt a couple of weeks ago were suddenly forgotten. He just knew they were in murky, dangerous territory, but he couldn't remember why. He knew there was a reason. What was it again?

It was dark there under the trees. Jeremiah broke free and looked around.

Amanda kept kissing him. "There's no one around," she whispered between kisses.

Yeah, there was a reason not to . . . but it . . . it was . . . not worth fighting for. Not in this moment. Not right now. He couldn't think. Didn't need to. All he needed to know was that there was a beautiful woman, and both she and he were feeling the need to celebrate the New Year together.

As closely together as humanly possible.

Consequences? Those seemed a long way off.

CHAPTER TWENTY-TWO

ADVICE FROM A FRIEND

Jeremiah had never expected himself to turn into some sort of sex fiend. Still, it kept happening over and over. For months, his relationship with Amanda became a repetitive pattern of slipping, having sex, feeling guilty, asking God for forgiveness, lying low while being hammered with guilt, getting back together with Amanda, promising to abstain and be good, slipping again.

Except after each slip, it hurt a little less. The guilt wasn't as bad. The shame not as oppressive.

Or maybe the shame and guilt were worse—maybe they never went away, so he got used to their weight. So each time he slipped, they piled on some more, but he couldn't tell because he was already weighed down.

For Amanda's part, she was often downright cavalier about their activity. A couple of days after their fourth or fifth time (Jeremiah had actually lost count), the two of them sat on the couch, alone in her apartment (how did he keep getting in these situations?), when Amanda handed Jeremiah a small box, wrapped with Christmas wrapping paper.

"Bit late for a Christmas present, isn't it, Amanda?"

She giggled. "Just open it, silly."

Jeremiah peeled back the label to reveal a purple box with a picture of a man and a woman in silhouette, leaning close to each other. "These are condoms."

Amanda narrowed her eyes and smiled a confident smile. "Exactly."

"Why did you give me condoms?"

She gave him a playful slap on the shoulder. "Better safe than sorry."

Well, that made sense. Except . . . "I thought condoms weren't a hundred percent."

"The only thing that is, is abstinence, Jeremiah. Didn't you pay attention in youth group?"

"Yes."

"But," she said, whipping off her glasses and leaning close to him to whisper in his ear. "I don't feel like a hundred percent."

Jeremiah had heard the term "come hither stare" before. He now knew exactly what it looked like—he had the ultimate representation in front of him.

"I don't know, Amanda . . ."

"Come on," she said, standing up and attempting to get him to do the same by jerking on his arm. "Don't you want to use your new present?"

Why didn't he break up with her? Call it off? He didn't know, exactly. Didn't matter. He knew the pattern.

He couldn't resist a pattern.

| | | | | |

Over those same months, Jeremiah's musical life was rocketing skyward. Under Michael's guidance, Knuckle Sandwich was getting huge in Tulsa, a city not known for cherishing original music. That they cherished Knuckle Sandwich was a miracle. Michael started getting them shows outside the Christian arena, and everywhere they played they made new fans. Soon they were selling out of their demo at each show and ordering more.

They made T-shirts and started selling those at their shows. Stickers, too.

The stickers were cool. They had gone a cheaper route and made them white with black lettering. Michael added a picture of a fist at an angle that looked like it was punching whoever was looking at the sticker. Jeremiah immediately put one on his Corsica.

Jeremiah freaked out one day in traffic on I-44 when he saw a huge camper van with tons of band stickers in the window—and there was a Knuckle Sandwich sticker, right there among stickers of actual bands like Cross-Eyed and Deathlife and Zippo.

The highlight of Jeremiah's spring came during spring break, when the band played a rare show that didn't conflict with his dad's schedule.

"I'm so excited to see you guys play," Jeremiah's dad said over breakfast that morning.

Jeremiah was excited to have him out, too. "It's going to be a fun show, Dad."

"Well, I'm just eager to hear how you guys pull off your demo live. I love those songs. Looking forward to hearing more."

The show went well, and afterward Jeremiah's dad said, "Well, whenever you guys get big and famous and start looking for opening acts, don't forget that everyone loves solo jazz."

Other than that, their spring semester passed quickly, with shows almost every weekend, all over Tulsa. Matt even set up some shows down in Oklahoma City, and they started driving down to spend the weekend playing rock 'n' roll for whole new audiences. Those shows started off with small attendances, but the more they played in OKC, the more fans they got, and the more people started coming to their shows.

It was at just such a show, at a little church-run venue called The Outer Café, that Jeremiah did a double-take as he sat watching the crowd file in. The café's so-dim-it-was-almost-dark mood lighting didn't do much for illumination, but he thought he spotted a familiar Oklahoma Sooners cap sitting atop a familiar frame.

He stood up to get a closer look. It could be.

"Dan!" he hollered, eyes intent on the Sooners cap.

It swiveled toward his voice.

"Dan!" he said again, waving his hands in the air with way too much delight.

"Jeremiah!" The Sooners cap—and Dan, the person resting underneath it—made their way to Jeremiah. The old friends were soon in a deep embrace, each of them giving a hearty, manly clap on the back to the other.

They separated, and Jeremiah was the first to speak. "What are you doing here?"

"Dude, I *live* here," Dan said. "What are *you* doing here?"

"Playing a show, man."

"*You're* in Knuckle Sandwich?" It was good to see Dan's wide CD eyes again.

Jeremiah just smiled. "Yeah, Dan. So's Matt."

"Matt from church camp?"

Jeremiah nodded.

"Boy," Dan said. "I had no idea I was in for so many surprises tonight!"

Jeremiah looked around the rapidly crowding room (which wasn't difficult; it wasn't much bigger than the living room where they'd played on New Year's Eve), spied Matt and Liz engrossed in conversation near the stage, and motioned toward them. "Come on, man."

Dan followed him over while Jeremiah hollered toward the pair. "Matt! Check it out!"

Matt looked up, bewildered.

"It's Dan!" Jeremiah said.

Matt still looked bewildered as Jeremiah and Dan sidled up. "You remember Dan, right?"

Matt extended his hand to Dan, "Yeah, you're . . ." he said as the two exchanged a handshake. "You're . . ."

"He was the lead singer of Teens Ablaze," Jeremiah said.

"Oh yeah!" Matt said, mockingly smacking his palm against his forehead. "Duh."

"It's okay," Dan said.

"So, what are you doing out here?" Matt said, pointing to the Sooners cap. "You go to OU?"

"Yeah," Dan said. "A lot of people on campus are talking about you guys, so I thought I'd come check it out." He gave Jeremiah a punch in the arm. "Didn't know I had friends in the band."

"Well, you do."

"Ahem," Liz said, pronouncing it just like a word and not like the throat-clearing noise that word usually represents. "Anyone wanna clue me in?"

"Sorry, Liz," Jeremiah said. "Uh, Dan, this is Liz, our drummer. Liz, this is Dan, my best friend in high school and former lead singer of the Teens Ablaze youth praise-and-worship band."

"Pleased to meet you," Liz said.

"Likewise."

Matt glanced at his watch, "Hey, gang—it's time to rock. Dan, it was great seeing you." He started climbing on the stage.

"Maybe we can hang out more after the show?" Jeremiah said, also beginning to ascend to his position for the evening.

"Sure thing," Dan said. "Hey, if you guys have a second, can I pray with you real quick?"

Matt and Jeremiah hesitated in mid-step. Liz had remained standing where she was.

"Sure," Matt said, stepping back down onto the floor.

"Yeah, absolutely," Jeremiah said, hopping down as well.

The four musicians gathered in a circle, joined hands, and bowed their heads.

"God," Dan said, "thank you for this reuniting of friends. I pray that you would embolden my brothers and sister to play their best, so that the people here would get to see a glimpse of you through them. And God, we're careful to give you the praise and glory for it. Amen."

"Amen," the other three said in unison.

Jeremiah opened his eyes to see that Dan still had his head bowed, his eyebrows lowered with intensity. He nodded his head slightly a few times, then finally lost his intense eyebrows and opened his eyes.

"All right, guys." Dan said. "Make me proud."

| | | | | |

After the show, and the subsequent time meeting fans, selling stuff at the merchandise table, and settling up with the promoter, Jeremiah and Dan sat down at a café table to catch up while Matt, Liz, and Michael packed up the equipment.

"Man, you guys sounded awesome," Dan said.

"Really?"

"Yeah."

"You're not just saying that?" Jeremiah said. "To be a friend?"

Dan shook his head dramatically. "No way." He leaned in. "Tell you the truth, I'm kinda jealous."

Jeremiah leaned back, slapping the table in jest. "Oh, come on."

"No, no," Dan said. "I think you guys really have something happening there. Matt's amazing. You sound great. And that drummer girl?"

"Liz."

"Yeah, Liz—she's so good."

Jeremiah nodded in agreement.

Dan leaned back and folded his arms. "So, how're things with you, hombre?"

Oddly enough, the first thing Jeremiah thought was not how great the band was doing, or how school was going, or how great it was to see Dan. No, Jeremiah's mind was flooded by Amanda.

Amanda didn't usually come on the weekend Oklahoma City trips, and this time was no exception. She wasn't there, and Jeremiah was grateful. But he was even more grateful for this chance to unburden himself to Dan, to let out the secret he'd been keeping for so long. Maybe Dan could help lift off some of this weight.

Apparently, Jeremiah thought too long about Dan's question, because Dan was looking at him with concern in his eyes. "Something wrong, Jeremiah?"

Jeremiah just nodded.

"What's up, man?"

Where to begin? Jeremiah looked around the room to make sure the rest of the band was nowhere near. He couldn't even see them.

He leaned forward. "Well, I met this girl. She's my girlfriend."

"That's good."

"And we really like each other, and so, you know, we'd like, kiss and stuff."

"Mm-hmm."

Jeremiah set his forearms on the table, leaning on them toward Dan. "So, one thing led to another, and now . . ." It was so hard to say. He hoped Dan would be understanding.

"Oh, Jeremiah," Dan said, exhaling heavily. He, too, darted his eyes around before saying, "Say no more, okay?"

Jeremiah gave a slight, slight nod.

"Just once?" Dan asked.

Jeremiah shook his head.

"A lot?"

Nod.

Now Dan nodded his head. "I see, I see." He studied Jeremiah's face for a moment, and Jeremiah began to feel worried about what Dan was seeing. He was looking right into Jeremiah's eyes, and Jeremiah found the gaze lovingly uncomfortable.

"Do you feel a little . . . trapped?" Dan said. "Like, you can't help yourself?"

Jeremiah's eyes went wide. "Yes!" he said in an excited whisper. "Exactly like that."

Dan looked away for a moment, concentrating on his next words. "Jeremiah, I know you don't need me to beat you up about this. You've beat yourself up already, I can tell. Just— " he looked away again, then back. "Just remember that you always have a choice, okay? And that's not me talking, okay? That's God. He said he'll always, always, always give you a way out."

"Everything okay, Jeremiah?" Jeremiah hadn't noticed Michael approach, so his voice was the first thing he heard.

Jeremiah whipped his head around. Michael was standing a good four, five feet away from the table. "Yeah, man." He pointed to Dan. "This is a friend of mine from high school—Dan."

Dan held out his hand, and Michael stepped forward to shake it. "How's it going?"

"Good. I'm Michael Weathers. I manage Knuckle Sandwich."

"Oh, cool," Dan said.

Michael turned his attention to Jeremiah. "Jeremiah, I just wanted to let you know we're ready to roll when you are."

Dan slapped his knees and went to stand up. "Yeah, I need to get back to campus, too." He reached out to shake Jeremiah's hand, and when Jeremiah took it, he found himself pulled into a hug.

"Remember it, Jeremiah," Dan said softly in his ear. "You always have a choice."

CHAPTER TWENTY-THREE

INDIANA CHANGES EVERYTHING

Summer arrived before Jeremiah knew it, and it was then, after rehearsal one night, that he and Liz heard a life-changing announcement from Matt.

"Dude!" Matt said. "Michael's a genius! He got us on the New Or Unsigned Band Showcase Stage at Wilderfest!"

"'Wilderfest?' Like 'wilderness'?" Liz said.

"Yeah," Matt said. "It's a Christian music festival on this huge farm in Indiana."

Liz rolled her eyes. "Why does all Christian stuff have to have a stupid pun for a name?"

Matt gave her an exasperated look. "It just does." He regained his composure and addressed the pair. "Here's the deal: Demon Wrecka had the slot, but his wife is pregnant and is due to deliver *that day*. So Demon Wrecka doesn't want to go and miss out on his kid being born, so Michael called up the festival and convinced them to put *us* in his place!"

"No way!" Jeremiah said.

"So, I guess this is a big deal?" Liz said.

"Yeah, it's a big deal, Liz," Matt said. "A huge deal. There'll be, like, 20,000 people there."

Jeremiah turned to Liz. "Yeah, I've heard a lot about Wilderfest. Just about every Christian band plays there. It'll be sweet."

"Really?" she said.

"Yeah."

"Is Cross-Eyed playing?"

Jeremiah's eyes got wide. "Holy crap, I hadn't even thought of that."

Matt put his hand on Jeremiah's shoulder. "They are, dude."

Jeremiah looked him dead in the eyes. "When is it?"

"Three weeks."

| | | | | |

To save on gas, Knuckle Sandwich, their manager, and their now-official roadie Amanda all piled into Michael's Grand Caravan for the long, long trip to the Indiana farmland that hosted Wilderfest. The trip was essentially without highlight, unless one considers numbing and cramping a highlight. Jeremiah spent most of the trip in the middle of the backseat, his feet propped up on an ice chest Matt had brought and placed between the two front seats.

Matt had taken a summer job at a small, nearly bankrupt bagel shop, mainly because he got to keep as many day-old bagels as he wanted. And he wanted a ton. He brought a huge bag of them to live off of during the four-day Wilderfest lineup. Sadly, half of them were "everything" bagels, which smelled richly of dried onions and garlic powder. Every time the ice chest was opened, the entire van was bathed in that smell.

Halfway through Missouri, Liz, Jeremiah, and Amanda all told Matt that if he opened the chest again, they would throw it out the window.

This is why Jeremiah propped his feet on it. Made it much more difficult to open.

The other reason for their cramped conditions was, in addition to all their equipment, they had brought minimal camping gear. The only hotels in the vicinity had been filled long ago, so, like the rest of the 20,000 or so music fans attending the fest, Knuckle Sandwich and crew would be camping out in the instant village that was Wilderfest.

Roughly fourteen hours after they left Tulsa, they pulled onto the Wilderfest grounds, a dusty, grassy (somehow it was both) patch of land that went on for acres and acres. Jeremiah was glad he only wore sneakers—looked like they would be doing a lot of walking.

They drove down a dirt road that wound through the middle of the grounds. The space was mostly open, free of trees. Huge circus tents had been erected here and there. Jeremiah examined them as they drove by; they all had enormous stages on one end.

"Which one's the New Or Unsigned Band Showcase Stage?" he asked Michael.

"I have no idea, Jeremiah," he said. "But we'll find it, don't you worry."

"Probably should find a camping spot first, don't you think?" Liz said.

"Girl, that's what I'm doing."

Other than the tents, Jeremiah was most impressed by the number of people there. The music started tomorrow, and already there were thousands and thousands of people. Tents everywhere. When he had heard that 20,000 people would be there, it had sounded like a lot. Now that he saw the whole scene, a ramshackle city constructed of pup tents and carnival-style vendors stretched over acres and acres of Indiana farmland, it blew his mind.

They finally pulled to a stop in a small, secluded section toward the corner of the property, a small enclave among some trees that would provide their tents with a little shade from the afternoon sun.

Soon they had their camping gear unloaded and erected in their little spot. There was a big, maroon four-man box tent for the men to share, and a small, blue two-man domed tent for Amanda and Liz.

It wasn't much, but it would be home for the next four days. Four very eventful days.

| | | | | |

Knuckle Sandwich had the opening slot on the first day of the New Or Unsigned Band Showcase Stage, which meant they were the first band to play at Wilderfest '94.

Their slot was at 1:30 on Day One, so they arrived at the appropriate tent (Michael had found it the night before) an hour ahead of time to set up. They only had a thirty-minute slot, so they were determined to make the most of it.

When Jeremiah had heard there would be 20,000 people at the fest, he just assumed that they—or at least a large majority of them—would all come to see them. He realized now that he had been doing some serious wishful thinking. Tons of other bands—signed bands—were scheduled to kick off at 2:00, and it didn't look like too many music fans were planning on hitting up the New Or Unsigned Band Showcase Stage, heading instead to see bands whose music they knew.

When 1:30 rolled around, there were maybe twenty or so people in the huge tent. Here Jeremiah was on this large stage, playing through a mammoth sound system, at the biggest Christian music festival in the world, and there was hardly anyone out in the audience. It was a definite letdown.

Just before they started playing, Matt came back to Jeremiah and Liz. "Hey, guys," he said. "I know there aren't many people out there right now, but if we rock it hard enough—" he pointed to the streams of people walking by the tent on their way to other tents—"we'll get some of those people in here."

Liz and Jeremiah nodded.

"You guys ready?" Matt said.

They nodded again.

"Then let's rock."

Matt turned around and approached the microphone. "Hey there, Wilderfest!"

The tepid response from the assembled onlookers did not fill Jeremiah with confidence.

"Thank you, thank you," Matt said, ignoring the smattering of applause, or at least treating it like more than just a smattering. "We're Knuckle Sandwich, and, uh . . . I'm going to shut up now and let the music do the talking."

And with that, they launched into "Coaltongue," which was now their standard opening song.

Jeremiah was shaky at first, letting the lack of crowd get to him. But, as usual, Liz calmed him, and the more he paid attention to her playing, the better he played. Eventually he gave up on checking out the crowd response and just focused on rocking it as hard as he could.

He went this way for a couple of songs, but by the end of the third (a newer song Matt had written called "Mount of Transfiguration"), he heard a much more thunderous applause than after the previous two songs. He looked toward the front of the stage and saw that the crowd had swelled to a couple hundred people. Looked like Matt was right.

So Jeremiah gave it all he had. He got loose. He started bobbing, feeding on the energy of the ever-growing crowd. And the more energy the crowd gave him, the more he gave back—both to them and to his fellow musicians.

He was in the zone.

They all were.

He stopped thinking and let his fingers take over for him. And his legs. And feet. And shoulders. And neck. And head. He felt the groove oozing out of every pore, infusing every muscle fiber and nerve ending in his body with pure musical passion.

Before he knew it, they had one song left in their set. As Matt hit the last chord to the previous song, he turned and hurried back to Liz and Jeremiah with the five-year-old-kid-candy look on his face.

"Jet Reed is here," he said.

Jeremiah's heart leapt into his throat.

"Seriously?"

Matt nodded like a bobble-head doll in an earthquake. "Right by the sound booth."

Jeremiah scanned the sound booth, and, sure enough, there was Jet Reed, the lead singer of Cross-Eyed, standing in the back in a simple black T-shirt and tight jeans, hiding behind a pair of aviator shades. His trademark handlebar mustache gave him away.

"Oh, man," Jeremiah said.

"Yeah," Matt said. "So, change of set. We're going to close with 'Stranded on Ararat.'"

"Matt—" Liz started to say.

"I know, I know—it's new, and we haven't played it a whole lot, but we have it down pat, and it's the best way to go out."

Liz gave him an unsure look.

"Come on. Trust me, baby."

She nodded. "All right. I don't like it, but I'll do it."

Matt pointed to Jeremiah. "You good, homey?"

Jeremiah nodded quickly. "Get back up there and say something, dude. We gotta play."

Matt hurried back to the microphone. "All right, we only have one more song left to play, and then you guys can all get on with the rest of your fest." He laughed at his little play on words. "This is a new one—well, I guess they're *all* new ones to you guys—but this one's new to us, too. It's about being stuck in a routine and waiting for God to pull you out of it. It's called 'Stranded on Ararat.'"

Liz clicked off the song and they began playing. And once again, Matt had been right to change up the set, because the crowd clearly responded to the opening riff and his intense vocal delivery.

Jeremiah identified with the theme of the song, because, like the titular mountain, his relationship with Amanda was something he felt stranded on. Stuck. Waiting, just like Noah, for something to happen so he could get out of the ark and off the mountain.

He fed off the tension, the frustration, and put it all into his performance. He left nothing within himself, instead pouring out every ounce of energy onto the stage, hoping it would spill into the crowd. All the way to the back.

All the way to Jet Reed.

Jeremiah's mind was turned completely off, reveling in the cathartic song. Instinctively, he hit the last note and let it sustain, but intellectually he was unaware the song was even over.

The crowd response brought him back to reality. They went certifiably nuts. Clapping. Cheering. Whistling. He heard an unidentified male yelling "Roooooooooooooock!" over and over. He thought he heard a female voice scream "You're hot!" in his direction.

"Thank you! We're Knuckle Sandwich!" Matt yelled. He looked skyward and pointed, as if recognizing God in heaven above.

Jeremiah was flabbergasted at the response.

Michael, who had watched the show from side stage, came up as they began to put their gear away to make room for the next band.

"Great job, guys," he said. "Phenomenal. Just phenomenal."

Matt pointed his thumb toward the sound booth. "Did you see Jet Reed back there?"

Michael shook his head, looking toward the back. "No."

"Yeah, he was there."

"Well, I hope he enjoyed the performance," Michael said. "It was edifying."

They finished trotting their gear off the stage and received a few accolades from the next band coming up, a punk band that appeared to be composed of teenage boys who decided to differentiate themselves by the primary colors they'd died their hair.

Jeremiah kept looking into the crowd, hoping to spy Jet Reed. He couldn't believe one of his heroes had been at his own show. He was so busy looking that he didn't see Amanda sneak up behind him and put her arm around his waist.

"Great job, Jeremiah," she said. "You guys were awesome."

"Thanks," he said, leaning over to give her the requisite kiss he knew she was expecting. "Jet Reed was here."

Amanda blinked her eyes rapidly as her jaw dropped. "Are you *serious*?"

Jeremiah nodded. "Yep. He was in the back."

"Whoa. That is so cool!" She smacked him in the arm. "I don't believe it!"

"It's true."

"Man," she said. "I wonder if anything'll come of that?"

||||||

At night, the New Or Unsigned Band Showcase Stage was used for regular, popular bands. Bands that were big, but not big enough to play on Wilderfest's "main" stage, reserved for the A-list.

Bands that didn't quite make the main-stage cut often played midnight shows on one of two stages, and such was the case with Cross-Eyed, performing two nights later on the same stage that Knuckle Sandwich had used to open the festival.

It goes without saying that Matt, Jeremiah, and Amanda were in attendance. Liz had been fighting sunstroke the past couple of days, so she went back to the tents to crash. Michael, not being a night person, always went back to the tents to crash.

Jeremiah had seen Cross-Eyed only once, on the *Eyes on the Prize* tour, the one where he'd gotten his Cross-Eyed T-shirt. He was supremely pumped to see them a second time, this time in a festival atmosphere. He had noticed that all the bands sounded really good at the festival, as if being outdoors refreshed them into playing well. Or perhaps there was some competition involved—every band, especially on the New Or Unsigned Band Showcase Stage, wanted to be the one that everyone talked about on the way home. So they all rocked it as hard as they could.

Such was the case with Cross-Eyed. From their opening number, the classic "Tomb Stumper" from *Funnel Vision*, all the way to their closing song (and Knuckle Sandwich cover favorite) "Kill Me."

Jeremiah didn't hear "Kill Me," though. Jet announced that they had one more song, and what it would be, and the crowd gave their expected groans of disappointment that the show was over. But the reason Jeremiah didn't listen to the song was because of what Jet said just before playing it:

"Hey, a couple of days ago, I saw this rad band on the New Or Unsigned Band Showcase Stage called 'Knuckle Sandwich.' Anyone else see them?"

Jeremiah was surprised, first of all, that Jet Reed even mentioned them, let alone labeled them as "rad." Secondly, he was surprised at the huge amount of clapping and cheering after Jet mentioned Knuckle Sandwich, which only added to the surreality of the moment.

"Weren't they great?" Jet said. More clapping and cheering. "Anyway, I have a big announcement to make here at Wilderfest." He looked back at his band members for a moment, as if to make sure they were cool with what he was going to say. "This fall, Cross-Eyed is launching something we've never done before—our own *record label*!"

The crowd went nuts, whipped into a frenzy by Jet's hollering of the words "record label." Jeremiah, on the other hand, began connecting the dots in his head and nearly fainted at the conclusion he was drawing.

"Anyway, I really liked what I saw from Knuckle Sandwich, and I wanna sign them to the label. I want them to be the first artist on Jet-Son Records!"

More clapping and cheering. Jeremiah felt Matt and Amanda both clamp onto him at this unexpected news. Apparently they had connected the dots in their heads, too, but hearing the dots connected for them by Jet Reed was almost too much to bear.

"If anyone out there knows how to get in touch with those dudes—whoa, they're not all dudes, they had a chick drummer—but anyway, if you know how to find Knuckle Sandwich, I'll be right down here," he pointed to the front of the stage, off to the side, "after this song. Come see me."

And that was that. Jeremiah stood stock still during "Kill Me," not hearing a note. He just ran what Jet had said over and over in his head. Over. And over. And over.

Matt began to elbow his way toward the front of the stage, leaving Jeremiah and Amanda in the mass of sweaty, dirty festival-goers.

Jeremiah snapped back to the concert. "Matt! Wait up!"

Matt barely turned his head back toward them. "Come on!" His arms at shoulder level and flailing, he looked as if he were wading through a rushing river.

Jeremiah snatched Amanda's hand and followed. "Matt!" he shouted over the powerful bleating of the festival's top-notch sound system. "We should get Liz! Or Michael!"

Matt just kept going. Jeremiah thought he heard Matt scream, "No time!"

As they moved through the crowd, Jeremiah's mind was flush with images of hacking through dense rainforest and fording deep streams. Amanda stutter-stepped along behind him, continually saying, "Excuse me. Sorry. Pardon us. Sorry, again. Excuse us, please."

The song ended, and, after a hearty "Thank you, Wilderfest!" Jet jumped down from the stage to his designated spot. Matt was almost there. Jeremiah and Amanda were three steps behind him.

But, too late. Throngs of people surrounded Jet, blocking him from Jeremiah's view. Matt pressed forward. Like a sunbeam making its way through a heavy cloud, Jet suddenly reappeared. His eyes widened, and he pointed directly at Matt.

"Knuckle Sandwich!" he said. "Knuckle Sandwich right there!" He motioned him forward. "C'mere, dude! Your band with you?"

Matt reached back and grabbed Jeremiah's shirt sleeve, making a little three-person train that was soon in front of Jet.

Jet pointed at Jeremiah. "Bass player!" He held up his hand for a high-five. "You *groove*, dude! I've been telling Lance all about you!"

"Really?"

Jet steamrolled on, pointing at Amanda. "You're a different chick."

Amanda took Jeremiah's arm in hand. "I'm his girlfriend."

Jet smiled. "Rock on." He turned to Matt. "Where's your chick drummer, dude?"

Matt gestured with this thumb in some random direction. "She's back in the tent. Not feeling too good."

"Aw, man. I was hoping to meet the whole band," Jet said. "Oh well." He looked at the gathered crowd of onlookers, who had formed a circle around these proceedings. "What do you guys think, huh? Knuckle Sandwich!"

The crowd applauded heartily, if somewhat under obligation.

Jet turned back to Matt. "So, you guys got a manager or what?"

"Yeah."

"Rock *on*," he said with a thousand-watt smile. "I *dig* you guys. You aren't afraid to rock hard, you know? You do your thing, and if the people wanna hear it, cool. You got good songs. You got good stage presence. You give it all you got." He exchanged his smile for burning sincerity and lowered his voice, saying everything deliberately. "You guys are exactly what I'm looking for. You got a handsome lead singer. You got a foxy chick drummer—that's a good hook. You got a bass player that looks like a freakin' sidewinder up there. And you got talent!"

None of them said a word. Jeremiah really wished Liz could've been there.

"Seriously, I want to do this deal," Jet said. He reached into the back pocket of his jeans and produced a business card. "This is my manager's card, all right? Give it to your manager and have him call after the fest is over, okay? Let's make this happen!"

Matt took the card and reverently put it in his back pocket. "All right," he said.

"Dudes, I gotta head back, but I look forward to hearing from you. Seriously."

And with that Jet Reed stepped out of the tent, the circle of fans either following him or dispersing into the night air.

Jeremiah couldn't wait to get back to the tents to tell Liz what had just happened.

CHAPTER TWENTY-FOUR

CHANGING OF THE GUARD

Six weeks later, Jeremiah burst through his front door holding a thick packet of legal documents that bore his signature. "Dad!" he yelled as he came bustling through. "Dad! Check it out!"

His dad hopped up from the sofa, where he was watching an *Ellery Queen* rerun. "Everything okay, Jeremiah?"

"Yeah, yeah," Jeremiah said, panting heavily. He showed his dad the papers. "Look!"

"Hey, hey!" his dad said. "Look at that! You're officially on a label."

Jeremiah sank down on the couch. "I can't believe it, Pop. This is crazy."

Jeremiah's dad sank down next to him. "I'm really proud of you, son."

"Thanks, Pop."

Jeremiah's dad settled himself into the couch. "So, what's next? Record an album?"

"Yeah, we're supposed to record in September and October, then hit the road for a while, I guess."

"What about school?"

Jeremiah cringed. "Um, yeah. Kinda needed to talk to you about that."

Jeremiah's dad laughed. "Son, I know what it's like. This is a once-in-a-lifetime opportunity, and if you don't take it, you'll kick yourself later." He laughed again. "Heck, *I'd* kick you."

Now it was Jeremiah's turn to laugh. "No thanks. I'll just take it and avoid all the kicking."

"What about Matt and Liz?"

"I don't know about Matt—I know he's quitting school, but I don't know what his parents said about it," Jeremiah said. "Liz is on her own, so she can do what she wants. She already quit."

"And the Armory?"

Jeremiah let out a slight chuckle. "Yeah, I already talked to Betty, and she was fine with me leaving for now," he said. "She actually told me I always have a place there if my whole musical group didn't work out."

Jeremiah's dad shared the chuckle. "Did she actually say 'musical group'?"

"Yeah."

"That's funny."

The two sat there a moment in silence, a natural pause in their conversation.

"So," Jeremiah's dad said, "where are you recording? In town?"

"Nah," Jeremiah said. "Jet owns his own studio in Nashville, so we're gonna head out there to record."

"You'll be in Nashville for two months?"

"Yeah, I guess so."

"What about Amanda?"

Jeremiah let out a slow breath. "Well, it's too much time for her to be gone, so she's going to just stay back here and work like crazy."

This made Jeremiah extraordinarily glad. The mere thought of taking a break from Amanda was a great relief to him. While Amanda was always the one who initiated their sexual encounters, Jeremiah was no better—he didn't even put up his mental fight anymore.

Dan had told him that he always had a choice, but the words that had sounded so comforting in Oklahoma City now felt miles away, as if they'd stayed there. In the heat of the moment, he had such difficulty resisting. His brain had become accustomed to just going along with the pleasure his body was craving, and, in the moment, his brain always did exactly what his body told it to do.

But in the moments when he was away from Amanda, he was being eaten away by guilt from the inside. Outside of Jeremiah's confession to Dan, which he hadn't told Amanda about, they had kept their sexual relationship a secret from everyone. His constant inability to tell anyone about it, talk it through with someone—anyone—made the shame even worse. He felt totally isolated in his sin.

So maybe a month or two in Nashville, away from the temptation of his beautiful girlfriend, would do him good. He could focus on making the record, maybe go see a band or two.

"Well, I hope you guys can weather that storm," his dad said. He kept his head pointed at Jeremiah, but his eyes darted away as he said softly, "Isn't easy, being apart."

"I'll be fine, Dad."

Jeremiah's dad looked back at his son and smiled. "I'm sure you will be," he said. "Hey, what about Michael?"

"He has to take care of his family, so he's going to drive out there with us, spend a week or two making sure we get off to a good start, then fly home."

"Sounds like a good plan."

"Yeah."

He gave Jeremiah's knee a squeeze. "I guess you got it all figured out, huh?"

Jeremiah didn't know what to say to that. He didn't have anything figured out. He didn't even know where to begin.

| | | | | |

"Guys," Matt said four weeks later, "we're gonna be huge. This is only the beginning."

The standard four and Michael were at Hideaway, finishing up a huge Paradise Pie (pizza with Alfredo sauce, chicken, bacon, and tomatoes) as a means of savoring a little bit of Tulsa flavor before leaving for Nashville the next day.

"I wish I could go with you," Amanda said.

"You'll be in our hearts, hon," Liz said, rolling her eyes toward Jeremiah. "Right, Jeremiah?"

Jeremiah was slurping in some stringy cheese, so while he intended to smile and say, "Right," he was afraid it came out far less cool than it did in his mind.

Michael pushed his plate away, licked his lips, and dabbed them with a napkin. "If I could have everyone's attention, please. I have an announcement to make."

Jeremiah finished with his cheese while everyone else stopped chewing to look at Michael.

"Demon Wrecka has been offered an incredible opportunity with a label in Japan. A secular label there wants to make him the country's number one rap star."

"That's great, Michael!" Liz said.

"The best part," Michael said, "is that he isn't going to change his message at all. It will be such an encouragement to the Body to hear that the gospel is going forth like that."

Jeremiah took another bite and got more cheese, a big string that flipped down on his chin. "Cool."

"Now, while this is a magnificent turn of events for Demon Wrecka, it does affect you greatly." Michael blinked a few times rapidly. "I'll be going with you to Nashville tomorrow, and I'll stay for a week or so, but after that, I'll be going to Japan with Demon Wrecka for at least a few months."

No one said anything for a long time. Jeremiah forgot about the cheese on his chin.

"What's that mean?" Matt said.

"It means that I'm in a tight position, here, Matt," Michael said. He swallowed. "I'm afraid I'm going to have to resign as your manager. The label's going to take care of you now."

Liz nodded slowly.

"I don't want to," Michael said. "But I've been with Demon Wrecka from the beginning. I had to make a choice—and I've known him longer."

"We understand," Liz said. "That's great, Michael."

"Yeah, man," Matt said. "Besides, you can just keep Japan warm for us until we get there."

Michael gave a hearty laugh. "Well, I'm glad you understand. It's been my privilege to work with such talented musicians as you."

The waitress came by with the ticket, which Michael scooped up. "I'll take care of this." He got up and headed to the register at the front of the restaurant.

Matt turned to the rest of them. "What do you guys think?"

"I feel okay about it," Liz said. "I've always felt that something like this would happen."

"Yeah, me too," Matt said. "Jeremiah?"

"Whatever you guys think. I wish him well."

"Glad we're all in agreement," Matt said, turning to Liz. "Let's see if we can agree on what to do for the rest of the night."

"Let's go to Woodward Park," Liz said, her eyes closed as she inhaled an imaginary floral fragrance. "I'd love a walk—stock up on Tulsa before we head to Nashville."

Matt smiled. "Sounds good."

The two of them hopped up from the table and departed with a "See you guys tomorrow" and a "See ya," respectively.

"Well, Jeremiah," Amanda said, taking Jeremiah's hand in her own and stroking the back of it, "I guess this leaves you and me alone, huh?" She leaned down and looked over her glasses, deeply into his eyes. "I think we need to head back to the apartment so we can say good-bye."

Oh, if only he could resist those round, deep eyes.

| | | | | |

It was all rote to Jeremiah by now. What had started off as a glistening, thrilling experience was now a mere biological function. But what else was he going to do? It was in his chromosomes, right?

But something was different this time. Afterward, lying in Amanda's bed while she went into the kitchen to get a glass of water, Jeremiah felt a voice in his heart he hadn't felt before. It wasn't anything audible, not something he heard in his actual ears. Just . . . something he knew.

Time to be a man and quit this nonsense, Jeremiah. You know better.

And right then and there, Jeremiah prayed.

He had prayed tons of times, especially after sex, asking God to make him feel better, or to take away his desires. But this time, he prayed differently.

"God, change me. Don't take the desires away from me, take me away from the desires. I'm sick of this. I want something better."

It's going to hurt.

"I know. I still want it. I'm tired of knowing *about* you. I want to know you. For real."

I want that, too, Jeremiah.

Jeremiah got dressed, and for the first time in a long time, he felt just a hint of legitimate peace within. He knew, without a doubt, that he was about to change for the better.

And he knew that this had been his last time with Amanda.

CHAPTER TWENTY-FIVE

A FISTFUL OF HOLLERS

Cross-Eyed must have been doing well, because Jet Reed had a nice house in Brentwood, a suburb of Nashville that seemed to be a hub for Christian musicians. Jet gave them the grand tour as soon as they showed up, after pumping their hands like he was Willy Wonka.

"Welcome, welcome," he said, gesturing around the expansive front room. "As you can see, I have plenty of space." He pointed up the stairs. "Couple of guest bedrooms up there, one for the gents, one for the lady." He motioned for them to follow him as he moved toward another room. "Through here is the kitchen—there's a bathroom back that way—and then, if we look down here . . ."

He opened a door, revealing a wide set of stairs leading down into what Jeremiah assumed was a basement.

"Come on," Jet said, "this is pretty sweet." He flipped on a light switch, motioned for them to follow him, then headed down.

The rest of them followed, and Jeremiah sucked in a breath at the sight. Stacks of drums, a dozen guitars hanging on the wall, maybe six basses, a huge area of amplifiers, and an old couch with '70s-era yellow lines and squares. And that was just the front room.

Beyond that, the rest of the basement was split into two rooms. The first was a control room with a huge mixing board and all kinds of processors and rack-mounted electronic whirligigs that did Lord knew what. The other room was large and open, with plenty of space for recording. Microphones and stands stood all around, and there was baffling on the walls, intricately woven rugs on the floor, and a huge drum set in the middle. The wall separating the two rooms had a huge plexiglass window

"This is where the magic happens," Jet said. "We recorded the last two Cross-Eyed albums down here."

"It's perfect," Matt said.

A long-haired, bearded guy in a Nirvana T-shirt and carpenter shorts came walking out of the control room.

"And this," Jet said, ushering the man over, "is Edward Donaldson, your producer."

"No way!" Matt said, reaching out eagerly to shake Edward's hand. "I love what you did with the Cross-Eyed albums."

Liz leaned over and whispered in Jeremiah's ear. "Should I know him?"

"He produces Cross-Eyed," Jeremiah said, matching her volume and slyness.

"Huh." Jeremiah could tell she wasn't impressed. "Well," she said, "I'm just happy to be here."

"I can't believe *you're* going to be our producer!" Matt said. He turned to Jet. "Dude, you must really believe in us or something!"

Jet gave a mighty, Santa-worthy bellow. "I better. You're launching my label, dude!"

Jeremiah felt a long, long way from Tongues of Fire.

||||||

They got started the next day, laying down rough live versions of all their songs so Edward could listen and get ideas. Matt took full advantage of Jet's arsenal of guitars and amps, messing around with them to find different tones and nuances.

Liz was impressed with the studio's drum kit, a DW custom number with more toms and cymbals than she could possibly use. The first thing she did was strip it down to a simple four-piece kit with a couple of cymbals.

Jeremiah was pleased to see a Fender Jazz Bass in the studio, and it became his instant friend. After playing so many shows with his T-40 weighing him down, the J-Bass felt like playing a ray of sunlight. He couldn't believe what he had been missing, but he vowed, on day one of recording, to use his part of their modest advance to buy one of these exact basses.

The first couple of weeks were a blast. For starters, Jeremiah had headphones the whole time—quite a step up from his first recording experience. He liked talking to Edward, and the thrill of being in a new city playing music nonstop was almost too much for him to handle.

That thrill soon wore off, though. As the days went on, the process began to feel monotonous, and Jeremiah thought that if he had to punch in one more part, he would stab himself in the eye with the headstock of his bass.

It didn't help that Matt became his recording-obsessed self yet again. Matt had an instant rapport with Edward, which made it even worse. Though Matt was a musician and Edward was a gearhead, they spoke each other's language, as evidenced by the conversation Jeremiah overheard the day they started tracking Matt's guitar on "God Only Knows":

[Matt] "Should I use the Strat or the Tele?"

[Edward] "I think that Tele will give you more what you're looking for."

[Matt] "But what if we get a 57 and work the angle on the cabinet? Won't that help?"

[Edward] "Eh, that might work. I prefer to use an 87 at a little more distance to get a wet room tone. And then, instead of running it through the board, I run it through the universal pre."

[Matt] "Makes sense."

| | | | | |

Matt and Edward spent almost all their time in the control room tweaking things and coming up with ideas, with Matt often running back and forth from the control room to the recording room to throw down something.

Jeremiah did his best to pay attention to all these goings-on, but the whole process started to interest him less and less, which left him on that '70s couch quite often, a piece of furniture he usually shared with Liz.

"Boy, Matt's really going for it," she said during their third or fourth week there. "He sure loves this stuff."

"That he does," Jeremiah said, exhaling slowly. "You notice how he doesn't even ask our opinion on anything anymore?"

"Um, yeah," Liz said in a voice that filled with pique.

"Honestly, it doesn't really bother me," Jeremiah said, turning around in the couch to face her, digging his arm into the back cushion. "This whole band was his vision, right? Might as well let him keep on top of it."

"I guess."

The two of them sat there for a moment, reflecting. Matt walked through, on his way from the control to the recording room, and he didn't say a word or acknowledge them. He just shut the door. A few moments later, Jeremiah overheard him on the studio monitors talking to Edward. "Hey, Ed?" he said. "Can you post-track the verb so it'll sound wet in the cans?"

Jeremiah shot a look at Liz, who just closed her eyes and nodded slowly.

"Hey," Liz said, "how many lead singers does it take to change a light bulb?"

Jeremiah smiled. "I have no idea."

"One—to hold it while the world revolves around him."

They both burst into a fit of laughter.

As it died down, Jeremiah rubbed his eyes in fatigue. "So, Liz," he said, "tell me about yourself. When did you start playing drums?"

"Eleven years old."

"Really?"

"Yeah," she said, nodding. "My mom was . . . not enthused. She wanted me to play French horn."

"Those are pretty different, yeah."

"A little." She took a deep breath, looked at the ceiling with a furrowed brow, then looked back at Jeremiah. "I was also a cheerleader for a year in high school."

"No way!"

"Yeah, not my finest moment."

Jeremiah laughed inwardly at the thought of tiny little Liz jumping around waving a pom-pom on the sidelines at a football game.

"What else, what else?" she asked herself. "Oh—I like peanut butter and olive sandwiches."

"That sounds flavorful," Jeremiah said, swallowing grotesquely as he said the word "flavorful."

"You should try it," she said, laughing. "Okay, your turn." She wiggled her fingers, as if to conjure up a question through magic. "Um, where'd you get the name Jeremiah?"

"My dad. He's a big Three Dog Night fan."

Liz let out a cackle. "So, was he hoping you were a bullfrog?"

"I think he just wanted me to be a good friend of his."

She laughed again. "What else you got?"

Jeremiah thought for a moment. "I have a few of Shakespeare's sonnets memorized."

"Really?" she said, her eyes perking up. "Let's hear one, hotshot."

"No, I don't remem—"

"Come on," she said, using her finger to needle him in the ribs. "We got nothing but time, brother. You can sit there and think up at least one."

"Okay, but I won't remember the whole thing."

"That's fine."

Jeremiah closed his eyes, searched his memory, and recited:

O me! What eyes hath Love put in my head,
Which have no correspondence with true sight;
Or if they have, where is my judgment fled,
That censures falsely what they see aright?

There were some more lines in there, but he couldn't remember them; he only knew the last two:

O cunning Love! With tears thou keep'st me blind,
Lest eyes well-seeing thy foul faults should find.

He opened his eyes, and the first thing he saw was Liz, sitting stock-still, looking at him with the corner of her mouth upturned. The second thing he saw was a pool of wetness forming in the inside of her left eye.

"That's so . . . beautifully sad, Jeremiah," she said, her voice hushed and cracking slightly.

Ordinarily, Jeremiah would've found such honesty and insight into an emotion other than happiness off-putting. But sitting here, talking with Liz so easily, unwittingly opening himself up with that sonnet, and seeing her go down that emotional road with him . . . it was so different.

It was almost like talking to a best friend.

"Amanda and I are having sex."

There. It was out there. It was out there, and it felt good to say it.

Liz shuddered, her eyes wide open, presumably shocked at the suddenness of the confession. She stayed that way for an instant, then her entire body language melted into sympathy, shoulders down, head to the side.

"I know, Jeremiah." He could barely hear her cracking voice.

The temperature of Jeremiah's insides dropped a hundred degrees. "You do?" he whispered, choking back tears.

Liz gave a slight nod. "Amanda and I are roommates, Jeremiah. Difficult to keep something like that from your roommate and best friend."

He nodded, promising himself he wouldn't cry. But oh, the relief that was flooding him now. She understood.

She understood.

Liz reached out and laid her hand on top of his in reassurance. She looked directly in his eyes. "For what it's worth, I told her you guys needed to stop. Is that something you've wanted?"

He didn't say anything. He just nodded. A single tear rolled down the valley between his nose and cheek.

Jeremiah heard the door to the recording room open and whipped his head around. Matt came through, already chattering to Edward, "That A-flat-minor-seven was just giving me such a hard time, but I finally . . ." His voice trailed off as he went back into the control room and closed the door. He hadn't once looked toward the couch.

Jeremiah turned back to Liz and saw that she had watched Matt walk through. She leaned toward him and said, "Well, as long as we're being honest, Matt and I have been . . ." She stopped and thought, as if choosing her words carefully. "Intimate. Several times."

Jeremiah withdrew his hand from under hers, not out of repulsion but out of shock. "*What?*"

She just stared at him, eyes pleading with him to maintain his composure.

He caught himself and mellowed his voice. "Really? I thought you guys were, like, super Christians."

Liz leaned back. "Jeremiah, no matter how much you love God, you can still wind up sinning. It doesn't make it right—it just makes you human."

"What—how'd this happen?"

"Same as with you. It's two people in love, or who at least *think* they're in love, getting too close and going too far. Listening to the wrong voice inside. Screwing up."

Jeremiah nodded. He knew exactly what she meant.

"We were together the night before we left for Nashville," she said. "And I told Matt then and there that it was going to be the last time, at least until we got married."

"You guys are getting *married*?"

Liz smiled. "Well, not yet. No one's proposed or anything."

She looked down at the floor, then at the control room. She stayed that way for a long time before she finally looked back at Jeremiah. "It's something we've talked about." She sighed. "We'll see. "

"Cool."

"Jeremiah," Liz said, reaching out and swatting his knee, "I think you and I need to make a little pact here, okay?"

Jeremiah's eyes bounced between Liz's eyes and the knee she just swatted. "What about?"

"I think we both need to be the ones to stand up for abstinence. You know, like our youth pastors used to tell us to do all the time."

"How so?"

"It's up to us to keep our relationships pure, man. From this point on, we're staying sex-free, and we're not giving in."

Jeremiah liked the idea of the pact—it might be easier if he knew someone else was committed to it, too. And would be checking up on him. "Yeah," he said. "It's a deal."

"Great!" Liz offered him her hand. "Shake on it."

They shook.

"Jeremiah," Liz said, "take good care of Amanda, okay? She's a sweet girl, and my best friend, and if you do anything to hurt her, I'll cram a drumstick down your throat."

He smiled. "Yes, ma'am."

She smiled back. "You're a good man, Jeremiah Springfield."

"Thanks."

Jeremiah had never really noticed this before, but Liz was pretty cute when she smiled.

||||||

The rest of their time in Nashville was, as Jeremiah would put it, unpleasant. Knowing what he now knew about the nature of Matt and Liz's relationship, he read new insights into the way Matt treated Liz. Matt was alternately short-tempered and indifferent to her. Before this, Jeremiah had chalked it up to Matt's obsession with recording—he just figured that was getting in the way of his better judgment. Now he realized that Matt was frustrated with Liz because he wasn't getting any. To use the vernacular.

It showed up in a discussion the three of them—along with Jet—had about the album title over dinner in downtown Nashville at San Antonio Taco Company, an a la carte Tex-Mex place that had a definite natural-wood vibe to it.

Matt had gotten the ball rolling after biting into a chicken fajita taco. "So, what are we going to call the album?" he said, a little bit of shredded cheese falling out of his mouth.

"I already got this one covered, Matt," Jet said, waving his hands regally. "The first single is going to be 'Ham-Fisted,' so that's going to be the title of the album, too."

The three members of Knuckle Sandwich looked at each other. No one said a word.

"Unless one of you three has a better idea," Jet said.

Jeremiah speared a piece of cheese enchilada with his fork. "I just figured we'd call it *Knuckle Sandwich*," he said, inserting said piece of cheese enchilada into his mouth, "You know, go the self-titled route."

"My goodness, you boys have no table manners," Liz said. "There is a lady present, after all."

Jeremiah finished chewing, swallowed, and said, "Sorry, Liz."

Matt took a huge bite of his taco, turned to Liz, and said, "Yeah, sorry," purposely shooting food debris toward her.

"So. Mature."

"Anyway," Jeremiah said, waving Matt off with his fork, "I

thought we could do it self-titled, and the cover would be a big fist—" here he made a fist, his fork sticking out from the middle—"between two pieces of bread. Pow!" He punctuated his pow with a punching movement at no one in particular.

"I don't know about that, man," Jet said. "It's a little obvious."

"For me, I always like long album titles," Liz said. "What about *Sparkling Blues of Water Pure*?"

Matt put down his chicken taco and rolled his eyes. "Come on, Liz," he said. "Be serious."

"For crying out loud, Matt," Liz said. "Show some respect to your girl. It's just an idea."

"Well, it's not a good one."

"I don't hear *you* suggesting anything, *Matthew*."

He ground his index finger into the table. "I have several ideas, *Elizabeth*, I just haven't settled on one."

Jeremiah looked down at his plate and fought the urge to arrange grains of rice into squares.

"Why don't you pray about it? Huh?" Liz was getting hot now, her hands becoming more animated, her posture leaning ever so slightly toward Matt. If she had been a cat, her ears would be pointed back and the hair on her back would be sticking straight up. "Or are you too cool to pray these days?"

"Hey! I don't have to pray with *you* all the time. I do it on my own!"

Jeremiah snapped his head up. "Matt."

"*What*?"

"Calm down," Jeremiah said.

"Matt, dude," Jet said. "Seriously."

"You shouldn't talk to Liz like that," Jeremiah said. "She was just suggesting an idea."

Matt swiveled his accusatory finger in Jeremiah's direction. "Well, I guess *you* would know how to talk to her—that's all you guys have been doing lately." He turned back to Liz. "I'm starting to wonder whose girlfriend you really are."

If Liz had been a cat, this would have been the moment she would have sunk her teeth and claws into Matt's nose and held on for dear life. Instead, she closed her eyes, took a deep breath—in through the nose, out through the mouth—set her fork down, and shook her head.

"Matt, that's enough," Jet said, fixing Matt with the most serious look Jeremiah had ever seen Jet give. "I think maybe the strain of recording is getting to all you guys here."

Matt kept staring at Liz. He finally wadded up a napkin and threw it on the table in disgust.

"I think," Jet said, "we just need to spend the rest of the night relaxing."

||||||

They went back to the house, where Liz went straight to her room with a terse, "I'm going to bed."

"Here, let's go into the living room," Jet said. "I feel like watching a movie. You guys?"

Jeremiah shrugged. "Sure."

Matt did the same. "Yeah."

Jet had an enormous movie collection, all on laserdisc, which Jeremiah found to be a treat. He was used to the fuzzy, slightly hazy picture of VHS; to see a movie in pristine digital treatment was especially nice.

The majority of Jet's collection seemed to be westerns, so they put on one of the Clint Eastwood/Sergio Leone pictures. It was a good one, and Jeremiah could tell that, after the tension in the restaurant, Matt was beginning to relax. Something about all the shooting, probably.

An hour and a half into it, Matt snapped his fingers in triumph. "I got it!"

Jeremiah and Jet both turned to look at him. "Got what?"

"The name of our record," Matt said.

"What do you got?" Jeremiah said.

"The perfect title!" Matt said, his eyes wild. "It fits with our name, it describes our music, and it's catchy."

"And it is . . ." Jet said.

"*A Fistful of Hollers.*"

Jeremiah and Jet were silent. In the background, Clint Eastwood shot someone.

"I like it," Jeremiah said.

"I love it," Jet said at almost the same time as Jeremiah. "That's awesome! I can see the cover already: a dusty, dry desert climate, with an open sky. Lots of brown. And in the center, a guitar leaning up against a microphone stand. With one of those old jazz singer mics on it."

"That's gonna look killer," Matt said.

"Yeah," Jet said. "Nice."

Jeremiah was disappointed there would be no fists in bread. Oh well. There was always the next record.

CHAPTER TWENTY-SIX

IN WHICH JEREMIAH TAKES A STAND

Once the album was finished, it was back to Tulsa for a couple of months of rest (and work), and then on the road with Cross-Eyed. Jet wanted to release the record in March to coincide with Christian Music Week and the annual QUAILS Awards for Outstanding Christian Music, but to get a buzz going for that release, Knuckle Sandwich was going to hit the road with the band that discovered them.

As soon as he got back into Tulsa, Jeremiah went to the Armory and talked to Betty. He assured her that, while his musical group was doing just fine, he still needed to get his old job back for the Christmas rush. Betty was true to her promise and hired him back to be register help for the excruciatingly busy Christmas season.

The second thing Jeremiah did when he got back to Tulsa was stop by Amanda's apartment to say hello. They had talked on the phone quite a bit during his time in Nashville, but he had yet to clarify the picture about future sexual activity—in other words, he had yet to live up to his end of the pact he'd made with Liz. Though he dreaded it, the time was now.

Amanda jumped into his arms and gave him a huge bear hug. Jeremiah almost fell over at the contact. She began smothering him with kisses, then, just before his knees buckled, she hopped down and led him into the apartment, hurriedly shutting the door behind them.

"Where's Liz?" Jeremiah asked.

"Down at Cracker Barrel," Amanda said as she locked the door. "She's trying to get a seasonal job there, and she has an interview in, like, ten minutes."

Jeremiah had walked into the living room and was standing in front of the couch. Amanda had her hair in a ponytail. She whipped the ponytail holder out of her hair, letting it fall loose. She took off her glasses and set them and the ponytail holder on an end table, then tackled Jeremiah onto the couch.

"I missed you so much," she breathed into his ear.

"I . . . missed you, too," Jeremiah said more loudly than he wanted to. He wriggled out from underneath her and sat up on the couch. "Hey, Amanda, I think there's something we need to talk about."

"I know. No more sex," she said. "Jeremiah, we've had this conversation a thousand times, and it just doesn't work for us." She put her arms around his neck. "Come on. We'll talk about it after."

He pushed her away and stood up. "No!" he said.

"Jeremiah!"

"No. I'm not going to do it anymore." He took a seat on a chair that sat opposite the couch. "Amanda, please. I don't want our relationship to be only about sex anymore. I want it to be about *us*."

"That *is* us. It's us, together."

"Well, I don't want to be together like that anymore."

She narrowed her eyes and burned a hole through him. "Okay."

"Okay?"

"Yeah. Sure. Fine. Whatever." Amanda clipped the end of every word, tight-lipped. She got back up from the couch and went to the end table to retrieve her glasses and ponytail holder.

Jeremiah leaned forward. "Amanda, listen—"

She put her hair in a reckless ponytail. "I heard you, Jeremiah," she said, tartness in her voice. "It's fine. Really." She threw on her glasses and stomped into the kitchen, opening the cabinets as if looking for something.

Jeremiah tried to think of some words to offer, something that would salvage the moment and bring their relationship back to where it needed to be—to where it had been.

Then he discovered the reason he was speechless.

There was nothing to say.

CHAPTER TWENTY-SEVEN

STOP FOLLOWING CHRISTIANS

Amanda stopped coming to Knuckle Sandwich rehearsals after that. It was awkward at first, mainly because Jeremiah was worried about Liz's drumstick threat, but once he saw Liz before rehearsal and explained what happened, she actually took his side.

"She'll calm down, Jeremiah," she said. "I'm proud of you."

"Thanks," Jeremiah said. "How are things with you and Matt?"

"Let's see," she said, biting her lip, "What's a good word to describe it? Frosty?"

"That bad, huh?"

"Yeah," she said. "I mean, I thought there might be some fallout in Nashville, but I think he was so focused on recording that he didn't even try anything."

"That's good, I guess."

"Yeah, I guess," Liz said. She folded her arms. "Although, I gotta tell you—I was a little hurt to play second fiddle to a guitar and a microphone."

Jeremiah laughed.

"Anyway, when we got back, I put the hammer down, and he reacted about how I'd expected."

"Well," Jeremiah said, laying his hand on her shoulder, "stay strong."

She laid her hand on his shoulder. "You, too."

They stayed there for a second, until Liz broke the silence. "I feel like we should have a secret handshake or something—just some way to end this conversation."

"We could just end it."

"Okay."

||||||

When the band wasn't rehearsing, they all worked. They'd gotten a modest advance when they signed their record deal, but it was nothing huge, and they still had bills to pay and stuff to buy.

Matt got a temporary job at Gap and took advantage of his discount to gear up for their future tour. Since he was no longer a student at ORU, and therefore couldn't live on campus, he started crashing at Amanda's and Liz's apartment.

"Dude, you can stay at my house," Jeremiah said. "My dad won't care, and we have the room."

"Nah, man," Matt said. "I'm kinda feeling bad about the way I treated Liz in Nashville. I'm trying to spend as much time as I can with her."

"Don't you think it kinda looks bad, though?" Jeremiah said. "A guy staying with two cute girls, and one of them is his girlfriend?"

Matt laughed. "It's all good, homey," he said. "Liz and I promised not to be there alone together. If Amanda ain't around, we're hanging out somewhere else."

"Okay," Jeremiah said. "Hope it works."

Liz got a job with Amanda at Cracker Barrel, but as a hostess, not as part of the waitstaff. She spent a lot of time browsing the kitsch shop; she bought Jeremiah a brainteaser made of horseshoes for Christmas.

Jeremiah called Amanda on Christmas day to wish her well. He realized later that Liz must have been priming the pump, because he was not prepared for the voice he heard.

"Jeremiah!" Amanda said, her chipper tone coming through the phone so clearly it nearly pierced his eardrum. "Merry Christmas!"

"Merry Christmas, Amanda," he said. "How are you?"

"I'm all right," she said.

"Just all right?"

"Yeah. I miss you—not, uh, *being* with you, you know? Just—I miss hanging out together."

Jeremiah couldn't resist smiling. "Yeah, I miss hanging out with you, too."

"Liz says you really like me and want to be with me and that you not wanting to have sex with me had nothing to do with me and everything to do with sex."

Jeremiah's mouth got progressively more open through Amanda's run-on sentence. He hesitated for a moment, waiting for something intelligent to come out of his mouth.

"Well . . ." he said.

"She also said that you're really great, and that I'd be stupid to be mad at you for wanting to do the right thing, and that I should say I'm sorry for getting mad at you, and that we should get back together and start over from the beginning and take it slower and so I think that's a good idea and I'm sorry Jeremiah and will you pleasepleaseplease forgive me?"

Wow. Way to go, Liz.

"You bet, Amanda. Of course I forgive you."

She squealed, once again nearly piercing his eardrum.

A week later, when midnight hit and 1995 came, they kept their celebration to a quick peck.

||||||

Two weeks later, it was time to hit the road with Cross-Eyed. Jet-Son had bought them a nice Econoline van to tour in. All their gear fit snugly in the back, and they all three took turns driving.

Touring was a new experience for Jeremiah, and he liked it at first. He liked going to all the different cities. He liked playing to new crowds every night. He didn't like the ten-dollar per diem the label gave him to live on, but he made the most of it by skipping breakfast, unless the hotel had a free one. In that case, he'd swipe a couple of extra muffins or pieces of fruit to make a dandy lunch.

The highlight of his tour, though, was seeing the Cross-Eyed guys, when he got the chance—although they tended to keep to themselves. Usually, Jeremiah got to interact with them around sound check, and that was about it.

Except Jet. He was always checking up on them, seeing how they were doing. "You guys are like my baby—and I'm a proud ol' papa!" he kept saying.

They played mostly mid-size venues. Not arenas, but not clubs, either. Places that fit a couple thousand people, sometimes concert halls, sometimes just large church auditoriums. Night after night. Getting to the venue in the afternoon, loading in their equipment, checking sound, eating promoter-provided food (usually pizza), playing their show, hanging by the merch table, meeting fans, packing their equipment back on the van, heading to the hotel, sleeping, hitting the road the next morning to do it all again.

Every. Single. Day.

| | | | | |

JUN-JUN . . . JUHHHHHHHHHHH-JUN!

With a squall of feedback, the song ended and the set was over. The assembled throng roared appreciatively.

How does one roar appreciatively, exactly? It depends on how many people are in the "throng" in question. In this case, Jeremiah estimated a good thousand or so people, cheering, clapping, and offering their personal variations on the vocalization "Woo!"

Jeremiah unplugged his bass and gave the crowd a wave as he made his way off the stage, carefully stepping around the cables, amps, guitars, guitar cases, and half-full 32-ounce convenience store drink cups dribbling condensation onto the floor. He rested his bass in a nearby guitar stand, the appreciative roars dying down, echoing against the bare concrete walls of . . . what was the name of this venue? Jeremiah couldn't remember. He didn't even remember what town they were in.

The repetitive nature of the road had finally gotten to him.

He made his way to the sparse backstage area, Matt and Liz following him while a couple of nameless teenage kids from the venue started striking gear in preparation for Cross-Eyed.

Jeremiah headed to a six-foot table in the corner of the already cramped backstage area, where a small desk lamp illuminated that evening's dinner fare: Domino's.

Again.

Jeremiah had never imagined that he could get tired of pizza, but three weeks on the road had done it to him. Nevertheless, he was more tired of being hungry right now, and his daily ten bucks had already been spent, so he reached for a slice of Italian sausage. He'd just taken his first bite when he felt a clap on his sweaty shoulder.

"Awesome show tonight, man!" Matt said. "They freakin' *loved* us!"

Jeremiah gave him a semi-enthusiastic nod. "Mm-hmm."

"Dude, we keep this up—we're gonna be the headliners soon," Matt said, wiping his hands through his stringy, shoulder-length black hair. He wore an army-green shirt with a big black star on the chest, his sweat soaking through the front in the shape of a cross.

"Right on," Jeremiah said through another mouthful of pizza.

Matt turned to look toward the back of the warehouse-like venue, easily seen from their vantage point. "I'm gonna go hang at the merch table. See how things are moving."

"Sure thing."

"See you at the hotel—I'm riding over there with Cross-Eyed."

"Whatever."

Matt hustled off, his Doc Martens boots clunking away on the hard concrete floor.

Jeremiah turned back to his pizza.

"Something wrong, champ?" Liz's voice came spilling from the darkness of backstage. "You're kinda distracted lately."

Jeremiah looked toward the voice and saw Liz approaching, apparently in search of a bite or two herself. One thing this tour had taught him: After every show, while he and Matt were drenched in beads of sweat, Liz only glistened, her short brunette hair slightly damp.

Jeremiah lifted up his now half-eaten slice of Italian sausage. "Pizza again."

Liz nodded, reaching for a slice herself. "Yup." She made a clicking noise with her tongue. "We gotta get one of those contract things that prohibits this stuff." She took a bite, then, through her pizza, said, "You know—brown M&M's only and that sort of thing."

Jeremiah chuckled. "I'd be happy with just 'no more pizza' written really big." He held out his pizza to Liz as if it was a piece of paper. "The only rule, Mr. Promoter, is no pizza. Sign here."

Liz gave a laugh. Jeremiah laughed along, but his died down well before hers.

"How's Amanda doing without you?' Liz asked.

"I don't know. I haven't talked to her today." He gestured toward the stage. "Too rushed."

Liz nodded in understanding. "Sucks."

Jeremiah nodded in time with her nodding. "Yeah." He took another bite, moving into a half-sitting/half-leaning position against the table. "So, what's up with Matt?"

"What do you mean?"

"Have you noticed how he hardly hangs out with either of us anymore? He's always hanging with the Cross-Eyed guys."

"Maybe he's hoping to trade up."

One of the nameless teenage kids shuffled toward Jeremiah, half the kid's face hidden behind a long shock of stringy hair. "Excuse me, dude?" the kid said.

"Yeah?" Jeremiah said, slightly amused at the older-person respect he was getting from this teenager who was probably only three years his junior.

"Well, sir," the kid said, scratching the back of his head, "um, we gotta move your bass and rig to make room for the Cross-Eyed rig."

"Yeah?"

"Well, do you want us to do that, or do you want to? I didn't know if you wanted us messing with your gear."

Jeremiah smiled and gave the kid a reassuring look. "I'll do it, man." He set his half-eaten pizza slice on the table and dusted off his hands on his jeans.

The kid gave a half-smile (whether the other half of his mouth smiled remained a hair-covered mystery). "Right on."

Jeremiah followed the kid back up to the stage, grabbed his bass off the stand, and turned his head to look for his guitar case. Unfortunately, his dusting-on-the-jeans job hadn't worked as effectively as Jeremiah had hoped. A slight amount of pizza grease and flour remained on his fingers.

This, reacting with the highly polished maple wood neck of his instrument, resulted in his hands being unable to contain the momentum of his bass as the time-honored principle of inertia took over.

To wit: His bass slipped out of his hand and headed in a perfect arc toward the unsuspecting crowd.

It all happened so fast that Jeremiah didn't have much time to react. But react he did. He spun all 155 pounds of his skinny frame to save his bass (and any crowd member who might be struck by it), but had the misfortune of stepping on one of those 32-ounce drink cups with sixteen ounces of drink inside it and two ounces of condensation outside.

His foot slipped on the puddle of condensation, back into a mess of cables that immediately ensnared it like a hungry weasel.

Down he went. Arms flailing.

The hand of his flailing left arm snagged the guitar strap in mid-flail. The unsuspecting crowd was saved!

Jeremiah, on the other hand, was not.

As his knees connected with the floor, his flailing arm whipped the bass directly toward his head, which hit the following things in the following order: the floor, his bass, the floor.

Before he knew it, everything was at rest. Jeremiah lay facedown amidst a pile of cables, a spilled drink soaking into his pant legs, the headstock of his bass laying across his neck.

Man, he hated pizza.

||||||

Two days later, Matt gathered Jeremiah and Liz onstage after they finished their sound check. "Hey, guys," he said. "Jet wants us to come to their bus after the show tonight. He has some news for us, he said."

Jeremiah did the best he could to jump for joy without moving his body. Quality time with Cross-Eyed—that's exactly what he needed to turn this tour around. "Sounds awesome!" he said.

"What's it about?" Liz said. "We're not getting fired, are we?"

"I think it has something to do with our record," Matt said. "I guess we'll find out tonight."

That night, post-show, they boarded the cramped bus to find all the members of Cross-Eyed standing in a cramped dinette-type area that featured a cramped bench, a few cramped chairs to go around a cramped table, and a cramped aisle between them.

"Hey, Knuckle Sandwich is on the bus, everyone!" Jet said, wresting cheers from the rest of the band. "And we have a big announcement for them, don't we?"

There was general merriment and revelry, Cross-Eyed style.

Jet turned to look at the three members of Knuckle Sandwich. "Gentlemen—and lady—we just got word today that your record has already shipped 10,000 units!"

Everyone cheered. Even Jeremiah joined in with Liz and Matt, though he had no idea what that meant.

"Is that a good thing?" Matt asked.

Cross-Eyed laughed. Jet put his arm around Matt. "It's nothing in the regular world. But in the Christian world, that's pretty dang good—especially for a buncha newbies like you guys."

"Great!" Matt said.

"Yeah, so let's celebrate!" Jet said. He went to the bus refrigerator, opened it and removed a couple of glass bottles. "Let's see, we got Foster's and, uh, Rolling Rock. And Pepsi for the underage crowd."

A needle scratched over a record in Jeremiah's head, like in movie trailers when something goes crazy. Beer? Cross-Eyed had beer on tour?

This . . . this was . . . Jeremiah didn't know what to make of this. Like sex, the *other* thing he'd been routinely cautioned against, growing up, was alcohol. Only, unlike sex, it was not something God created for marriage; it was basically the devil incarnate. Pure evil. It ruined lives. It destroyed souls. It sent teenagers to hell.

This was the gist of what he'd been taught.

He thought he should rightfully be shocked by seeing his favorite band—a Christian band!—partaking of alcohol.

Basically, though, it just weirded him out.

He felt something cold in his hand and looked up. It was a Pepsi. Jet had placed it there.

Liz was sitting on one of the cramped chairs at the cramped table, holding a Pepsi bottle and looking out the window.

Matt was sitting on a bench between Jet and Lance Stanley.

"I did—I didn't know you guys were drinkers," Jeremiah said to no one in particular.

The band members laughed.

"I mean, Jet, we were with you for, like, two months in Nashville and I never saw a thing."

"Jeremiah," Jet said, standing up and sidling toward him, "we aren't trying to get drunk or anything. We just enjoy a good brew on a celebratory occasion." He clapped Jeremiah on the shoulder. "Hey, in a couple of years, you'll be able to celebrate with us."

The other members of Cross-Eyed raised their bottles to toast. Matt followed suit. Liz left hers on the table.

Jeremiah ambled toward her and sat down in the little available spot next to her at the cramped table.

"Everything okay?" she said. "You look a little shell-shocked."

He leaned toward her and hissed through his teeth, "This is kinda weird, don't you think?"

She shrugged and took a swig from her bottle. "I don't know." She looked around. "I guess it means we're in."

"In what?"

"In the insider's world of the industry. Or something. I don't know."

The cramped atmosphere was starting to be too much for Jeremiah. It was so stuffy. And getting hot. The air was growing stale. Could he crack a window or something? Get some air movement in here?

One look at the windows told him that wasn't a possibility. He turned to Liz. "I'm gonna head outside and get some fresh air."

He stood up. "Good night, everyone," he said. "Thanks for the Pepsi."

"Good night, Jeremiah," they said.

He stumbled down the stairwell and out the doors of the tour bus, into the fresh, night air. It brought him clarity.

His mind suddenly felt better. He closed his eyes, sighed, and slumped against the side of the tour bus. He could hear laughing inside.

Then he heard steps coming down the stairwell. He heard someone walking toward him. He heard Liz's voice. "You don't look so good."

He opened his eyes and looked at her, the moonlight adding a comforting glow to her face. "Yeah, I just . . ."

"Not used to alcohol?"

He shook his head. "I just . . . you know, I've been taught all my life that beer is bad. My dad hears it all the time—he plays bars and stuff, and people in the church are always giving him a hard time about it. He never drinks because he wants to 'keep up his witness,' you know?"

Liz nodded.

"It's just weird," Jeremiah said. "There are all these people that I've looked up to—Matt, Jet—and I've always looked at them as really spiritual, really grounded people."

"Yeah?"

"Well, not Matt so much anymore, but you know what I mean?"

"I think so."

Jeremiah looked up at the moon. "And now, I'm finding out that these people have some sort of hidden side, some secret they keep to themselves."

Liz didn't say anything. She leaned against the bus, next to Jeremiah, her shoulder touching his arm.

"I guess it just makes me disappointed," Jeremiah said. "That's all."

"Well, they are human beings—just like you."

"That's true."

"Jeremiah, I think you'll be a whole lot happier if you stop looking at them—or yourself—and start looking at Jesus. Stop following Christians and start following Christ."

Looking at the moon, listening to Liz, something suddenly fell into place. It was as if his entire life was an arch under construction, and Liz had just given him the keystone—the thing to hold it all in place. "Why haven't I ever thought of that before?" he said, mostly to himself.

"Thought of what?"

"I've been trying to follow God on my own. I've been white-knuckling my way through life, just doing what was expected of me."

Liz elbowed him in the ribs. "It's an easy thing to do, Jeremiah."

"I'm just thinking about all this: the band, and Amanda, and everything, and how I've just been letting it all happen to me." He pointed to the moon. "That moon? And the stars? That's been God to me. Always there, but always distant. Just another thing to take for granted."

"And now?"

Jeremiah looked back at Liz. This was God in action. God, taking an active role in his life. God, reaching into his mess and inviting him to a better, smarter, easier way of living. "God is beautiful. And I'm going to follow him."

Just follow Christ.

How simple.

| | | | | |

"Jeremiah? Jeremiah?"

Jeremiah looked up from his reading at the sound of Liz calling his name.

"Huh?"

"We're almost there," she said.

"Wow," he said, looking out the window. "That was a short drive."

Liz let out a cackle as she eased the van off the highway onto the first exit ramp in Peoria, Illinois. "Jeremiah, we've been on the road for three and a half hours."

"Really?"

"Yeah. You must be digging that Bible."

Jeremiah held up the book in question. "Yeah, it's really interesting," he said. "I've always had it, but I've never *really* read much of it. It always felt like schoolwork or something."

"Yeah, I know what you mean."

"But now—like, what do you think the world was like when Jesus was on it, you know?"

"A lot different from this one."

"I bet. I mean, he was really here, man! It's kinda weirding me out."

Liz followed the Cross-Eyed bus, turning at a stoplight, then moving into the left lane, leaving her signal on.

Jeremiah continued: "I've always thought of Jesus as this vague concept, or notion, or, you know, bearded white guy on the flannelgraph board in Sunday School."

"With the white robe and blue sash?"

"Yeah!"

Liz turned left into a parking lot. "I think that's the standard flannelgraph Jesus."

Jeremiah laughed. "You might be right."

"Hey, you're the one who worked at the Christian bookstore."

"True," Jeremiah said. "Anyway, Jesus wasn't like that, you know? He was a living, breathing, bleeding human being."

"Yeah, exactly," Liz said as she pulled the van neatly next to the bus and parked it. "It's so easy to forget that if you're surrounded by it all the time. I forget it."

"And then, check this out," Jeremiah said, flipping his Bible back open. "I found this psalm today. The last one. It talks about praising God with all these different noisemakers and instruments like cymbals and trumpets and harps and stuff like that. Basically, if you have an instrument, you could use it to praise God." He closed the Bible with a snap, setting it on the dashboard with a flourish. "How cool is that?"

"Jeremiah, I'm a drummer, and I'm a Christian," Liz said, taking off her sunglasses and slipping them under the sun visor. "That verse is, like, the first thing you learn. It's like one of the rudiments."

Jeremiah laughed.

Liz's face lit up. "Hey, Jeremiah, I just got an idea."

"Yeah?"

"Yeah. Let's do that psalm tonight when we play. Let's praise God with our instruments."

Jeremiah smiled. "Deal."

||||||

"Hey, we're up." Matt was standing at the doorway to the green room.

"Oh, okay." Jeremiah stood, reluctant to leave the couch, a comfortable black pleather number that made a great place for praying. Liz was already standing near the door.

"Come on, let's rock," Matt said, taking off toward the stage.

"Hey, can we pray first?" Jeremiah said.

Too late. Matt was already gone.

"I'll pray with you, Jeremiah," Liz said. "Just make it quick—I think Matt's about to play a solo show there."

Jeremiah grasped Liz's hand in a handshake motif, and the two of them bowed their heads. "Lord, help us to worship you with our instruments, just like you said we could. Bless Matt as he sings, and may you get all the glory. Amen."

Liz gave him a single nod. "Great. Let's go worship God."

They hurried out to the stage, where Matt had just walked out. Jeremiah grabbed his bass and threw it on, doing his best to focus on his Psalm 150 Mission. He tuned out the cheering from the audience.

"Thank you, thank you," Matt said. "We're Knuckle Sandwich, and we're excited to be here to play some of our music for you."

He picked out a couple of bars of a nondescript riff. "Look for our first album, coming out in a few weeks on Jet-Son Records. This is the first single—you can request it from the radio now. It's called 'Ham-Fisted.'"

He looked back at Jeremiah and Liz and gave them a quick wink. Then he threw himself forward and began playing the intro riff.

Jeremiah looked at Liz, who gave him a quick wink of her own. She mouthed the words, "One, five, oh," at him.

He smiled. Okay, God. This is for you.

Jeremiah began to play, and his fingers took on a life of their own. He found melodies he hadn't even known existed, things he hadn't played before. He was playing for God and God alone, and it unlocked a player in him he had no idea was there.

He turned his back to the audience for the rest of the show. Not out of spite—he didn't want anything to distract him from this moment with God. It was just the two of them. Jeremiah grooving, playing more stoutly than he'd ever played before, his body liquid and at his command, his fingers flying across the fretboard in symphonic harmony with everything Matt was doing on the guitar.

He got the distinct feeling that God was smiling on him. That God saw him, and that he was good.

Before he knew it, the show was over, and he was sad that it had to end.

They gave their standard waves to the crowd and stepped off the stage, Liz rushing to Jeremiah almost immediately.

"Wasn't that awesome? You were really having some kind of God experience there."

Jeremiah was so content, he didn't say anything.

Matt hurried up to him, too. "Dude!" he said. "Whatever you were doing just then? Keep doing it, okay? That was killer!" He slapped him on the back and took off for the green room.

Liz gave him a thumbs-up and followed Matt into the green room.

It was then that Jeremiah realized he'd been so into God during the show that he hadn't once worried about whether he was locked into Liz's beat.

Even better: He realized that that thought didn't scare him.

CHAPTER TWENTY-EIGHT

IN WHICH JEREMIAH AND LIZ TAKE BACK THE BAND

Three weeks later, the tour was over and Knuckle Sandwich was back in Tulsa. Life could get back to quasi-normal, but only for a month — they were scheduled to go to Christian Music Week in Nashville, a huge music conference-type thing where the Christian music industry celebrated itself in style. It culminated every year in the QUAILS Awards for Outstanding Christian Music Ceremony, where all the best — or most popular — Christian music artists received accolades for Quality, Uniqueness, And Individualism with a Loving Spirit.

Most people just called them "the Christian Grammys."

But that was a month away, and until then, Knuckle Sandwich focused on resting up and recuperating from their tour. They didn't take any jobs; they all just wanted to hang out, and they'd made enough money on the tour to do just that. Barely.

Two weeks after they got back, Jeremiah tried to call Amanda one morning but got Liz instead.

"Hey, Jeremiah, what are you doing?"

"Nothing. Just wondering if Amanda's there."

"She's still asleep. Matt, too."

"Oh."

"Want to get some coffee? I'm bored over here—I can't do anything 'cause Matt's taking up the couch."

"Sure. I'll meet you at Java Dave's over on 81st?"

"See you there."

A few minutes later, Jeremiah and Liz were sitting down, sipping two cups of Colombian Supremo.

"So what's up?" Jeremiah asked.

"Not much," she said. "How're things with you and Amanda?"

"Oh, you probably know better than I do, being the roommate."

She laughed. "Probably so. She's really glad you're home."

"Yeah, me too."

"And you guys have been, uh," Liz searched for the words as she took a sip, then swallowed, "faithful to the pact?"

"Yeah, yeah. She really hasn't brought it up since Christmas."

"That's good."

Jeremiah took a sip. "What about you and Matt?"

She rolled her eyes. "Well, we're fine on the pact, but I'm about to give up on him. He's really changed a lot."

"No kidding," Jeremiah said, clinking a spoon into his cup just for the fun of it. "He's really letting the band get to his head, I think."

Liz snorted—and somehow managed to do it in a lady-like fashion. "Oh, my. What was your first clue? The constant mugging for applause or the stage dive in Roswell?"

"That looked kind of fun, actually."

"Okay, you're right."

"Still," Jeremiah said, raising his cup to his lips. "It's just so sad—he has so much potential, and he's frittering it away." He blew on his coffee, then took a sip. "I mean, I looked up to him so much, and now I feel like I'm looking down on him. I don't like that feeling."

"Yeah, exactly."

"I don't know," Jeremiah said. "It's messed up."

Liz stirred her coffee absentmindedly. "You know what bugs me? How much he used to love using his talent for God, and now to see him using it for himself. It's such a waste."

Jeremiah drummed his fingers on the table. "Is there anything we can do?"

Liz drummed her fingers in time to Jeremiah's.

They both sat there, drumming, thinking, and sipping coffee.

"You know what?" Liz said, suddenly looking a little angry. "We're just as much part of the band as him." She pointed at Jeremiah for emphasis. "We should go talk to him. Right now."

"Seriously?"

"Yes, seriously," Liz said, leaning forward. "This band is getting off-track, and it's up to us to put it back on."

Jeremiah studied the table for a moment, considering. Finally, he gave the table a light smack. "All right—let's do it."

| | | | | |

The morning sun had finally warmed what had been a chilly March morning. Jeremiah and Liz stood in the parking lot of her apartment complex, looking at her front door. Jeremiah inhaled the fresh morning air, then turned to Liz. "Okay, we're just going to go in, wake him up, and tell him we have to talk."

"Right."

"And the key word, I think, is 'love,'" Jeremiah said. "I think if we look like we're coming on too strong, it won't work."

"Right."

"We should probably say a prayer, huh?"

Liz didn't bother with taking hands or bowing heads or any other prayer formalities. She kept her eyes focused on the door. "Lord," she said, "I pray that your will be done here. Give us strength and boldness to say what we need to say."

"And God, please help us to operate in love," Jeremiah said, sneaking a glance at Liz, who was still locked onto her front door. "Amen."

"Amen."

They walked the short distance to the front door, and Liz unlocked it carefully. "I don't want to wake up Amanda," she whispered. She turned the knob slowly, and they walked into the living room.

The couch was empty.

Jeremiah heard whispers coming from one of the bedrooms. Giggles, too.

Amanda's bedroom.

He closed his eyes as the realization hit him. His legs went numb. A shiver ran through his whole body; his palms immediately began to sweat. He felt tiny pricks in his fingers.

His heart—his poor heart—was clamped in a vise. He clenched his teeth and sought to manage the flood of emotions that began boiling over in him. Anger. Jealousy. Hatred. Bitterness. Betrayal.

It all happened in an instant. He knew.

He knew.

Liz knew, too. “That son of a—” she said, marching to Amanda’s bedroom door. She flung it open, and Jeremiah heard the unmistakable voices of Matt and Amanda:

“Liz!”

CHAPTER TWENTY-NINE

"TRUST ME"

Jeremiah had never been confronted with a cheating girlfriend before, so he didn't know what to do. Liz had run out of the apartment, crying madly, and straight to her car. Matt had run after her, draped in a sheet.

Jeremiah watched it happen. Watched Liz run out; watched Matt run after her. Amanda came to the door of her room, hiding behind a comforter.

"Jeremiah?" she called softly.

He couldn't bring himself to look at her. He stared at the carpet instead. Slowly, dreadfully, like a man on death row, he turned and made his way to the front door, which Matt had left open on his way out.

"Jeremiah? Please?" Amanda called, louder.

He didn't turn back.

He just kept walking. He was determined to maintain his composure.

He was composed all the way to the door.

He was composed all the way to his car.

He was composed all the way home.

As soon as he hit his room, he lost it.

| | | | | |

Jeremiah was prostrate on the floor of his bedroom, twenty years old, bawling like a baby. Saliva running into the carpet.

His dad must have heard him crying. That's probably what brought him to the door and into Jeremiah's room. That's probably why he was lying down on the floor next to his son, his arm around him, holding him tight.

That's probably why he wasn't saying anything. Just holding him.

Jeremiah had never been so glad that his dad didn't have a day job.

| | | | | |

Jeremiah let it all out to his dad. All of it. After he had spent himself on the floor, after his eyes had been emptied of tears and his nose had been emptied of snot. After his voice was so raw from crying it sounded like a dull saw blade. After his dad had helped him to a sitting position, leaning against his bed. After his dad had brought him a glass of water, which helped.

After all that, he told his dad every secret thing he'd been holding in for the past year and a half. About sleeping with Amanda. About how much he had grown to hate playing in the band. About what had just happened in that apartment.

About Liz.

Everything.

"Dad, I'm so sorry. I'm so sorry."

"Sorry for what, son?"

"I'm just sorry."

The shame was overwhelming.

"Dad, I—I drove Amanda to this. This is my fault."

"Son, I don't— "

"I should never have done it in the first place," Jeremiah said. "I should have been strong. I should have been a better witness."

Jeremiah's dad gave his son the most serious, most matter-of-fact, most righteously indignant look Jeremiah had ever seen.

"Listen to me, Jeremiah," he said. "I want you to get this. Amanda and Matt are responsible for their actions. Not you. You are only responsible for your own, and you did the right thing."

"But why does it hurt so much, Dad? Why am I so ashamed?"

"Because you sinned, son. You're a sinner, just like the rest of us."

Jeremiah said nothing. He just blinked back more tears and wiped his nose with the end of his shirt.

"Jeremiah, look. Part of your shame is just because you sinned. You did the wrong thing, and that hurts. But the devil is ruthless. He hates you, and he's ruthless. He tempted you in the first place. He used your body against you, tried to tell you that it was okay to sleep with Amanda. And then when you did, he told you how badly you screwed up and made you feel ashamed and guilty. Right?"

Jeremiah's eyes widened. This was something new.

"Dad, I thought all that guilt and shame was because I went against God."

His dad reached out and put his hand on Jeremiah's neck. "No, Jeremiah. That's not God. That's more of the devil. He tempts you, gets you to sin, and then condemns you for doing what he told you to do in the first place. He's brutal."

Jeremiah started to cry again.

"But Jeremiah," his dad continued, "with God, there is no shame. You don't feel condemned. You feel bad for doing something wrong, but it's a hopeful kind of badness. God helps you feel like you can maybe do something right for a change."

Jeremiah breathed in heavily. He nodded. "Thanks, Pop."

His dad smiled. "You're welcome, son."

"I love you, Dad."

"I love you, too, son."

| | | | | |

Later that morning, after his dad had left him alone with his thoughts, Jeremiah sat at the edge of his bed and said a prayer.

"Hey, God. I guess we're all screwups. I guess we all need you. I need you. I need some hope right about now, God. This rejection really sucks."

Whether it was God speaking directly to him or just a realization that struck him in the back of his brain, Jeremiah couldn't say, but he thought about how God—Jesus—maybe knew a thing or two about rejection.

"I don't want to hurt anymore."

A Scripture leapt into his head: *My yoke is easy and my burden is light.*

"God, that Scripture doesn't make sense. Being a Christian is hard. I feel like I've just been going through the motions, and if I really want to live for you, it's going to be the hardest thing I do."

A thought clobbered him over his head. There's still a yoke. There's still a burden. God hadn't promised an easy life—he had promised a better life than one without him.

“So what do I do now?” Jeremiah wasn’t sure if he was praying out loud or just inside his mind. Either way, he was suddenly overwhelmed by a sense of peace, like a thick, heavy, soothing liquid pouring over his backbone.

Deep within, he kept hearing two words over and over:

Trust me.

CHAPTER THIRTY

A FINDING OF FRIENDS

An hour later, Jeremiah was lying on his bed reading his Bible when he heard a knock on his bedroom door. He took a deep breath, exhaled, and prepared for a visit from his dad. "Come in," he said, his voice still scratchy and weak.

The door swung open. It was Liz.

"Hey, Jeremiah," she said. He wondered if his eyes were as red and splotchy as hers.

He sat up on the edge of the bed, smoothing the blue gingham sheet on his way. "Oh, hi," he said, waving her into the room. "Have a seat."

She sat down on the edge of the bed with him, pointing to his Bible. "At it again, huh?"

He smiled slightly and nodded. "Yeah," he said. "I figured it was, um, a good time for it."

She blinked rapidly and drew her mouth tight, giving a curt nod. "You okay?" she asked, her voice on the edge of losing it.

"Yeah, yeah," Jeremiah said, maybe a little too quickly. He lowered his head, like a doctor examining a patient. "How are you?"

Liz started blinking again, then just closed her eyes as the tears began to flow. She brought her hands up to cover her face, her shoulders moving erratically up and down.

Jeremiah scooted next to her and placed his hand on her back. He closed his eyes and began to say a prayer for her, silently.

She leaned into his arm, then rested her head against his chest. Her sobs lessening slightly.

"Matt caught up to me," she said, the words muffled as they came through her hands. "I told him I couldn't do this." She sniffled. "I can't."

Jeremiah reached his other arm around and hugged Liz around the neck. "It's okay," he whispered. "It's okay."

"I know it's going to change everything, but I can't. I can't, I can't."

"It's okay."

"I knew something was wrong. I've known it. I can't."

Jeremiah shushed her, closing his eyes as his own tears began to fall.

He had no idea how long they sat there, crying.

The next thing he knew, Liz was pulling away from him, sitting up straight. She wiped each of her eyes with the back of her hand, took a deep breath, and looked straight at him with a half-smile.

"I'm so glad I have a friend like you, Jeremiah."

EPILOGUE

Matt called Jeremiah two days later.

"Dude, I need to know that you're still good to come out to Nashville for Christian Music Week."

Jeremiah was glad Matt said that over the phone. Had he said it in person, Jeremiah could not have been responsible for his actions. "No way, Matt."

"Come on, man. Liz isn't going to come, but I need you there."

Jeremiah snorted. "Are you kidding?"

"No—Jet still wants us to come out and get all this worked out." Jeremiah couldn't hear a hint of apology in Matt's voice.

"Work it out yourself, Matt," Jeremiah said.

"Oh, are you quitting like Liz?" There was no apology in Matt's voice, but there sure was hostility.

"Yes, Matt," Jeremiah said. "I hope you have a good time in Nashville."

"Come on, Jeremiah—this won't be the same without you, brother."

"Goodbye, Matt."

Matt kept talking, but Jeremiah hung up the phone without listening to another word.

||||||

Knuckle Sandwich still played their showcase at the Ace of Spades in downtown Nashville. Except it was just Matt, with Lance Stanley and Mick Dillard from Cross-Eyed on bass and drums, respectively. The show was the talk of Christian Music Week. Everyone was buzzing about Knuckle Sandwich.

A Fistful of Hollers released on March 21, 1995, the first day of spring. It sold well initially, but when Matt hired a drummer and a bass player to go on tour to support the record, the band never gelled like Jeremiah and Liz had, so their live shows were no longer able to live up to the word-of-mouth hype. Fans began to feel let down, and sales tapered off.

Matt changed his name to Matthew Righteous and embarked on a solo career as an adult contemporary artist. He is now a three-time QUAILS award winner. He has also been divorced twice.

||||||

Jeremiah and Amanda never made up. She moved out of the apartment that day and into her mother's house. She never made it to college, and the last Jeremiah heard, she was a customer-care rep for a budding Tulsa company that specialized in on-hold marketing.

||||||

Jeremiah and Liz started hanging out together, and even began to fill in with Jeremiah's dad on some of his bigger gigs. Jeremiah especially got a kick out of playing music in non-Christian venues, taking his Psalm 150 attitude everywhere he went.

One time, after playing one of those shows, Jeremiah and Liz went out for coffee. Sitting there, finding patterns in the half-and-half swirl in his Americano, he thought about how awesome it would be to marry his best friend.

"Liz, I have a question for you, and I want you to answer me with complete honesty, okay? Don't tell me what you think I want to hear."

She was stirring her coffee with a spoon. She stopped, mid-stir, looking nervous. "Okay."

"I'm pretty sure I'm in love with you. I want to sign the dating papers. Become a couple. How do you feel about that?"

Her eyes lit up with surprise. She smiled so big that her cheeks were almost level with her forehead. "I think it's great! I feel wonderful!" She leaned over the table and punched him hard in the bicep. "For crying out loud, what *took* you so long?"

They were married within six months.

Jeremiah quoted Shakespeare to her on their wedding night:

Those lines that I before have writ do lie,
Even those that said I could not love you dearer:
Yet then my judgment knew no reason why
My most full flame should afterwards burn clearer.
But reckoning Time, whose million'd accidents
Creep in 'twixt vows, and change decrees of kings,
Tan sacred beauty, blunt the sharp'st intents,
Divert strong minds to the course of altering things;
Alas! why, fearing of Time's tyranny,

Might I not then say, 'Now I love you best,'
When I was certain o'er incertainty,
Crowning the present, doubting of the rest?
Love is a babe, then might I not say so,
To give full growth to that which still doth grow?

ABOUT THE AUTHOR

ADAM PALMER is a freelance writer, video/film producer, and musician who spent his early twenties playing in a variety of bands. His previous works include *Mooch* and *Taming a Liger: Unexpected Spiritual Lessons from Napoleon Dynamite.* He lives in Tulsa, Oklahoma, with his wife and six children, none of whom would actually like listening to Knuckle Sandwich.

Read more about Adam Palmer on his website, www.adampalmerauthor.blogspot.com.

CHECK OUT THESE OTHER GREAT TITLES FROM THINK BOOKS!

Mooch

Adam Palmer

ISBN-13: 978-1-60006-047-2

ISBN-10: 1-60006-047-1

Jake Abrams has mastered the art of the handout. From turning a job waiting tables into his own personal buffet to crashing company parties for the freebies, he has a knack for making the most of every opportunity. But his life takes a turn for the weird when a local big shot suffers a fatal heart attack.

From Bad to Worse

Todd and Jedd Hafer

ISBN-13: 978-1-57683-970-6

ISBN-10: 1-57683-970-2

What starts as a simple shared ride between friends becomes an excursion with unexpected curves as Griffin deals with deep personal wounds and his hidden feelings for Amanda. As he nears his final destination, Griffin must once again confront his fractured family and a secret from the past.

Maggie Come Lately

Michelle Buckman

ISBN-13: 978-1-60006-082-3

ISBN-10: 1-60006-082-X

Maggie McCarthy is more than ready to be just a regular teen. Ever since her mother's death, Maggie has found herself acting as a mother to her two younger brothers and serving as the resident housekeeper. All of that changes after she rescues a classmate and rival from sexual assault and becomes an accidental hero and celebrity at her high school.

NAVPRESS®
BRINGING TRUTH TO LIFE
www.navpress.com

To order copies, visit your local Christian bookstore, call NavPress at 1-800-366-7788, or log on to www.navpress.com.
To locate a Christian bookstore near you, call 1-800-991-7747.